A HABIT
OF
HIDING

LJ HEMMINGSON

To Greg & Marta

Make a "habit" of friendship!

LaVonne (LJ) Yoder

Create Space
4900 LaCross Road
North Charleston, SC 29406
USA

Publisher's Note: This is a work of fiction. Names, characters, places, and incidents are a product of the author's imagination. Locales and public names are sometimes used for atmospheric purposes. Any resemblance to actual people, living or dead, or to businesses, companies, events, institutions, or locales is completely coincidental.

A Habit of Hiding/LJ Hemmingson
ISBN 9781548121655

For my mother

Hattie Taute

CHAPTER ONE

"Where are we?" she begged.

"You know I can't tell you exactly where we are for now," he responded.

Opening the driver's door, Sam climbed out to the sound of crunching gravel under his feet. He stretched his long frame, arching his back while rolling his neck from side to side, mostly to loosen the tight muscles, but also to make certain they were as alone out here as they felt. As he looked into Abby's fearful face, he pulled her out of her seat and escorted her to the front door.

"It won't be as bad as you think, Abby," he said in his low slow voice. "And it's not forever."

She squinted up at a cupola atop an old stone four story fortress, visible above the stockade fence that surrounded it. The stones of the massive structure were of a grayish weathered hue, adding gloom to the already apprehensive feeling that had taken residence within this young girl. There was not a shrub or tree to lend any shade to the bare ground. Her heart pounded wildly.

Apparently someone knew they were coming, as the fence gate was unlocked. Walking toward the heavy front door of the big house, Sam reached for the bell.

"Don't be frightened, the warden isn't as bad as she may seem," he tried to joke.

A woman pulled the door open, quickly glanced at the tall Indian, and ushered the pair inside. She was dressed in a black uniform complete with sturdy walking shoes and a heavy belt around her waist. At only seventeen, Abby was no judge of age, but she guessed this woman to be in her early sixties, or maybe older. Even though the woman's face remained impassive, there was a hint of some emotion deep in her eyes. Swinging from the belt was some sort of wooden or metal object, and Abby could only think of the book she had recently read, "Flowers in the Attic," and a scene of that grandmother's wickedness hovered shadowy in her memory.

"This is the girl I told you about on the phone," said Sam. "You'll check her in and take care of the rest?" Sam seemed acquainted with this matronly woman, who confidently replied,

"Of course, we know how to take care of young women here. You know that."

At that, Sam lowered his eyes and said a hurried good bye, abruptly retreating to the parking area.

He climbed into the Crown Victoria, started the engine, and turned the car around. Heading back out onto the main road, Sam's next visit was heavy on his mind. After pulling onto Hwy 377, he threaded his way back up to I 90 E. One of the few places to grab a meal while crossing this part of the state was one of Sam's favorite stops on the east side of the river. Easing the car up to a pump, he slipped his credit card through the reader and picked up the nozzle. The car's gas tank guzzled its share before Sam pulled into a parking spot in front of the old iconic family style restaurant and slid into a booth upholstered with faded red plastic. This place was nothing fancy by big city standards, but these country cooks sure did know how to satisfy a man's hungry stomach. After enjoying his favorite buffalo burger and fries, he pulled the Ford from the parking lot and was back on his way east.

CHAPTER TWO

Come with me, Ms. Williams. Is it Abigail?"

"I prefer Abby, ma'am," she managed to squeak. The older woman's gaze scanned the frightened young girl with long auburn hair tied up in a ponytail. Her large hazel eyes darted around the room while she nervously sucked in her bottom lip.

"Then Abby it shall be," stated the woman matter-of-factly. They walked down a long corridor with doors on either side. The floor was of a blackish gray terrazzo, well-worn with years of use. The walls were lined with pictures of somber looking older women, all in uniform. At the end of the first hall the woman climbed a flight of stairs, with Abby trailing. Down another hallway they marched, then through a locked door into yet another section. No keys were necessary. There was a code to punch in at each floor. It would seem that this old building might be full of spider webs and dust, but instead Abby saw gleaming polished surfaces everywhere. Even the window sills were free of any grime or debris. So far no other people had been visible anywhere, but when they rounded the next corner, there was an open door, and what appeared to be women being lectured in a meeting.

Again, they were dressed in black uniforms, but these were young women. They sat up so straight that Abby thought a metal rod couldn't stand more erect. Several glanced at the newcomer as she was trailing the stout woman, but no one smiled or acknowledged her presence.

Eventually the pair came to a row of tiny cubicles on the third floor.

"Here is your cell, Abby."

A cot, a sink, a chair, and a rod with four metal hangers shared this cramped space. A small simple locker sat on the floor. The word "cell" uttered by this woman fueled Abby's worst fears.

"The restrooms are down this hall, and you won't be needing much room for clothes. We will see to your wardrobe tomorrow," stated the woman. "Oh, and you can call me Mother. Everyone does." Abby flinched at her use of the word.

Suddenly alone in this confining space, despair flooded over the young teenager. Thoughts of "Will I ever get out, and who will rescue me?" tormented the teenager. She lay down on the thin mattress covered with a gray blanket and put her head on the scant pillow. Abby began to sob uncontrollably.

After several minutes she heard a gentle voice say, "May I come in?"

Jumping to her feet and dragging her sleeve across her tear-stained face, Abby stared at a pretty young woman. She was slightly built, maybe only five feet two inches tall, and had large blue sympathetic eyes. Ginger colored hair was pulled back from her face, which was void of any makeup. A sprinkling of freckles danced across her nose. She was wearing the same uniform as the others.

"Hi, I'm Sarah, and my cell is right next to yours."

"Are we locked in here then?" asked Abby.

"Oh no, we are free to move about the building, but the doors to outside are always locked. We are pretty safe here," she smiled. "It's close to dinner time and Mother asked me to bring you with me. Remember, there is absolutely no talking during meals. Keep your eyes on your food and try to eat whatever they serve. Just don't expect pizza and milkshakes. Later you will be assigned a duty, and it may be in food service. I've worked there before, and it's not a bad job. They like us to feel that we are one big family. They keep pretty tight control over us though. It's not a prison, but sometimes it does feel like one. I heard Mother call you Abby, is that right?" Abby nodded.

Following Sarah through the halls, around the turns, and down the stairs to the cafeteria, Abby noticed several other women coming out of their cells, or out of other common rooms. She supposed they were all on their way to dinner. Sarah introduced her to a few by name, but as they approached the dining hall she put her finger to her lips and winked at the new girl. They filed through a cafeteria style line with plenty of choices of food, although Abby's appetite had abandoned her.

After the meal was over, there was an hour of free time. Sarah led her new charge to a game room, where some were playing ping pong, reading or chatting. Sarah introduced Abby to a few young girls and several older women. Each of them seemed friendly and some welcomed her to their 'home,' although one or two of them seemed to look her up and down, dressed as she was in jeans and a blue sweater.

At her cell door, Sarah suggested, "Get some sleep, as we will be awakened early by a ringing bell."

Sam had tried to explain why this place would be the best under the present circumstances, but Abby was perplexed by the peculiarity of it. Oh, how she missed Mom and Dad. Where was Dad now? What was his life like?

The next morning Abby was summoned to Mother's office.

"Here is your uniform, Abby. I'll get you a second one as soon as Beverly gets it finished. After that, when you require new clothing, you will learn to sew it yourself. Now go to your cell and put it on."

As yet, this bewildered newcomer didn't know her way around this imposing structure. However, Mother, anticipating that problem, had called another woman to accompany her back up the flights to her cell. This one appeared to be more the age of Abby's mother, and exhibited gentleness about her.

She introduced herself as Catherine, and asked, "How long do you expect to be here?"

"I have no idea," came Abby's choked reply."How about you?"

"Oh, I was born here. This is my home."

Abby pulled off her clothes and struggled into this uniform, which was yards of black cloth, floor length, wide sleeves, and flowing. Catherine demonstrated how to hook it shut, as there were no buttons, snaps, or zippers. Across her bed had been placed a pair of heavy black stockings and an ugly pair of clunky shoes sat waiting on the floor. Surprisingly, they were the correct size. The uniform was a little long, but Catherine assured Abby that Beverly could shorten it up in a jiffy.

Now that Abby was properly clad, she was to attend an orientation session. Mother's assistant was a tall thin woman, older than any of the women observed so far. Piercing brownish green eyes were set beneath thick, drooping eyebrows, and a bird like nose rose like an arrow from the center of her face. Fear gripped the new guest, as this woman also had that wooden and metal device hanging from a belt.

"I am Mary Louise and I am going to give you the rules which you must live by. Please sit down." This was a command, not a request. Perching on the edge of a hard wooden chair, Abby waited for her introduction into this new life that she was being forced to accept.

"You will be assigned to work four hours a day at a job of my choosing. You will not speak with your superiors unless they speak first. We observe the Grand Silence here. Therefore, breakfast will be eaten in total silence. Any infraction of that rule will have you sitting in a corner of the dining hall finishing your meal alone.

You are expected to eat what is given you. Common rooms are for socializing and your cell is your private area, although I will make periodic inspections. You will find that some of our family members are friendly, and that some are not. Do you have relatives to whom you wish to write? If so, give me your letters in unsealed envelopes, and I will post them for you. We will not allow you visitors during your stay with us, for reasons that will be obvious to you later.

We do have a school here, and you will be able to finish your studies. Every afternoon you will have an hour of exercise before classes. There is an exercise yard behind the building. You are expected to get fresh air daily. Personal conversations are not encouraged, as many of our family members do not wish to share their past with others. Remember, discipline is the pathway to virtue. Be wary of forming 'particular' friendships. They can become a stumbling block. Do you have any questions?"

Trying to absorb all this information while holding back tears, Abby simply shook her head, as she couldn't trust her voice to answer.

"Alright then, let's get you started on your first assignment."

CHAPTER THREE

After a couple hours of evening driving, Sam had taken the exit into the city. He found an inexpensive motel room for the night, and fell off to sleep, with worries about both Abby and his next encounter heavy on his mind.

As he drove north on the main thoroughfare through the city the next morning, he marveled at the growth and changes that had happened here over the years. On the north side, near the actual falls, what used to be a hangout for drunkards and drug addicts now had been cleaned up into a beautiful park. It had a few little shops and photo opportunities of the city's namesake, the falls of the Sioux River.

Sam always made a quick stop here to soak up the strength his soul so desperately needed before he made his next visit. Then, sliding back into the seat, he again started the engine and headed up to the destination he dreaded. Parking the car in the state penitentiary lot, Sam slowly exited his car and made his way to the front of the building. After checking in and heading through all the locks, he was escorted to a table and chair designated for visitors. He sat there a few moments clenching and unclenching his fists, trying to swallow the acid that was rising within him. Closing his eyes he took a few deep breaths. A scraping sound of chair legs on the rough cement floor alerted him to the presence of someone on the other side of the glass partition. Picking up his phone, he heard Eddie's voice,

"Hey Sam." He slowly raised his eyes to stare at the familiar drawn face of the man facing him.

"Hey yourself, Eddie." Sam managed.

“What are ya doin’ in my neck of the woods?” ventured Eddie with mild interest.

“Can’t I just stop by and see how you are without an explanation?” responded Sam.

“Sure, you can, but do you? You’re always on your way somewhere.”

“OK, you win. I just made a delivery out west,” admitted Sam.

“Another one, same kind? You get paid by the piece, or what?” Eddie tried to provoke Sam.

“You know better than to say a thing like that,” shot back Sam.

“I guess your fancy big city job must pay pretty well. You’re lookin’ good,” commented Eddie. “Have you seen Ami lately?” After a brief pause, Sam shook his head and answered a slow,

“Naw.”

“Well, neither have I,” said Eddie, with a laconic smirk.

CHAPTER FOUR

Catherine reappeared and escorted Abby down three flights of stairs into a basement, and stopped in front of a door marked "Laundry." Inside were two other fairly young girls, busy pulling black uniforms from the huge washing machine and hanging them on cords tied across the room above their heads. A third woman was guiding a uniform through a set of rollers that pressed out the wrinkles.

"This is our newest family member, Abby. She will be working with you in laundry," stated Catherine.

Turning to Abby she asked, "Have you used a mangle before?"

"No," was the reply.

Catherine addressed a young girl who was lifting black cloth out of a tub of hot water. "Emily will show you how, won't you dear?" The tall girl with large brown eyes turned to smile at Abby. She too was dressed in a long black robe. Her dark brown hair was tied back from her face with a simple piece of black cloth.

"Sure I will," came the reply.

"When your shift is finished, please bring her to me and we will get her enrolled in classes beginning tomorrow." At that brief introduction, Catherine turned and left.

It was so hot in the room, perspiration was beading on Abby's face just standing still. This suffocatingly long robe only made matters worse. She could feel sweat trickling down the back of her neck. The others seemed to be used to it, and kept up a good pace with their work.

"When did you arrive?" asked Emily.

"Just yesterday," Abby answered.

“Don’t be afraid. It isn’t so bad after you get into the routine here.”

“I don’t really understand what is expected of me or how long I have to be here,” Abby responded while choking back tears.

“Then it wasn’t your choice to come here?” asked Emily.

“Of course not,” answered Abby.

“How old are you?”

“Seventeen.”

“Hey, so am I, and I’m finishing my classes here, so we will be together every morning as well as afternoons. I can show you the ropes.”

Abby tried to force her face into a smile as she struggled to absorb all that was happening.

That night she lay awake trying to process all that had happened since her fifteenth birthday. Mother, Dad and she had lived in a modest house in Chicago, not far from her school. Dad owned a small restaurant in the city. He wasn’t a chef, but had a good head for management, and spent most of his time in his office in the back, analyzing income and expenses. Antonio did most of the ordering in addition to the cooking. He put together the best prosciutto pizza ever tasted.

Mom was not fond of all of the clientele that came in, as she knew some of the mob would stop by occasionally for Antonio’s baked ziti alfredo or his chicken piccata. But Dad always said, “You treat ‘em right and they’ll treat you right.” He loved to walk among the tables and make sure his staff was taking good care of all his customers. Mom didn’t work in the restaurant. Instead, she worked in a high end dress shop uptown. Dad would say, “OK, Diane, I’ll feed ‘em, you clothe ‘em.”

But then memories of the rest of that year flooded back, and Abby squeezed her eyes shut to block out the horror of that scene she could not forget.

The next morning Sarah met her in the hall outside their cells and the two girls walked to the dining hall together. Everyone obediently seated themselves and got at the business of eating while two women Abby had not seen before moved among the tables, listening for any evidence of conversation. The shorter one was as round as a muffin, with rosy cheeks. Her plump sausage fingers were about all of her that could be seen, draped as she was in her voluminous black uniform. The other reminded Abby of a pinched little lizard with a permanent scowl attached to her face. She seemed to slither from row to row without a sound.

Sarah leaned closer and whispered "Beware the Gestapo!" Just then a frail little old woman, who was trying to seat herself while carrying her bowl of oatmeal, tripped on the hem of her robe and fell to the floor, breaking the bowl of gooey porridge.

The muffin shaped woman quickly helped her to her feet, but the lizard grabbed her by the elbow and hissed, "Joanna, you clumsy thing, get to the corner."

The poor old woman shuffled over and took a seat at a small table. Muffin brought her remaining breakfast over and placed it in front of her.

Glancing at Sarah, her eyebrows rose in disbelief. Abby received the slightest shake of her head from her companion, and looked down at her food.

This was the first day of classes and Abby was relieved to be able to focus on schoolwork, rather than the bizarre behavior of those surrounding her. Were they here by choice, or was everyone else a victim of circumstances as she was?

The first order of the school day was a form of group therapy, but really seemed more like group confession. The leader turned out to be Martha, the one Abby remembered from breakfast as permanently scowling. She was just as volatile in the classroom as she had been in the cafeteria. Insisting that each student "confess" what she had done wrong in the past twenty-four hours, she gave each of them the stink eye until infractions were volunteered. How could you have committed a wrong doing, when you were kept under such tight control? Abby hoped Martha couldn't read her mind, as by now she had plenty of thoughts to confess.

The classes were held in a separate wing from the cells. Abby thought she heard a child's voice that first day, but surely there were no young children in this place. As she and Emily were walking back from classes, Abby told her what she thought she had heard.

"Oh, yes, there are some," she replied. "Some of the women here were pregnant when they arrived, so there is actually a nursery, in addition to a school for the little ones."

"But Catherine said that she was born here. Why didn't she leave when her mother left?" Abby questioned.

"Not everyone leaves here," was the reply.

CHAPTER FIVE

Back at his desk in Chicago, Sam sat sipping his morning coffee while Will strolled in carrying his coffee with three sugars and a glazed doughnut, stuffed his body into the nearest chair, and casually asked,

"So, how did things go with that girl you took out west? And did you see anybody else familiar?"

Glancing up at Will, Sam remarked, "It went as well as it could, considering she is only seventeen and scared to death. And as far as seeing anyone familiar, of course I checked her in with Marguerite, as usual. I assume that's what you mean, Will?" countered Sam.

"Sure, Sam, sure, that's all I meant." Will pulled himself out of the chair, licked frosting off his sticky fingers, and headed to his own office.

CHAPTER SIX

The days turned into weeks. Abby wrote letters to Dad weekly, pleading to get her out of this place. His letters always repeated the same thing. "Abby, you just have to be brave. I'm working on the problems. Also you have to understand that you can't expect our lives to ever be the same again." Every time Abby received a letter from Dad, she dreamed again of that terrible night when her mother had gone away for good.

As sad and lonely as Abby was, she began to realize that not everyone here shared her feelings. Some of the women seemed to be very content, even happy. As Halloween approached, the women began to talk among themselves, laughing and plotting, it seemed. Then an announcement was made that there would be a costume party in one of the common rooms on Halloween day. As the day drew near, Sarah urged Abby to find or make some kind of a costume. There was a box of props pulled out of storage for such use. Abby saw some of the girls carrying masks. When they arrived at the party room, they donned their disguises and there was a contest to guess who was under each face mask. Of course, it was fairly difficult to distinguish people, as everyone had on the identical black robe. There was also a contest by popular vote to choose which woman had the most realistic costume. One of the women in disguise wore a face mask of a stern looking woman, and suggested that she should win as she was portraying the Mother and was wearing the complete costume! Everyone laughed as the winner was revealed as "Mother" herself. Donuts and cider were served and candy was even passed out. The children from the nursery and school had been invited and were entertained with games. Abby discovered that maybe, just maybe, she could have a little fun while here.

She really didn't even know where she was. She and Sam had driven for hours on the way here and Abby had slept much of the way. She had remembered leaving Chicago, and heading what she thought was west on that terrible day when she had told her dad good bye. He had held her close as tears ran down his face.

"Why do I have to go? Why can't I stay with you?" she had begged.

"Abby, I wouldn't do this if it wasn't absolutely necessary, you know that. I have things to take care of and then we'll see what's next."

Sam had tried to make small talk to cheer her up, but her throat closed up when she tried to reply. There had been a road sign for I-90 W. The fields along the highway were ripe with their grains and farmers with huge equipment were beginning their harvest. Abby thought to herself, "This land looks full of life. I feel dead inside."

The landscape was very flat. Rows of huge windmills sliced through the sky as if they had a job to accomplish, while others meandered in a lazy way. It was windy here and Sam told Abby how the farmers had planted large groves of trees decades before. There were rows of evergreen trees standing tall at the edges of fields, acting as sentinels. Sam explained that they were wind breaks. They passed a farm where children were playing a game of tag. Abby wondered if her life would ever again be carefree and filled with wonder and adventure.

They drove on a long bridge to cross a large river. The landscape immediately changed from row crops to rolling hills. Cattle grazed in the pastures and there were a few horses. She had slept fitfully the night before, with fear that she may never see her family and friends again. What would her best friend Beth think had happened when she had just disappeared? Soon her eyelids began to close like window shades, and before she knew it she was dozing. She had awakened when Sam turned off the highway and Abby heard the sound of gravel under the car tires. All these memories circled inside her head like a whirlpool.

CHAPTER SEVEN

It was dusty here. The yard was covered with sparse grass and rocks. A few shrubs were trying to grow but didn't look any happier to be here than Abby did.

Walking with her one day was Catherine, who seemed to have taken a special interest in the teenager. "Do you know the reason this house is here, Abby?"

"I know that it feels like a prison, even though Mother says it isn't and that I need to be here for awhile until things get sorted out at home and I can be with my dad again," she replied.

"Abby, don't you know yet what this place is?"Catherine searched the young girl's face with a quizzical expression.

"I have been wondering if this is part of an Amish Community," she hesitantly stated. Catherine burst out laughing.

"I suppose you could say there are some similarities. This is a convent and we are Sisters. We do often refer to ourselves as a community. Some people still call us nuns. And Mother is our Mother Superior in charge. She is also sometimes called the Prioress." Abby stared at her in disbelief. Her brain was as hazy as a foggy morning.

"Do you mean like a religious convent?" she frowned.

"Of course. What did you think?"

"The cells and uniforms and rules sure seem like a prison or boot camp to me," Abby countered.

"Actually," Catherine pointed out, "a convent does have strict guidelines to live by. They help us keep our vows intact."

"Vows?"Abby pried.

"We'll talk more later, and I'll try to clarify some details for you," Catherine said with a slight grin at her bewilderment.

"So are you Sisters or nuns?" Abby ventured.

"In most convents every woman would be called a Sister, but we have some special circumstances here and it would be inappropriate to call everyone by that designation," Catherine replied mysteriously.

"Do you know why this house was built on this particular location? It's because of Native American lore. Don't you feel an eerie mystique about it?" questioned Catherine.

"I feel eerie about it, that's for sure, but I don't think it is a mystique," she retorted.

"Give it time, I think you will when you understand more about this place," explained Catherine.

"Don't you miss your family?" Abby probed.

"My family is here. I don't know any other family," Catherine volunteered.

"You said you were born here, so what happened to your mother?" she ventured.

"She is with me all the time, even though I don't see her every day. Someday you'll understand."Abby turned to look at Catherine, who now had a slight smile crossing her face. Leaving it at that, she asked no more questions. Abby could understand Catherine's feeling that her mother was with her all the time, at least in memory.

CHAPTER EIGHT

Sam was on his way west again. This time his cargo was a fifteen year old girl from Chicago. Hannah was a runaway who had been picked up by the vice squad and eventually turned over to Sam for appropriate disposal. She had grown up in one of the poorest, most squalid neighborhoods of the city. Sam was delivering this girl as a favor to the agency that had rescued her.

Sam had Danielle, one of the women from the Chicago office, accompanying him to his drop off. They were afraid that Hannah would try to run when they stopped in Sioux Falls overnight, and Sam hoped maybe he could leave Danielle and Hannah at the motel while he ran out to see Eddie in the morning.

"Are you two hungry?" asked Sam.

"Of course" replied Danielle. "I don't live on burgers, sodas, and candy bars at home. I could do with a nice restaurant meal."

"How about you, Hannah?"

"Sure" was the only reply.

Once inside the restaurant, Danielle took Hannah to the rest room before they were seated. Danielle glanced at herself in the mirror and ran a comb through her sleek straight brown hair cut into a swingy bob. Her black slacks and tailored pink shirt on her slender frame accented the young professional that she was. "Aren't you going to wash your hands before you eat?" questioned Danielle.

"Oh, yeah, sure," replied Hannah with a sideways look at Danielle. She took a quick look in the mirror. Staring back at her was a teen-aged girl with unkempt brown hair, wearing an old pair of jeans and a grimy gray tee shirt. But the eyes carried the telltale truth that she harbored a lifetime of pain.

They slipped into the booth where Sam was waiting. He had been scanning the menu for one of those huge pork tenderloin sandwiches that he favored, with lots of mustard. "I guess not many places make them anymore," he lamented.

"Sam, have you ever thought about trying a salad?" smiled Danielle. She decided on a chef salad with extra shrimp. Sam stalled with his decision, while eyeing Hannah out of the corner of his eye. He suspected that she didn't know anything about ordering from a menu.

"Hey, Danny, why don't you make it easy and order for our young friend too?" Danielle quickly took the hint and suggested to Hannah that she might like the burger and fries. With a grateful nod, Hannah almost smiled. Sam finally gave the waiter his order for meat loaf, mashed potatoes, slaw and baked beans. Danielle wrinkled her brow and shook her head. While they waited for their food, Hannah's eyes darted from one patron to another, as if she feared she would be recognized. Sam, noticing her nervousness, casually said, "Ladies, we are a long way from home and nobody knows us out here, so we can eat all the greasy food and sweets we want." Danielle burst out laughing.

"Right on, Sam," she countered.

After they had finished the meal, the waitress came back and said, "Can I interest you in any dessert tonight?" Sam did not hesitate.

"You can bring me a piece of blueberry pie with ice cream, and my young friend here would like an ice cream sundae. Our other friend of course would not care for any dessert. She is still savoring her shrimp and lettuce." Danielle just rolled her eyes.

When Sam and Hannah had finished their desserts, the trio climbed back into the car.

"Sam, will you swing by Wal-Mart please? I think Hannah could use a new pair of PJ's." Once inside, Danielle propelled Hannah over to the girl's clothing section and helped her pick out a teenage sleep shirt, some underwear, and then suggested they take a look in the girl's blouse area. All that Hannah had come with was the cheap pre-pack of toiletries provided by a community rehab group in Chicago. Although hesitant, Hannah took Danielle's cue and browsed through the hangers of teenage tops, settling on a soft blue and white stripe shirt.

When the trio got to the motel, Sam checked them in, mentioning to Danielle that she and Hannah could sleep late in the morning if they wanted, since he would like to make a quick visit before heading out of town. With no further explanation, he retreated to his room. Danielle and Hannah were sharing a double room adjoining Sam's. Danielle suggested that Hannah take a shower and try on her new PJ's. She obediently followed the suggestion, flipped on the TV. Danielle took her time in the bathroom, and emerged in a soft pair of sleep pants and top while brushing her shiny hair. "I thought you'd be asleep by now, Hannah," said Danielle. "We have all had a long day, with another one ahead of us tomorrow."

"Ain't that Indian man comin' in here for sex tonight?" Hannah's question was so bluntly stated that Danielle stared at her with her mouth gaping.

"Do you mean Sam? I believe he prefers to be called Native American, Hannah. And is that what you think all men do to young girls?"

"Ain't that why you wanted me to take a shower?" the girl countered.

Danielle realized just how hurt this poor young girl had been, and how much work was going to be required by Sister Catherine and the others. She approached Hannah and wrapped an arm around her shoulder. She gently smiled at the teenager. "You aren't going to have to live that life again, Hannah."

In the morning, eyeing the dirty tee shirt draped over a chair, Danielle suggested Hannah wear her new shirt. "You are going to be meeting some nice women today who want to help you. I know you will think it all strange at first. I did myself," explained Danielle, as she remembered her first visit. But eventually you will find that their way of life is all for a good purpose. And remember, you don't have to always stay there. We are just hiding you for awhile." They walked across to the restaurant and had breakfast while waiting for Sam. When he arrived back at the motel, Hannah climbed into the back seat while Danielle greeted Sam with a "Good Morning." Sam's only reply was a nod. They pulled out of the parking lot and back onto the highway heading west.

Danielle had been across this state a couple of times before. It was such a refreshing change from the big city noise of Chicago. After leaving Sioux Falls behind, the landscape became more flat, and the city gave way to quiet countryside. Hannah stared out the window. Even though these two adults said they weren't kidnapping her, and they did act very kindly toward her, she couldn't help wonder about their motive. For a girl who had never been outside of Chicago, this trip across Iowa and now South Dakota was as foreign as if she were being taken to China. And how did she know where they might leave her?

CHAPTER NINE

One evening Catherine stopped by Abby's room for a short chat.

"Abby, I just wanted to see how you are doing by now. I know this is not easy for any of our guests."

"I'm OK. I am glad, though, that Emily is here too. It sure helps to have a friend. Have you spent your whole life right here, Catherine?" Abby asked.

"I was born here, and grew up here, but I left to go to college. Wow, what a shock that was. I wanted to see what life was like away from the convent, so the Mother Superior suggested I leave the convent to go to college. Of course, she wanted me to get a faith based education. I had never been to the eastern side of the state, much less to an environment outside our walls. She assumed that I would take religious studies and return to the convent to teach religion classes to novices. There were so many new and exciting topics to study. I took a couple religious courses, but really, I could have taught them," Catherine laughed. "My whole life so far had been prayer, obedience, work, Mass, and studying Catholic doctrine. I met some fun and interesting students who taught me plenty about the world. You know, they were just as curious about my world as I was about theirs," she continued. "After a couple years there, I transferred to the University, where I could take some different courses."

"Then what was your major study if it wasn't religion?" Abby questioned.

"That's the interesting part. I got my degree in Criminal Justice. You should have heard Mother when I told her I refused to change it into a study of her choice," chuckled Catherine. "But I was pretty persuasive and was able to convince her that I could serve God by offering stability to society through a career of my liking.

That hadn't been the convent way back when she was getting her education. Most of the young nuns had to follow a career determined by the Mother Superior. However, she became a teacher in a convent elementary school and says that she was pleased with her vocation, even though she was trained as a high school science teacher!"

"Are all convents just the same?" wondered Abby.

"Our order is not contemplative. Rather we believe in being active in society as a way of serving God. The college I attended was actually founded by a contemplative order, but I am glad that this order is not. That is part of the reason I enjoyed the freedom after transferring to the University. I do so enjoy the career I have," smiled Catherine.

"Where is the University?" Abby asked.

"It is in the eastern part of South Dakota, about three hundred miles from here," Catherine disclosed.

"South Dakota, is that where we are? No one would tell me exactly where I was being taken, so I quit asking," she revealed with frustration.

"I didn't realize that you still didn't know where you are. But it doesn't matter since you are so well hidden," Catherine commented.

"So, if we are in South Dakota, and you went to college in the eastern part of the state, we must be on the western side, right? Are we near the Black Hills?" Abby wanted to know.

"We are about 50 miles from the Black Hills, near a town called Scenic," Catherine explained.

"But I've never seen any city here."

"Oh Abby, we are hidden in the country. Scenic is mostly an abandoned town now, but it has a wonderfully rich history. We are right on the edge of the Badlands. You are familiar with the Badlands, aren't you?" she challenged.

"We studied about them in U.S. history and Dad was going to take Mom and me on a road trip across South Dakota to see the Black Hills this summer. But that won't happen now," she lamented with a catch in her throat.

"When your ordeal is over, I'll take you for a drive through the landscape. Maybe I can even talk Mother into letting you off the grounds before that.

The Badlands are broodingly beautiful. The sunrises and sunsets are like no other. There is a primeval quality to these unique formations, a desolate beauty," Catherine stated, with a faraway look in her eyes.

CHAPTER TEN

By now Abby had spent several weeks working in the laundry. At first she was assigned to those black cloaks that everyone wore, which she now knew were called 'habits'. Putting them through the mangle was like wrestling a bed sheet, but she finally managed to figure out how to get them through without too many wrinkles. Gradually she was given a variety of laundry and learned how to put linens through their boiling baths and rinses. The weather was starting to turn cold but the laundry staff was still required to hang most laundry out on clotheslines.

Abby had read history books about women using clotheslines in the early 1900's, but really, in this century? Her mother certainly had not dried their clothes in the backyard in Chicago. She and Emily usually worked this project together. Wires were strung between sturdy poles spaced several feet apart and the wet laundry was lifted out of tubs one by one and flipped over the wire line, then fastened up with clothespins. These were wooded two pronged pins about five inches in length that fit over the cloth and the line securely. By the end of November it was so cold that some days their fingers nearly froze working with the wet fabric. The only advantage to this method of drying laundry was that in addition to saving the electricity of running a clothes dryer, the pieces, she admitted to herself, did dry much more quickly, thanks to the wind.

Oh, yes, that wind. It nearly whipped the sheets out of their hands as they struggled to heft them up to the lines. Several batches of laundry could be hung to dry in a day, as the wind blew away all moisture in a short time.

Sometimes while putting bed sheets into the water baths, Abby saw blood stains. She asked Emily where the blood was coming from, but she didn't know and answered that there were things here that it was just was better to not know.

"Emily, I don't really understand about the Sisters here. Some are called a Novitiate, but others aren't. Some of this is so confusing. I am embarrassed to let Catherine know that I don't understand much about being Catholic. Are you a Novitiate, or a Candidate?" questioned Abby.

"I'm not either one. My mom explained some of it to me before I came here," said Emily. "I guess first when a girl is questioning whether she might want to become a nun, she spends time with nuns, maybe even living in the convent. That step is called a Candidate. Then if she decided to join up, she becomes a Novitiate, and probably goes away for more training to a different type of school. Then eventually, she can take her temporary vows, and finally her Final Profession. Then she is really one of them. And no, Abby, I am not any of that. And I don't intend to be either."

"I once heard that nuns actually get married to Jesus, is that true?" ventured Abby.

"I think they call it becoming the bride of Christ. My mom said she has seen photos of nuns wearing a wedding dress and actually celebrating a marriage, complete with a wedding ring. It does seem strange, doesn't it? But I guess if you were always a Catholic, you would understand it better," supposed Emily.

"Are you happy here?" Abby wanted to know.

"Actually, it isn't so bad when you get used to it," replied Emily. "At least, it makes me feel safe."

CHAPTER ELEVEN

After a few hours' drive from Sioux Falls, Sam took his usual exit from the interstate and followed the now familiar roads. In minutes he drove into the gravel driveway and parked in front of the big house. One of his passengers glanced around at the familiar surroundings. The other peered out the window apprehensively. Danielle slid out and opened the door for Hannah.

"Here we are, kiddo," said Sam.

The trio walked up to the door and Danielle rang the bell. When the door was opened, Sam said "Hello, Marguerite," to the same matronly woman who had met Abby at the door. She was already giving Hannah a cursory look.

"Hello Sam," was the reply.

"I've brought you another one from Chicago. She is a little skittish. Try to go easy on her," requested Sam.

"Sure, Sam, sure," said the woman. After a quick good-by from Danielle, Hannah was turned over to the convent. According to the usual procedure, Catherine was summoned to escort the girl to a cell. Catherine gently led Hannah up the flights to a cell on the floor near Abby.

Catherine tapped quietly on Abby's door and whispered, "I just brought a new girl up. Her name is Hannah. Would you introduce yourself and bring her along to dinner tonight?"

Later that evening when they had gone back up to the third floor, Hannah whispered to Abby, "Why are these rooms called cells? My uncle is in jail, but it don't look like this."

"Oh, it's very confusing and strange when you first come here, but actually, this style of living is all part of the convent Sister's vows of poverty, chastity, and obedience. They really aren't as bad as you probably think."

"Yeah? How long have you been here?" Hannah asked.

"Sam brought me here in the fall," was the reply.

"How often do you turn tricks for him?" ventured Hannah.

"What are you talking about?" Abby asked.

"You know, sex."

"Never! He just brought me out here and left me," frowned Abby.

"I know, he tries to seem nice, but most of 'em do. He didn't expect none from me in the motel room, but sometimes they try to fool you into thinkin' they are your boyfriend. Then the next thing ya know, you're turning tricks for 'em, and they own you," sighed the newcomer.

"Hannah, I don't exactly know what you are talking about, but it isn't anything like that here. After someone new arrives, she just has to learn the rules and do her job. We really aren't being held against our will. Catherine has explained to me why some of us are here. The nuns are trying to hide us and help us. And besides that, there aren't any men here. All women. That's all I have ever seen, except for deliverymen."

The following evening after dinner Abby tapped on Hannah's door to ask her to join the rest of the girls in the common room for an hour of free time. Hannah's eyes darted around the tiny cell, searching for a hiding place. As Abby pushed open the door, Hannah was shoving something into her locker. She quickly turned at the sound of Abby's voice, closed her cell door, and joined Abby.

As Christmas approached there was an air of festivity in the hallways. This was something totally unexpected. The week before the big day new faces began arriving. Most were middle aged women, more Catherine's age. They seemed to bring with them a cheeriness not otherwise felt here. They didn't wear the uniform, but instead dressed smartly in sweaters and skirts or tailored trousers. Most came by themselves or in two's, bringing luggage with them, laptops slung over their shoulders, and sometimes a briefcase of papers.

"Who are these women?" Abby asked Sarah.

"Oh they are the women who live out in the workforce and come home for holidays," she answered.

"Why does Mother let them live away from here? How are they safe out there? Don't they have to follow the same rules like we do?" she wondered.

Having never been to the top floor of the building, Abby hadn't realized that there were several more sleeping rooms up there. She noticed that some of the women came in pairs.

"Do they live together?" Abby whispered.

"Uh, yes. Some of them have lived together for years. There is jealously between them if a third Sister is asked to join them in their apartment," she revealed. "Sometimes Mother thinks it is a money saving effort to expect them to live in larger groups like we do here, but in the long run she usually regrets it as she has to act as a family counselor," Sarah remarked.

Abby still wanted to know what these women did when they weren't here. "Sarah, just what do these Sisters do if they don't live here with us? Do they have jobs?"

"Of course. They are the cash cows. Some are teachers, and some work in churches. Some teach in Native American Schools. They live normal lives like you probably did before you came here."

While the out of town sisters were visiting at the convent, the cooks baked favorite breads and cookies, and many meals were followed by a special dessert. When Abby and Emily left the dining room one evening, Hannah told them she would catch up in a minute, as she lingered at the table. Glancing around, she quickly shoved something up the sleeve of her habit.

At the beginning of the week before Christmas as Abby was on her way to classes, she noticed a young woman waiting nervously in Mother's receiving room. With her was a slightly older man. Could this young woman be coming to join us in the same way I had, she wondered. Maybe the man with her was checking her in much as Sam had deposited her here. Mother appeared and approached the couple with a slight smile. "Come on in to my office and we will finish the paperwork. Then we can make the exchange and you can be on your way," she indicated. Was the man receiving money to bring girls to this place? Had Sam been paid to deliver her here? "Oh, Dad, why don't you come rescue me?" Abby brooded.

One afternoon later in the week Hannah was summoned to Mary Louise's office.

"Hannah, I was making an inspection of your cell today, and upon checking your locker I found two cookies, a piece of cake, and some fruit stuffed inside. You know that no one is allowed to take food back to their cells. Rules are rules. Food is to be consumed in the cafeteria only. Now I will have to tell Catherine about your infraction."

As a trembling Hannah reported to Catherine later that day, Catherine gently said, "Have a seat, Hannah. Let's talk about this. I understand that Mary Louise found food hidden in your cell. Is that right?"

Hannah nodded.

"Don't you get enough to eat in the cafeteria? You know you can have as much as you want. We don't ration food here," Catherine smiled.

"I just am afraid of bein' hungry. I don't want no belly ache again. I only take one little thing at a time. One day there ain't gonna be enough," stammered Hannah, "and then I'll have extra stored up in my room."

"We will always have enough food here for you, Hannah."

Catherine, realizing that this street girl had stayed alive by stealing and hiding food, rose from her chair, crossed to Hannah and gently put her arm around the frightened girl. "You are not in trouble. You are here so we can protect you and help you. In the future eat as much as you need at mealtime, but please don't take food from the cafeteria.

Your locker might get bugs in it, you know," she grinned. Hannah stood and brushed the tears running down her nose, while Catherine handed her a tissue. "Now go on to your cell and wash your face before dinner."

One day when Emily, Hannah and Abby were returning from the classrooms, Hannah spoke up, "I still don't understand why they make us live in cells if this ain't no jail."

Emily replied, "When I was a little girl and I would see Sisters in their long black robes, that they called habits, walking on the street, I would ask my mom lots of questions. She said that when a girl gives her life to God, she wants to spend her whole life serving Him, and she gives up the kind of stuff the rest of us want."

"What kinda stuff do you mean?" asked Hannah.

"You know, a husband, children, a nice house, a nice car, pretty clothes, and things like that," explained Emily.

"That stuff ain't real. It's just in movies. I never knew nobody who had things like that," retorted Hannah. Emily and Abby looked at each other.

"Where did you live?" posed Abby.

"Mostly on the streets. When I was little we lived in an apartment, but there were lots of other people there too. I had to sleep on the floor. There was never enough food. When my older sister was twelve, my dad made her start turnin' tricks for money. Then when I was eleven, he told me I was old enough too. He would force us to go out at night. I hated it, and so did my sister. But she got knocked up when she was thirteen and somebody forced her to have an abortion. She died. That's when I ran away."

Emily and Abby both were too shaken to think of anything to say. Hannah continued, "Some old woman on the street showed me places to sleep at night and how to steal food from dumpsters behind restaurants. But I was always hungry, and still had to turn tricks for 'nough money for food. Once I did live in a house with some other people, but they was always drunk or shootin' up, so I left."

"Didn't anybody notice and try to help you?" Abby asked with a frown.

"I was pretty careful about where I was seen, always tryin' to stay out of sight of the cops. Then one day a cop did pick me up and sent me to a recovery house. I even had a social worker try to help me. She knew Sam, and the next thing I knew, they were bringin' me out here. But you ain't answered my question. Why do we live in cells if this ain't a jail?" Hannah persisted.

Emily tried to explain. "Catherine says that when you are a Sister, you have to follow the promises of being obedient, chaste, and living in poverty. But that being obedient really only means not deciding to follow your own plans. They have strict rules so that the girls learn to be obedient. And they live in a tiny room so that they realize they don't need worldly possessions. That's why they all dress alike too. No comparisons, no jealously. And the promise to remain chaste means they don't have relationships with men."

"Then I guess that means I can't never be a nun," Hannah snickered.

Writing to Dad at least once a week, Abby always asked when she could come home. Little by little his letters revealed some underlying activities that had nothing to do with her. He finally told her he was being "protected" but in a different way than Abby's isolation. He was being guarded by the government until a particular case came to court.

"Dad, what have you done?" begged Abby in her letters.

"It is nothing I did, I assure you, Abby, but sometimes we get into situations that are beyond our control. Do you remember when Carlo and Frankie and Tommy used to come into the restaurant?" he wrote. "I knew they were not exactly law abiding citizens, but in Chicago you learn to keep your nose in your own business, and they were good customers for the restaurant.

They brought in large parties of businessmen, and had plenty of money to spend. Sure there was a lot of drinking, but they were always polite to my staff, and threw their tips around like their money grew on trees. Some of our staff would get excited when they knew 'the boys' were coming for an evening. They brought high energy and plenty of bravado into the place. Even our regular customers seemed to enjoy the spectacle and sometimes would ask if our 'special guests' were going to show up. They were one reason that your mother didn't work in the restaurant. She was never very comfortable with the situation. Late one night last September, when we were closing down, the only person left besides me was Antonio. He was in the kitchen finishing plans for the next day and I was in the front of the restaurant locking up. Carlo, Frankie and Tommy had just left when I heard a gunshot. Tommy lay in a pool of blood on the sidewalk. I unlocked the door and ran out when Frankie turned and saw me. I realized that I was now dispensable. The only witness to a mob killing, my life was now in danger.

I didn't dare tell Antonio what I had seen. For a brief time I actually thought I could pretend that I had seen nothing, but of course that was not to be.

I went home, terrified that something might have happened to you, but you were safely asleep in your room, and Emma was ready to leave for the night.

I faked being sick for two days, hiding out at home, trying to think this mess through. My biggest fear was that they would threaten to do something to you, to keep me quiet."

As Abby read this letter, she began to cry and her hands were shaking so she could hardly hold onto the pages. "Oh, Dad, what will happen now?" she worried.

"Is this why I am out here? Are you hiding me? Where are you, Dad?"

Abby fired all these questions back to him in another letter. She wasn't allowed to make or receive phone calls for safety reasons, so letters were her only contact with Dad. He assured his daughter that he was as safe as she was. He was going to testify as a witness against Frankie, so the government was protecting him. "I have twenty-four hour protection from the U.S. Marshals and I am safely hidden, just like you are. We have to get through this and eventually everything will be alright again, Abby. Different, but alright," Dad assured her.

CHAPTER TWELVE

Now that Christmas had come and gone, Abby admitted to herself that celebrating Christmas here had actually been a pleasant experience. Everyone joined in singing Christmas carols, lots of hymns, and some of the younger girls added some contemporary tunes of their own. There was a party for the children and Mother had even passed out little gifts for each one. This celebratory atmosphere lifted the hearts of many, and the older ones seemed very content to participate in a religious experience. She noticed as the months went by that some of the younger women were missing. No one mentioned anyone as they simply seemed to slip away unnoticed. However, the older women all seemed to stay in their roles, and quietly continue their days.

Something the girls noticed during this season was that there were whispers among the women that elderly Joanna had taken to bed and was being cared for in the infirmary. She had recently been seen less and less at mealtimes and was sleeping most of her day away. Joanna was in her nineties, and had been a very active and devoted nun since she had come to this place as a teenager. She was from a large Catholic family on the east side of the state and coming to this convent to receive an education was the best opportunity for her. She had left her family at the age of fourteen to attend the school here, and had never left. Joanna had not attended college, but stayed on, taking her vows and working in the kitchen and eventually becoming the head cook. A very kind and gentle woman, Joanna had been a favorite of many. Now her body had worn out, and she was approaching her death. The Sisters took turns sitting vigil with her night and day until one evening she slipped into heaven.

Rather than a sadness blanketing the women, eternal life with Jesus was their fondest wish. There was a sense of jubilation as each woman closed her earthly life. These nuns welcomed the step beyond and rejoiced when one of them passed to the other side. This was a surprise to Abby.

A week later, toward the end of December, another of the older ones also passed on from this life. This time it was quite sudden, and a surprise to many, although Anna also had been in frail health for months. Abby learned much about this attitude of surrender to death while witnessing the rituals that accompanied their vigils, receiving of the body, sharing stories, and eventually the funerals.

The women who had come "home" for Christmas were preparing to go back to their jobs away from here. There seemed to be a tension and curiosity in the air following the funerals. "With two deaths, there will certainly be a trip to Sioux Falls for a few of us," mused Betty, a young Sister who was teaching school in the middle of the state. "I don't know if I am prepared for that step yet."

Abby overheard bits of these conversations, leaving her in deep confusion.

CHAPTER THIRTEEN

As the days moved on, the temperature began to drop and snow had begun falling. Abby thought about how she used to love this season. But winter in this place was different. The wind always blew. Hannah took every opportunity to look through a window at the accumulating snow. She felt safer here than anywhere she had ever been in her short life, but somehow the howling wind caused a fear of the unknown that she couldn't dispel. Abby, sensing the girl's nervousness stood beside her and gently put her arm around Hannah's shoulders.

"Winter has always been one of my favorite times," she shared. "At home my friend Beth and I would pull on coats, hats, scarves, gloves and boots and hurry to the ice skating pond not far from our street. In the warming house we would change boots for skates and compete to see who could get out onto the ice first. It was cold, and I thought my nose might stick shut, but we had such fun racing around the frozen pond with our friends. Sometimes a certain boy in my class would fly by and try to trip me, but I knew he would be the first to help me up if I did fall."

"You sure did have a nice life, Abby." Hannah quickly wiped a tear away.

"Yes, Hannah, I did, but everything is so different now. At least we are both warm and safe here. I'm glad we aren't out in this storm."

The lights flickered twice as the girls stood watching the snow pile up. The wind was now lifting the fluffy white stuff and dropping it in drifts against the building.

After dinner Hannah and Abby joined the women as they gathered in the largest common room. The power had been out for a couple of hours, and the generator only powered the kitchen area. Mother, Catherine, and others of the staff had found flashlights and candles to distribute to the group. A fire had been lit in the common room fireplace, and its orange flames danced as logs crackled. Aware that some of the young girls might be apprehensive, Mother had sent the cook down with old fashioned popcorn poppers filled with kernels ready to be held over the fire. Soon everyone was laughing and sharing popcorn, songs, and stories. Emily had lived in South Dakota all of her seventeen years and always thought a snow storm was a great adventure.

"This might turn into a real three day blizzard," she suggested.

Sister Judith, one of the older sisters who had come here to attend the convent school when she was just fifteen, piped up.

"Have you girls heard the story of Sister Claudia and the blizzard of 1888?"

"No, I don't know anything about Sister Claudia," replied Emily. "What was so special about that blizzard?"

Judith began her story in a shaky voice. "At Christmas time of 1887 the young nuns who were the first to be sent out here celebrated two full years of life in this convent. One of those young women was Sister Claudia. She was teaching school in a one room school only three miles from this convent. It was a January day, the twelfth, I believe, and there had been a little lull in the otherwise cold winter. That particular Thursday the temperature had climbed to a comfortable January thaw by noon. Early settlers of course had none of the warning systems we do now. People were out on this relatively mild winter day, going about their duties. Schoolchildren were finishing up their day in the one room schoolhouses so common on the prairie then. Three brothers who lived farthest from the school had begun their walk home and others were still in the schoolhouse when a sudden dark wall of blowing snow came rushing down from Canada, through Montana and into Dakota Territory. When Sister Claudia realized that the boys who had already left the building to walk home were out in the storm, she grabbed her woolen cloak and shouted over her shoulder, 'Don't you dare leave this building. Gather around the stove and, Missy, I want you to read a story to the younger ones.' Those were her last words.

With these final instructions she pulled open the door. Snow pelted in, carried by the ferocious wind. Two of the older boys ran to the door and together managed to slam it shut against the punishing blizzard. Sister Claudia then pulled her hood over her head and bent forward, trying to trudge through the accumulating drifts."

"Did she find those kids?" asked Hannah.

"No, she didn't. The icy needles shooting at sixty miles per hour were able to even freeze eyelids shut. There had been no reason to fear a snowstorm on this day, so children weren't even bundled up as warmly as most days. There was no time for most people to get to safety. Sister Claudia lost her way, stumbled and fell. Fighting her way back onto her feet, she took a few more steps, then fell again and tried to crawl forward. But of course the skirt of the long habit she was wearing only made that impossible too."

The young women sitting around Sister Judith now sat very still.

"Did somebody find her when they came to the school to pick up the children?" asked another young nun.

"You don't seem to understand the brutality of the blizzard. When the wind died down, and it had quit snowing, neighbors moved snow away from their doors and managed to stumble into the blindingly white world. The sun was shining on the sparkling snow, turning the outside into a fairyland."

"That sounds pretty," mused Hannah.

"Ah, yes, nature can provide surprises. It did look pretty, but this story does not have a happy ending. Sister Claudia's frozen body lay half buried under a snow drift less than a mile from the schoolhouse. You see, the temperature had dropped far below freezing."

"Oh, no," exclaimed Emily. "What about the children?"

"Many people were found frozen to death a short distance from a building, but had not been able to see it in the blinding blizzard. Some turned over hay racks and huddled under them. The three boys who had left the school building were found alive, hiding as far into a haystack as they could push themselves.

Sister Claudia's body is buried right here in our cemetery, on this property. A photo of her hangs downstairs. She was the first nun from this convent to die. She was only twenty-two years old."

Realizing that she may have added a sense of foreboding to the girls' already uneasiness, Judith turned to Sister Sapphira.

"Why don't you tell our young guests about your grandparents' homesteading adventures?"

"What exactly is homesteading?" asked Cathy, one of the young Postulants.

Sapphira looked around at the younger women and leaned forward, eager to share her stories. "This was a long time ago to you young people," she began. "In the late 1800's the United States government gave people free property if they would clear the land and build their 'homestead.' My grandparents decided to try claiming some of this free land that was being given to homesteaders. Gold had been discovered in the Black Hills in eighteen seventies. That was another big reason so many people came west, thinking they would become rich. But homesteading was much harder than they realized. Many were young and excited to have a great adventure. Others were families who wanted to own their own land and the promise of free land seemed too good to be true.

The town of Scenic was settled in 1906. My mother Bess was nineteen years old and a newlywed in 1910. She and my dad wanted their own land too, so they moved even farther west, and settled near here. Oh, the stories she told us kids about those early years. Actually one of the funniest was when they were on the move out as part of a wagon train. The men had gone ahead scouting for the best route, and looking for water. The women were left with the small children and a few tents that had been pitched. They decided they may as well set some bread dough to rise, from their 'start' of yeast. Shortly after the dough had been kneaded, a terrific wind came up. The tents blew down. The women were unable to put them back up. I asked my mother, 'What did you do then?' 'We did the only thing we could do,' she replied. 'We sat and watched our bread dough rise!' " Sapphira chuckled and continued her tale. "Ma spoke kindly of the prairie. They had come in the spring, and the prairie flowers were in bloom. You could see for miles on the flat land, and it was fresh and exhilarating. This was before the women would feel the loneliness and monotony of the endless prairie."

"Wait a minute," interjected Emily. "Where did they live? There weren't enough trees out here to build houses, were there?"

"Their first house was a soddie."

"A what?"

"A soddie. You are correct, Emily," replied Sister Sapphira, as her wrinkled old face crinkled into a grin. "When the settlers arrived, they did not have the luxury of lumber available to build houses. However, the prairie grass was tall and thickly rooted. When it had rained the soil was the easiest to cut. The sod would be cut in long thin strips with a 'sod cutter' pulled by horses or oxen. Then the men would chop it into pieces resembling bricks, and begin to build their houses."

"Are you kidding? They made houses out of grass? Didn't they freeze in them in winter?" asked Emily.

"Actually, no," was the reply. Sapphira continued, "The sod walls could be made so thick that the soddies were warmer in winter and cooler in summer than some of the wooden houses that had no insulation. The wind could blow through those, but not through the sod houses.

Hardships were many. She told us about how sometimes when they were out of coffee, she would put molasses and cornmeal in a skillet and burn it until it was crisp. Then she would crumble it and brew it into something they called coffee!"

“Oh, that sounds terrible,” said Abby. She was again thinking about the great coffee Dad had served in the restaurant.

CHAPTER FOURTEEN

Abby sat staring out the window of her classroom, wondering why a convent would ever have been built out here, when there wasn't even a town close by.

When afternoon classes were over, she decided to make a stop at the library to see what she could discover.

Scanning the shelves in the History section, her eyes landed on a book titled "History of the Territory of Dakota from 1861-1889." She began reading.

"Back in the late 1800's when North and South Dakota were still part of Dakota Territory, a Catholic bishop came west with a desire to convert the Native Americans to Christianity. He built an Indian School and soon a handful of nuns were sent out to staff the school. Soon more arrived, and eventually there were enough nuns in the area to set up a convent for their housing. The Lakota Sioux Indians considered this land to be a 'holy site' and the bishop felt that nothing could be more fitting than to build a convent in this sacred landscape. The convent was established in 1885, shortly before South and North Dakota were separated from Dakota Territory into two states. The Free Homestead Act of 1863 brought more and more settlers from the east to claim free land."

By now Abby had heard the town called Scenic mentioned more than once. This old library still recorded the locations of its books through a card catalog, so Abby flipped through one of the little drawers until she found a card marked Scenic. There were three books listed. One was a history of the establishment of the town, one was about colorful characters from the past, and the third was called, "Catholic Convent comes to Scenic." She glanced at a few chapters until she came to one explaining why young girls chose to live in a convent.

“The town of Scenic, although a ghost town now, was actually established in 1906, after the convent was thriving. In those days there weren’t many vocations for women. If a girl didn’t get married and spend her life as a wife and mother, she would either stay at home with her parents or perhaps teach school, and even then she would usually board with parents of the pupils. There were not many options for a single woman to be independent. But the convent and religious life offered an opportunity for a woman to live in community with other women with likeminded ambitions. Many young girls came to the convent as teenagers and completed their schooling there.

An all-girl’s grade school and even a high school were established on the property. Often the girls would leave to go to a college, usually a religious based school, but not always. After graduation, when the Mother Superior had determined the girl’s career choice for her, she would be moved to her destination and begin her life’s work.”

As Abby closed the book, she realized that girls a hundred years ago didn’t always get what they wanted for themselves, either.

CHAPTER FIFTEEN

Danielle tapped on Sam's open office door. The door was never closed unless necessary.

"Hi, handsome. Where have you been? Out making deliveries again, I suppose, even though you didn't ask me to come along this time."

Sliding into a chair, she crossed her legs, folded her arms, and tilted her head to get a good look at Sam.

After a few seconds, "I repeat, where have you been?"

"I didn't know I needed to report to you, Danny," he joked.

"I miss our little chats when you mysteriously disappear. You do look rested though. Was this a long needed vacation? Maybe you went home for a change and actually visited your family?"

Sam eyed his colleague with a mixture of curiosity and mischievousness.

"If you must know, I did take a little vacation time. I went out west again. And I did visit my big brother."

"Oh, where does he live?" Danielle asked with interest.

"He resides in Sioux Falls. I doubt if you could call it living."

Sam delivered this bit of information without sarcasm, but with a hint of uncharacteristic bitterness. Danielle continued to watch him, waiting for any indication that he planned to share details.

"What? Do you want more?"

Sam leaned back in his chair, crossed his long legs, and began to drum his fingers on the edge of his desk.

"Only as much as you want to tell me, Sam. I bet I can out wait you though!" He threw back his head and laughed that deep throaty laugh she had learned to appreciate.

"I have a better idea. How about we have dinner tonight and I'll tell you the whole story. It's about time I got this off my chest."

"You're on, my friend. How about a salad at the Chop House?" she suggested with a smile.

"How about a steak at Pete's?" he retorted.

"You win. I'll be there at 7:00," Danielle conceded. When Danielle walked into the steak house, she spotted Sam already tucked into a corner booth with a half empty glass of root beer in front of him.

"You got here early?" she raised her eyebrows in question.

"Not only that, but I ran five miles on the gym track when I left work. A quick shower, and back down here before 7:00. But I knew you couldn't beat me here, with all that fussing you do," Sam teased.

"And you don't like to look good, Sam? Working out to keep that over forty body fit, that hair neat and shiny, and you even smell good," she retorted.

"I do it for my job. I don't want to scare the young girls when they have to get into a car with me and be driven across state lines."

Signaling a waitress, he asked Danielle what she would like to drink.

"Mineral water, please," was the reply. Sam rolled his eyes.

"Shall we order so you can begin grilling me without interruption?" asked Sam.

"Sounds good to me," laughed Danielle. As was expected, Sam ordered a steak with baked potato, sour cream, and topped with onion rings. He did agree to have a small house salad too, while Danielle ordered baked salmon, broccoli, and a spinach salad, dressing on the side.

"Okay, mystery man, let's hear what deep dark secrets you are hiding," coaxed Danielle.

Sam rolled his neck, stretched his biceps, shrugged his shoulders, and replied, "How much do you want to know?"

"All I know about you is that you grew up somewhere 'out west' as you always say, and that you apparently have an older brother. You have told me that you were recruited for this job after college, and have lived in Chicago for fifteen years."

"You've got that much right, Danny," he interjected.

She continued, "So let's begin at the beginning, Sam. Exactly where are you from?"

"I was born on the Pine Ridge Indian Reservation in western South Dakota."

At this, Danielle's eyebrows shot up, but she knew better than to interrupt now.

"My dad died when I was two years old. Mom tried to keep body and soul together for herself, my big brother, and me, but she didn't do a very good job of it. She began drinking and eventually my aunt Amitola took over most of our care. In my language, Amitola means rainbow, and she was truly a promise of something better for us. She liked the old Indian ways, and taught Enapay and me lots of our old customs."

"Is that your brother?" asked a surprised Danielle.

"Yes, he was the firstborn, and was given a traditional Native American name." Sam unfolded a napkin and pulled out a pen, writing E n a p a y on the paper.

"When we were old enough to go to school, Indian children were being taken from the reservations and forced to attend boarding schools. The idea was to force the 'savage-born' children to transfer from their culture into the so called 'civilization' of the white people."

At this, Danielle squirmed in her seat, but tried to keep her face impassive.

"This practice had begun back in 1869, when the U.S. government decided to pull Indian children from the reservation and strip them of their language, culture, and customs. In 1879 the first boarding school sanctioned by the federal government was opened in Carlisle, Pennsylvania. It was named the Carlisle Industrial Training School. This school for children was actually patterned after a prison school that had been begun for Indian prisoners of war in Florida.

Within thirty years, five hundred of these schools were in existence. Most of these were run by churches, particularly the Catholic Church. Now I don't want to sound bitter toward the Catholic Church, since I have become a Christian, but I do struggle every day with the memories of what happened to my brother and me as a result of the boarding school we attended.

Enapay is five years older than me. The government tried to take him away when he was five, but my aunt Amitola fought for us and refused to let him go. She managed to keep him on the reservation until I reached the age of five. By then the government was punishing families by withholding food rations when they discovered parents who were hiding their children. We were both taken away to a boarding school in another part of the state. We didn't get to see our families for most of the school year. The last thing my mother and Aunt Amitola told Enapay was that he had to watch out for me.

I'll never forget that day. Enapay hung on to Mom with tears running down both of their faces, and I wrapped my arms around Aunt Amitola and screamed and cried and cried. Even at five years old I knew this was not going to be good. We were two little boys clinging to each other and sobbing for our home."

Danielle pulled a tissue from her handbag and dabbed her eyes, but could not manage to say a word.

Sam had a faraway look in his eyes as he recounted his story. Sometimes he would change his focus and stare into Danielle's eyes, searching for her reaction. At other times he seemed to be reliving his memories of a faraway time.

"Now I know you are quite aware of the Catholic Church scandals currently going on," Sam continued. "But what most people don't realize is how far back the abuse began. Some of these schools were run by the Bureau of Indian Affairs, while the rest were managed by the churches. Of course, the schools were all run on small budgets. Children were forced to work to help raise money for staff salaries. Some were 'leased out' during summers to work on farms, or as domestics, not being allowed to spend their summers back on the reservations with their families."

"Sam, you don't have to tell me all this. I didn't dream that you had lived a childhood like you are describing. I only wanted to know a little more about you," Danielle offered.

"It's okay, Danielle. It does me good to talk about it once in a while. I guess they call that cathartic," he smiled.

Continuing on, Sam told her about some of the daily life at the boarding school.

"We were really prisoners there. Both priests and nuns inflicted abuses. I'll never understand how people in nurturing positions can turn on their subjects and do some of the things these people did. Enapay was separated from me most of the day, since we were in different classes, but they did let us share space in a sleeping dormitory. He would always ask me if I had been hurt that day. Because I was so young, I never thought to disobey anything the priests or nuns said or did.

Of course, the first thing they did to us was to change our names. Punishment was meted out if a nun heard a child using an Indian word. Our names were changed immediately to Eddie and Sam. Do you know how hard it is for a five year old to suddenly be told that he has a different name, and that he will be punished if he calls his brother by his real name, or tells anyone what his own Indian name is?

Eddie told me stories about older kids who had their mouths scrubbed with lye or chlorine solutions, or made to eat a bar of soap for using Indian words. I didn't know what lye or chlorine were, but Eddie made it sound so bad that I was scared to death to answer adults. When I didn't answer a question, a nun would grab me by the shoulder and shake me until my head snapped back and forth. Some kids had to stand in a line for hours without moving as punishment. Others had to scrub the floor with toothbrushes."

Again, Danielle didn't utter a word, but instead put her hand over her mouth to stifle a gasp at being told of these cruelties.

Sam leaned forward and lowered his voice even more as he shared the following. "I have been researching some of the cases that have been brought before courts recently. There are records of over one-hundred thousand Native American children over the years who were forced to live at these boarding schools. There are reports from former students in some of the boarding schools about violence inflicted upon them. The punishment was horrific. One person remembered a Sunday night ritual where the Indian kids who had tried to run away that week were lined up, stripped, and given lashes. It's hard to accept that this kind of stuff was happening right here in our United States within the last fifty years, isn't it? Some of the schools had fences of barbed wire around the perimeter, and some even had the wire over the top, enclosing the children in a pen when they were allowed outside."

By now the waitress had cleared the table and for the first time Danielle noticed that Sam didn't have an appetite for dessert tonight.

"Would you like something else to drink?" the waitress offered.

"I'll have black coffee," replied Sam. "I doubt if my companion drinks the stuff, though," he mentioned, with a teasing glance at Danielle.

"Actually, I believe I will have a cappuccino tonight," she said, with a shy grin at Sam.

When they were settled with their after dinner coffees, Sam continued his narrative. "Eddie and I were there for about five years. We usually got to go home during the summer for short visits with Mom and Auntie Amitola. These were some of the best memories a boy could have. Especially with Auntie. She was such a good person and knew how to spoil us. She tried to make up for the months that we had spent away. Even though we were not allowed to speak about anything Native American at school, she never failed to teach us the old customs and dances." Sam's eyes twinkled as he said, "I bet you didn't know I can dance the ribbon dance, did you? And I am pretty good at it if I do say so myself."

Danielle had no idea what he was talking about. "Really, Sam, a ribbon dance?"

"Yes, it's a very fast paced dance. It helps me to stay in shape too," he joked.

"And just where do you dance this dance? In your front yard?"

"It is very popular at pow wows. Actually, I attended a pow wow last week when I was on vacation. But that's another story." Glancing around the restaurant, he realized that most of the customers had left.

"It looks like they would like to close up for the night. Have you heard enough now, Danny?" he wanted to know.

"Oh, no, Sam. I have so many questions. Can't you tell me a little more?"

"If you really want to hear more, how about we go over to my place and I'll try to tell you the whole story. It's a little too public here anyway."

"I'll come if you promise I can trust you," she teased. "Is your apartment very far from here?"

"I don't live in an apartment. Not after the years I had to spend in a boarding school. Too confining. I have a little house a couple of miles away. You can follow me with your car."

Danielle walked out into the night air and shivered. She didn't know if it was from the slight chill in the air, or from the story Sam had been telling her. Sam jogged toward his car and motioned for her to follow.

They pulled up in front of a neat little white house with dark gray shutters and a deep burgundy front door. Sam unlocked the door and stepped aside for Danielle to enter. Instead of walking into a bachelor's disarray, she stepped into a snug living room with a matching chocolate brown leather sofa and recliner. At either end of the sofa were tables with sturdy lamps carved from dark wood. The lamp shades were a translucent material decorated with shadowy wildlife images.

As her eyes roamed the room, she noticed brightly colored ribbons sewn together hanging over the back of a chair. "Whose is this?" Danielle asked as she raised an eyebrow. "Am I intruding?"

Sam laughed and explained that she was holding his ribbon dancing regalia.

"You've got to be kidding me. You actually wear this?" giggled Danielle.

"I told you I had been to a pow-wow last week. And yes, I actually wore that. Contrary to your assumptions, we Native Americans can be a colorful lot when we want to. But you'd have to observe me in action to fully appreciate my talents. Maybe someday," he wiggled his eyebrows and winked. To cover her blushing, Danielle tried to change the subject.

"You are a man of many talents, Sam."

She couldn't help but stare at the collection of Native American artifacts Sam had tastefully displayed on the walls. A bookcase was filled with history books and crime mysteries by popular authors. The legs of a large old round oak table had been cut down to make a low coffee table and filled the center of the room. The table had been sanded to a silky finish and stained a dark mahogany.

"Why, Sam, this place is beautiful!" murmured Danielle.

"Have you done this yourself, or do I detect a female influence?"

"What? Don't you think I have any taste? I have gradually filled my place with objects that are a comfort to me. I did refinish the table myself and I'll show you a clock in my dining room that I built."

"Where do you do that kind of work?" she wanted to know.

"I have a basement with a small workshop where I spend evenings puttering when I'm not reading. Go ahead and make yourself comfortable. Would you like a cup of tea now? I actually do have some Earl Grey around here somewhere."

"Sure, that would be great, thanks."

Sam went to the kitchen to fix the tea while Daniele settled into a corner of the sofa, tucking her legs up under herself.

Sam returned with a mug of steaming tea and a bottle of root beer for himself.

"Are you sure you want to hear more?"

"Yes, you know I asked you to tell me the whole story," she pointed out.

"Okay," Sam replied, as he took a deep breath.

"But first, Sam, I need to understand something. Sometimes you refer to yourself as an Indian, and other times you use Native American. Which should I use?"

Sam grinned. "It isn't that big a deal to me. When I was a kid our school was called an Indian school, you white kids played cowboys and Indians, and the government maintained the Bureau of Indian Affairs. Sure, it's probably proper to say Native Americans, but I grew up being an Indian. Have you ever heard of kids playing cowboys and Native Americans?"

Danielle smiled.

"I know that you are very aware of the sexual abuse by Catholic priests that has been exposed recently," Sam continued. "This was going on as far back as the nineteen fifties at least. Even in the forties a religious order was organized to treat Roman Catholic priests who were involved in sexual misconduct and alcoholism. High ranking leaders in the Catholic Church were even warned about instances of pedophile priests. Even after specific cases were presented to Rome, and a long investigation had followed, priests were still only pulled from their positions, moved around, and established in another setting which often again involved children. Enapay and I were together at boarding school from nineteen seventy until nineteen seventy-five. It's hard to believe this stuff was still happening in the seventies, isn't it? At first, or course, I wasn't aware of anything sexual going on. I didn't even know what that meant. I just thought some of these women in the funny clothes were mean to us kids. Some of them were very nice, though, and I tried to obey and please them. There were priests there too, and again, some of them were very kind, and some pretended to be taking good care of us. I think the nuns did most of the teaching. The priests seemed to be in charge, but maybe weren't as strict as the women. I think now that the priests were trying to be our friends, to get us to trust them. That way we would cooperate with whatever they wanted.

Even though Vatican II was over, and the nuns no longer had to wear habits, the ones at our boarding school still did. I think this was probably to keep us scared of them. I can tell you, at five years old, I sure was scared of the women walking around in long black robes with funny things on their heads, and only their faces showing. Aunt Amitola had tried to prepare us by explaining how the nuns dressed, but her descriptions were nothing compared to actually seeing all the women at the school dressed like that. In addition, they had a way of staring us down, so we were afraid of our own shadows. I have read a report made in the sixties from one of the schools to the Church leaders regarding abuses by nuns. This report documents a couple of nuns 'excessive interest' in older Indian boy students. So you see it wasn't just the priests. And it wasn't just the girls they were abusing.

Enapay and I had been there for most of the five years when he started telling me to be careful when around certain priests. He said to tell him if I thought that a priest was showing too much attention to me, or saying things that I knew he shouldn't be saying. Enapay was now fifteen, and had heard a lot of stories from the older boys in the dormitory about a couple priests who would take a younger boy with him to a private room. One day this very thing happened to me."

"Stop, Sam, I don't think I want to hear anymore," grimaced Danielle.

"Now that I have told you this much, I have to finish the story. You need to know what happened to my brother," Sam continued. "The first time Father Tobias took me into a room with sewing machines on some tables. He said that the women who sewed quit working every afternoon at 3:00 and the room was nice and quiet for our little talk. He just offered me a candy bar, something we never got at the school. He pulled his chair close to mine and put his hand on my knee while he asked me about my family, and my studies. He also wanted to know what my favorite candy was. Then he led my back to the door and said, 'I have enjoyed our little chat, Sam. Maybe we can do this again real soon. I'll bring your favorite candy next time.'

That night in our dorm I told Eddie what had happened, and he got really angry.

'Don't you realize what he is doing? He is trying to make you trust him so he can do other stuff to you later. Find an excuse and don't go with him next time, Sam.' Eddie also asked me what room Father Tobias had taken me into and I told him it was the sewing room where the nuns made their clothes. After that I noticed that Eddie was keeping an eye on me when I wasn't in classes. I would see him slip around a corner or watch to see if I was alone. I think he also followed Father Tobias sometimes. A few days later Father Tobias told me he had found my favorite candy, and that he had hidden it in the sewing room, just for me. I thought I would leave as soon as he gave me the candy, so I followed him down the hall. Eddie had seen him talking to me, and had slipped through the maze of hallways to get there ahead of us. Somehow Eddie had stolen a key to that room. He has never told me how he got it.

When Father Tobias and I were inside the room, Father went to a drawer and pulled out the candy bar. He sat down on a chair and waited for me to finish the candy. Then he told me to take my pants down. He had already unzipped his pants. I just stood there not knowing what to do. Eddie was watching us through a crack in a wardrobe closet where the extra material was stacked for the habits. He had grabbed a dressmaker's shears, which have a long blade and were kept very sharp. Just when Father Tobias took a hold of me to pull my pants down, Eddie charged out of the wardrobe, and plunged the blade of the scissors into his stomach."

CHAPTER SIXTEEN

One day when she had some time with Catherine, Abby decided to ask her more questions.

"Why did you get to choose your own career when nuns in the past couldn't? I sure wouldn't want to be told what I had to do for the rest of my life," stated Abby.

"Have you heard of Vatican II?" asked Catherine.

"Vatican II, what's that?" asked a puzzled Abby. "I thought there was only one Vatican, in Rome."

"Vatican II doesn't refer to the building, or even the institution, but instead was a meeting of Catholic hierarchy who were trying to modernize the Catholic Church. There had been a Vatican I meeting back in 1869 and 1870, and they also were trying to deal with issues in society and the church.

Vatican II met in Rome, at the Vatican, from 1962-1965.When it was over, the Second Vatican Council issued 'The Documents of Vatican II.' "

"Did they make new rules?" asked Abby.

"Actually, the results were that some of the strict rules for Catholics were relaxed, and convents also reaped those benefits. Nuns were to 'Serve where there is the greatest need.' The nuns in the United States took that very literally to mean they should leave the confines of their convents and venture into the world of the poor, administering any assistance they could."

"How was that different from all the time before the sixties?" questioned Abby.

"Nuns used to be required to wear the full habit, live in the convent with other nuns, and follow all the rules, hour to hour. There were specific times for prayer, meals, work, study, singing, and speaking."

"Speaking! Rules for when you could speak?" asked a perplexed Abby.

"Yes, even speaking." disclosed Catherine. "Their goal was supposed to be to achieve perfection and holiness by being set apart from the world."

"But that's kind of your goal here now, isn't it?"

"Not really. To a degree it is, but later you will understand that we have a very specific mission in this convent, and some of the outward visible things we do are done only to make the outside world realize that we are indeed a strict convent," revealed Catherine. "Actually, we follow the silent meal times mostly to train the new postulants what we mean by obedience. It isn't really important that we don't talk at meals, but we still need, for other less obvious reasons, to maintain the impression that we adhere to the established rules."

"It sounds like you have rules that aren't necessary."

"That's true. However, we need to be taken seriously by Rome," explained Catherine.

"In many convents what happened was that some of the nuns who stayed got rid of their habits, and moved out into their own apartments, while getting jobs in other professions besides teaching. Some became community activists, lawyers, counselors, hospital chaplains, nurses, church secretaries, and even Midwives. The end result was that many nuns actually left the convents, deciding that they could serve God and the poor better on their own. And of course, women's lib helped push them along too."

"Women's what?" asked Abby.

"In the nineteen sixties there was a movement called 'Women's Liberation.' The purpose was to gain for women equal social and economic status with men.

And then along came the sexual revolution and the pill. All of these changes in society contributed to the sought after freedom by some young nuns to live their lives free from the previous constraining rules of the Catholic Church regarding women."

"So you are saying that nuns liked Vatican II's new rules, right?" Abby interjected.

"Yes and no. There is a down side to all of this. Convents no longer gained new Postulants. Some convents closed, and some had to join together to be large enough to sustain themselves. There were some who simply moved to a more active convent.

Our convent had a long and proud history, having been founded back in eighteen eighty-five. The governing council of the convent didn't want to close its doors, and they were so isolated geographically that they couldn't very well join with another convent. But these were a strong group of women, who surely didn't rely on men to solve their problems.

Remember what I told you about settling the Dakotas? If a woman came out here, and actually stayed, she was of pretty hearty stock! After a lot of discussion, they hit upon a method of sustaining their membership. Although it wouldn't have been approved by the Catholic Diocese, these women were able to pull it off without their methods being discovered.

Sometime I may share a couple of the ideas that they implemented to generate income and remain viable," Catherine stated, as she began to unravel some of the mystery.

CHAPTER SEVENTEEN

Emily's Story

My older brother is just one year older than me. When we were little we were playmates and had so much fun together. But when he was in his early teens, he started to look at me in a different way. Sometimes when we were horsing around, he would try to touch my chest. Sometimes he even put his hand between my legs, when I had my jeans on.

At first I tried to excuse it, thinking those instances were just accidents. One day when he was fourteen and I was thirteen, we were home alone. I was listening to music in my room with my earphones on. Something touched my shoulder. I turned around and there he stood, with his pants unzipped. I was so shocked. I had never seen a boy's private area, and I stared. I was frozen numb. He shoved me onto my bed, and pulled down my jeans. Then he put his hand inside my underwear. He started touching me down there. I was terrified. Suddenly he was on top of me and pushed himself inside me. I screamed for him to stop, but no one was home to hear me. It hurt so much. When he was finished, he left my room and said nothing. I cried and cried. Then I ran to my bathroom and took a long shower, sobbing the whole time.

I couldn't tell anyone. A couple of weeks later, he came into my room after I had been asleep awhile, and did it again. I tried and tried to push him off. I didn't want my parents to hear me scream. That was the beginning of months of abuse by my brother. He did start using a condom, so at least I didn't get pregnant. My grades started to slip. I didn't feel like seeing my friends. I hardly spoke at mealtimes.

My parents started to worry, and couldn't figure out what might be wrong. Finally my Mom said either I needed to talk to her, or she would make an appointment for me with the school counselor. I couldn't let anyone at school know, not even the counselor. So I told Mom what had been happening. Needless to say, my parents were shocked and mortified. But you know, a family is a family. They loved my brother too, and decided to send him to counseling. Of course they didn't want to press charges. A scandal like that would have devastated our family. Mom wanted me to talk to our family priest, but I just couldn't.

I talked to a Christian counselor for a while, but I couldn't relax and live in that house anymore. Mom had heard of the school in this convent, where I could finish high school. It's hard to have a secret like mine. If I tell anyone, I'm afraid no one will be my friend, even Abby.

CHAPTER EIGHTEEN

Judy's Story

Emily, what's wrong? Don't you feel well?" Catherine stopped by Emily's cell one day after classes. "I saw you in the hallway this afternoon, and you looked like you had been crying."

At that, Emily began to sob. "It's just that I thought I was handling my situation okay, but when I hear Hannah talking about what her life has been like, it brings it all back to me."

"Why Emily, I'm so sorry. I thought you had dealt with the incest months ago."

"So did I, and I confessed to a priest, even when it wasn't my fault. But I still feel like I can't forgive myself."

"There is someone here that it would be good for you to talk to. I know you may not think that she will be compassionate, but I believe you will be surprised.

Marguerite's job as prioress is to be a Mother to all the rest of us, and she does that job very well. I'll set up an appointment for you and explain a little about what happened with your brother. I'm sure she will be able to make you see that whatever has happened in your life, you can be forgiven."

Emily timidly knocked on the Prioress's door. Marguerite offered a warm welcome and invited the teenager to have a seat. The older woman crossed the space between her desk and Emily in a few steps and sat down beside her, gently reaching for her hand.

"I'm so glad you have come to have a little visit with me, Emily. Sometimes just talking out our problems puts them into proper perspective. I understand that you have been through a very traumatic time at home. Even though it was several months ago, it probably manages to remain at the front of your mind. Catherine has explained to me some of what you have experienced. The easiest way for us to cope with our problems is to share them. One of my favorite Bible passages is Jeremiah 29:11, 'For I know the plans I have for you, declares the Lord, plans to prosper you and not to harm you, plans to give you hope and a future.'

Would you like to share with me how your brother's behavior makes you feel?" Marguerite silently handed Emily a tissue.

Tears began to flow as she haltingly told the Prioress as much as she could manage about the months of sexual abuse by her brother. "The hardest part of all is that I can't forgive myself. Even though I know it was not my fault, I still feel so dirty and sinful for what happened to me."

Marguerite gently took Emily's face in her hands and looked deeply into her eyes. "You are forgiven. God forgives you, and I forgive you. Now you must forgive yourself.

Let me tell you a story about how a woman's life can be changed by the influence of the religious life," Marguerite began.

"In the fall of nineteen sixty-four a girl named Judy was a junior in high school with great prospects for her future. Fairly popular, she was on the cheerleading squad, a member of the varsity chorus, and played girls' basketball. In addition, she joined various clubs and had a wide range of friends. By the end of the school year she even had a boyfriend. Judy was a tall girl, with rather pretty sculpted features, and beautiful blonde hair. She had attracted the attention of a senior named Jim who was one of the really popular boys in school. They made a striking pair and were the envy of many of Judy's classmates. Judy's naivety was no match for Jim's sophistication. Jim's dad was a professional business man and they had a standing reservation at the local country club, along with other doctors, lawyers, and business entrepreneurs. His mother was a typical stay at home mom of the sixties, spending her time making a beautiful home for her family. Jim and his sister were used to going to Colorado on ski trips over Christmas vacation, as well as summer trips to the Florida beaches.

Judy had caught Jim's eye and was giddy when he asked her to accompany him to a movie. Judy's parents were an average middle class family. She wore box pleated skirts and twin sweater sets to school with her penny loafers. She and Jim listened to Beatles music on his car radio. During the week, after her homework was done, Judy could watch TV with the family. Of course, no teenager had a TV in her bedroom. On weekends, Judy looked forward to dates with her boyfriend. She would spend a great deal of time rolling her flip hairdo, and teasing or backcombing to get the bouffant look Jim liked.

The following summer brought many dates, spending time with friends and spending many hours alone together. Jim had graduated from high school in May, and was heading to college at South Dakota State University in the fall. The summer was filled with swimming parties, roller skating, and drive in movies. Judy thought she must be in love. Jim, on the other hand was just enjoying his last summer before college.

Judy's mother was worried as any mother would be with her sixteen year old daughter spending so much time with an eighteen year old boy, but of course his family was well known in the city, and attended the same Lutheran Church in Sioux Falls that the Bjorgs attended. By the middle of the summer, however, Judy no longer protested Jim's insistent kisses and surrendered her body and will to his on her seventeenth birthday. By the time Jim was getting ready to leave for college in August, Judy began to panic when she realized she must be pregnant. It didn't take Mrs. Bjorg long to notice something was wrong, and confronted her daughter.

"Mom, I am so sorry," sobbed Judy. "I just love him so much." In the sixties, I'm sorry to say, pregnant unwed mothers were not yet allowed into high school classrooms, and instead were hidden away in special residential homes, termed 'Homes for Unwed Mothers.'

There was such a home in Sioux Falls, and it was even sponsored by the Lutheran Church, but the Bjorgs were mortified that their 'good girl' daughter had become one of those girls. It was a different time, and attitudes were more rigid. Instead they cast their net farther away for a location where Judy could disappear with the least amount of questions. Fortunately for the Bjorgs, Mr. Bjorg had a sister living in Rapid City. However, she had five children of her own, and regretfully explained that she just did not have room to take Judy in for the duration of the pregnancy. Then an idea struck her. There was a Catholic convent about fifty miles away, and they had upon occasion taken in unwed girls. The Bjorgs were none too happy to send their precious Judy to be cared for by Catholic women, but the convent did seem to be the perfect answer. They could tell their friends and fellow church members that Judy's aunt in Rapid City needed help with her large family and Judy would be close enough to her in case of emergency. They could even bolster their lie with the suggestion that Judy may start college classes early in Rapid City. This would give the Bjorgs an excuse to take a trip across the state. So arrangements were made and when school was beginning in September, Judy was deposited in the convent here at Scenic, when her friends were starting their senior year of high school back in Sioux Falls.

Judy had been on several trips across the state to visit her aunt and uncle and cousins in Rapid City, and the family had spent many happy vacations touring the beautiful Black Hills. Even though she was heartbroken over her circumstances, she was familiar with the beauty of this treasured vacation spot. One of her favorite memories was of being surrounded by the fresh smell of pine trees. She remembered how she had always loved driving with her family from Rapid, as the locals called the town, out onto Needles Highway, Mount Rushmore, and all the scenic twists and turns throughout the Hills.

But when her dad took the exit off the freeway that headed toward the Badlands Loop, Judy exclaimed, "I thought this was near the Black Hills, Dad."

With his jaw firmly set, Mr. Bjorg continued driving. The next sign indicated a road toward Saddle Pass. "Saddle Pass! Where exactly are you taking me?" demanded Judy. Half a mile past Sage Creek Rd. Mr. Bjorg turned off onto a gravel road which wound back close to a mile and opened up into a hidden clearing. Looming in front of them was an imposing old stone building mostly hidden by a tall stockade fence.

"Honey, it will only be for the school year," Mrs. Bjorg declared.

"Are you talking about this convent?" asked Emily.

"Yes, Emily, it was this very convent." Marguerite continued with her story.

"In the spring of nineteen sixty-six Judy gave birth to a baby girl in the convent. Fortunately, the nuns had experience with babies who were put up for adoption. The baby was kept in the convent nursery while Judy attended classes in the convent school. She had no trouble keeping up with her studies, and was able to finish her senior year by June. Mrs. Bjorg told Judy, "Now you can come home for the summer, and get enrolled into college in the fall, and no one will be the wiser."

"What about my baby, Mom?" questioned Judy.

"Of course it will be put up for adoption. Your dad and I have already spoken to the Prioress about that," answered Mrs. Bjorg.

"Adoption? No way Mom," Judy shouted at her mother. "I am keeping Carrie. She is mine and I love her more than anything."

"And just how do you plan to do that? It has always been our wish for you to have a college education, and you can't manage that with a baby. Your dad and I will pay for your college expenses but we certainly will not help you raise an illegitimate child. And what would our friends think? What would the church members say? What would your high school friends say about you? We so carefully have covered this entire thing up so that none of us have to go through life tainted by your behavior," Mrs. Bjorg firmly retorted.

"You still have a chance to clean up your life and save your family from disgrace, Judy."

"Just leave and let me stay here at the convent for a couple more weeks. I can't say goodbye to her yet," sobbed Judy, as she stubbornly refused to pack up and leave.

The Bjorgs reluctantly drove back to Sioux Falls without their daughter.

Judy sat in her room and brooded for hours. After the tears subsided, she walked over to the nursery and picked up her baby girl. Judy held little Carrie close and kissed her and whispered, "You're mine, and you will stay mine. I love you to the moon. No one is going to take you from me."

The next morning Judy asked for a meeting with the Prioress. "Good Morning, Judy," smiled the Prioress. "I saw you with your parents yesterday. I know you are getting ready to leave us and get back to your own life. The paperwork has been done for the adoption of the baby, and I have prospective parents coming tomorrow to meet her. Soon this will all be a memory that you must banish and get on with your education."

"Please, please, isn't there some way you can help me to keep Carrie?" begged Judy, tears streaming down her cheeks. "Can't I just stay here? Can't we live here with the nuns?"

"Judy, you aren't even a Catholic!" exclaimed the astounded Prioress, Sister Evangeline.

"What do I have to do to be a Catholic then?" Judy posed the question.

"You would have to leave the protestant faith and go through Catholic instruction. Then you would become a Candidate, then a Novice, and after a few years you would profess and take vows of poverty, celibacy, and obedience," the Prioress carefully spelled out. "There is no quick fix."

"Is that what the nuns here did?" asked Judy. "If they did it, I can too."

"I don't believe we have ever had a protestant girl become a Catholic nun, Judy. It would be very unusual, and a lot of studying. I doubt if you even understand the ramifications of poverty, celibacy, or obedience for that matter," the Prioress declared, with a firm look at Judy. But Judy had over the past few months made quite a favorable impression on the Prioress, who had watched her diligently keep up her studies, slip into the nursery on every free moment, and fulfill her housekeeping duties as assigned to her by Sister Evangeline. Baby Carrie was a favorite of all the older nuns, who also slipped into the nursery on free time. Her big blue eyes, strawberry blonde curls, and eager smiles filled the hearts of many childless women with a maternal love that had been denied them. The Prioress knew she should have pushed harder for an adoptive couple to take the baby, as she had in previous situations, but something in Judy Bjorg's determination and maturity kept her from taking the adoptive steps sooner, even though Judy's parents fully expected her to assist in the adoption and trusted her to carry it out as soon as possible. They were after all very generous with the financial arrangements that had been made to the convent to keep Judy during her pregnancy. Judy also displayed a real curiosity about the Catholic faith, attending mass and prayers with the nuns and making friends with the young Catholic girls attending the convent school. Her faith had come to life while participating in religious classes and she particularly loved the chants and hymns.

Sister Evangeline mulled this proposal of Judy's over for days, discussing it with the local Priest and some of the older nuns. Finally she called Judy to her office and questioned her on her determination to become a Catholic nun.

The Prioress raised the question, "How will you convince your parents that they should let you do this?"

"I'll be eighteen in July and then they can't force me to do anything."

That summer was the beginning of Judy's immersion into the spiritual life of the convent. She officially became a Candidate, then a Novitiate, made her temporary vows, and made her final Profession in the fall of 1969.During this time little Carrie was cared for by the entire house full of women. She attended the convent school while her mother left the confines of the convent to attend college. When Judy graduated from college, she returned to the convent, serving in a teaching capacity. Most young nuns, when they had completed their Final Profession, left the confines of the Mother House, as it was also known, and moved out to a "mission" as their positions or jobs were commonly called. Usually it was to a church in another small town, teaching catechism to the youth, visiting the sick, and any other duties as needed. This was a most unusual situation, for a nun to be raising her own child, but the Prioress had pulled a few strings and to outward appearances, little Carrie was just another child of an unwed mother, or perhaps a boarding school child at the Convent school. The Prioress felt that it was in the best interests of all concerned that Judy stay close to her daughter, as some of the other nuns were getting too attached to the child.

Outwardly, however, I did not acknowledge that I was Carrie's mother, and eventually the nuns began to forget the unusual circumstances of this beautiful girl's childhood.

My name, when my final profession came, was changed to the religious name, Marguerite, which I will use for the remainder of my life."

Emily's mouth fell open and she sat staring at the Prioress. "You are Judy?"

"Yes, Emily, I am Judy."

"You had a baby here? What happened to her?"

"She grew up to have a good life too. After finishing her high school education here, she went away to college to prepare for a job, just like most of the nuns have done. My daughter took her final vows and is a dedicated and wonderful nun. So you see, regardless of what happened in my past, what I did wrong was forgiven, and I have a very fulfilled life. The same can happen for you."

CHAPTER NINETEEN

"I know it's getting late, Sam, but now you have to tell me what happened to the priest and your brother," coaxed Danielle, as she sipped her second cup of tea. Sam glanced at the clock.

"After Eddie realized just what he had done, he grabbed me and shoved me toward the door.

"Run to the dorm room right now," he hissed.

I took off as fast as I could with him right behind me. We were running pell mell toward our hallway when Father Peters stepped around the corner. I ran blindly into his chest.

"Whoa there, boys," he called. "What is the hurry?"

"Oh, nothing. We were just racing," Eddie tried to convince the priest.

"Now you know better than to run in the halls. Take it outside," he scolded.

"Yes, Father," said Eddie.

"Yes, Father," I echoed.

"Of course, it wasn't long before we heard an ambulance speeding down the road, its siren blaring. Eddie and I hid in the exercise yard as long as we could. We saw the ambulance attendants slide Father Tobias through the open ambulance doors."

"Do you think he is dead?" My chin trembled when I looked at Eddie. He wiped a couple of tears from his face.

"I don't know, Sam," he choked.

"Oh Sam, how awful for you boys," said Danielle as she dissolved into tears.

Sam continued, "When the bell rang for supper, we knew we had to go in or there would be punishment for sure. Once through the door, Father Peters grabbed both of us by the arms, one in each of his hands. I probably don't need to tell you anymore, Danny. It was obvious that we were running from something and even Eddie wasn't a very good liar. He told the truth. But the truth did not set him free. The reservation got him a lawyer. A good lawyer from Rapid City. But the Catholic Diocese could afford the best. Their lawyer pointed out that Eddie was a poor Indian kid who already had to be taken from his home and put into a boarding school. That was so unfair. All Indian kids were taken from their homes. And he had stabbed a priest.

'A priest, for God's sake,' the lawyer banged his fist on the table.

Who was going to sympathize with an Indian kid who stabbed a priest? Especially when the priest was only giving his little brother a candy bar. Yes, the lawyer actually said that in court. No one would acknowledge that there was any truth to the accusations by kids. They tried to charge him with attempted murder.

Our lawyer argued for self-defense, which can be used when the person reasonably believes that it is necessary to protect either himself or someone else. The problem was that the person must use no more force than that which appears reasonably necessary to the situation. Eddie had a six inch long sharp dressmaking shears and the priest had no weapon.

However our lawyer got it reduced to assault with a deadly weapon. Eddie was only fifteen, so he was sent to a Juvenile Detention Center. There was a lot of publicity about the case state wide. I suppose most people sympathized with the priest, since in the seventies who would have thought a priest would sexually abuse anyone, much less a child. But there were supporters for Eddie too. A protest was staged in front of the court house when he was sentenced and there were a lot of coffee house discussions for a few weeks. The local newspaper was full of letters to the editor and editorials. Then the furor died down and Eddie was locked up."

CHAPTER TWENTY

A new assignment came Abby's way. Now she was to work in food service. She had helped her mom in the kitchen since she was really young, so she found this job to be much better than the laundry service. The prospect of handling food that others might appreciate was a far better thought than handling other's dirty laundry. As a little girl, she used to stand on a stool in the kitchen and sneak the chocolate chips from the package while Mom mixed up the cookie dough. Sometimes she would slip under the table while nibbling chocolate. "Where is Abby?" Mom would tease. "Is she hiding? I can't find her. Abby, where are you?"

By the time she was thirteen, there was no need to hide while she sneaked treats. She was proud of the fact that she had learned to mix and knead bread dough almost as well as Mom. Sometimes she had made a nuisance of herself at the restaurant asking Antonio questions about cooking. Because of this background, she didn't feel as intimidated starting this new assignment as she had her first week in laundry.

Abby still longed for the days when she had dropped by the restaurant after school and Dad had stopped whatever he was doing to spend a few minutes talking with her. She was his only child and he loved having a daughter to show off to his customers. "Abby, when you finish college you can join me as my partner and then take over the restaurant on your own when you are ready," he'd grin. "So keep up the grades, and be especially attentive to your math skills. That's what keeps us profitable. Oh, and of course a great chef helps too," he would wink at her as Antonio shot him a look.

Sister MaryAnn started Abby off washing dishes, but it wasn't long before she was moved to preparation work. While peeling potatoes, slicing carrots, shredding cabbage, or chopping peppers she would drift back to the happy times with Mom in their kitchen. Even though she hadn't worked in the restaurant, she was an excellent cook and loved preparing a good meal for Dad and Abby.

"How can I compete with Antonio?" she'd ask Dad.

"Oh, Diane, your food is packed with love," he'd reply, "while Antonio's food is packed with cream and butter!"

The longer Abby worked in the kitchen, the more curious behavior she observed.

Some of the food from each meal was dumped together and pureed in a large blender until it became a grayish concoction. About thirty minutes before the Sisters arrived for a meal, MaryAnn would divide it into smaller containers marked B or E. A few of these she would mark RE.

All of these she would set on a rolling cart and tell Anna to take this order to the infirmary. Once she asked Anna what this mixture was used for in the infirmary. "Their meals, of course," was the reply. "It is just nutritious food pureed so they can eat it, just like a smoothie."

"Why is it pureed?"

"The B containers are for the babies who need soft food, and the E's are for the elderly who are not well enough to chew their food. It gives them nourishment without effort," she clarified.

"What about those marked RE?" Abby probed. She had noticed that these were a much thinner mixture. "I am not sure, but I think they are for the really elderly who don't need as much food for each meal," Anna guessed.

CHAPTER TWENTY-ONE

Abby bit her lip trying to hold back the tears as she remembered that evening when Dad and she had left the restaurant to pick up Mom from the dress shop.

It was still winter and one of those Midwestern nights when it was so cold the snow squeaked with each step. The street lights did their best to put on happy faces in spite of the cold. Holiday shoppers were hurrying along with their warmest coats, boots and mittens. Scarves were twisted around heads and necks to block out the wind. As they had approached Mom's street, they saw her huddled in her new fuchsia wool coat, waiting outside the shop with packages in both hands. "Looks like your mom is taking advantage of her employee discount again," Dad laughed. Mom had become quite the urbane clotheshorse with all the tempting outfits surrounding her each day. Tied around her throat was a teal and fuchsia scarf with one end pinned to her lapel with a jazzy brooch. She had a little teal tam perched jauntily on her head.

A huge smile crossed her eyes when she spied them. Dad slowed the car for a red light and she stepped off the curb to cross the street. One of her parcels must have blocked her view momentarily. Abby shuddered as she remembered how just as Mom took her second step onto the roadway a car came speeding in the left lane of traffic, running the red light and slamming into her.

CHAPTER TWENTY-TWO

One February morning before breakfast, the girls followed Sarah from their cells to the Chapel. There the tradition of Ash Wednesday was being observed. The women were lined up, and each kneeled before one of three nuns who were using their thumb to imprint dry ashes on the forehead in the sign of a cross of each Sister present. Sarah had told the young girls that it was a sign of repentance and they were welcome to receive the symbol.

Sister Leah's classroom was always a comforting haven for Abby, Hannah, and Emily. This nun was a pleasant young woman in her mid-twenties with a round friendly face and a ready laugh. As a child Emily had attended mass with her parents and had been active in a youth group until the dark and terrible secret began. She had begun finding excuses to stay away from her friends, and stayed in her room after school. "Maybe if I pretend I'm not a part of the family anymore he will leave me alone," she reasoned. Emily was afraid that she might say something to one of her friends that would reveal her secret. Attending her local Catholic church only made her feel more and more filled with sin. There was all the talk about confession, but how could she confess something that her brother was doing to her?

Abby's family worshipped in a local Protestant church in her neighborhood, but she didn't know much about Catholicism.

Sister Leah quickly realized that Hannah had no understanding at all of religion. The girl had lived a degrading life on the streets of Chicago, and the only times she heard about God or Jesus was when her father was using them in a profane way. Her perception of a father was of a terrifying authority who could force you to do whatever he wanted. Sister Leah loved history, and was able to kindly and gently work into her lesson plans the history of Christianity. Hannah listened with curiosity, then began to ask questions. She realized even she could be forgiven and maybe even someday have a safe and beautiful life like Sister Leah.

This gentle young nun explained that Lent is the season lasting forty days, not counting Sundays, between Ash Wednesday and Easter when Christians repent of their sins and prepare for Easter. She asked the girls if they would like to begin worshipping with the Convent Sisters on Sunday mornings in their chapel.

On the walk back to their cells, Emily remarked, "I sure like Sister Leah. She has a cute dimple, doesn't she?"

"I hadn't noticed. Just one dimple?" asked Abby.

"Yeah, funny isn't it? Just one dimple."

As Easter approached, the snow melted and the days began to get longer. The freshness of spring, the birds, and the warmer weather all helped buoy up Abby's spirits, as she continued to write letters to Dad. He now explained that he was meeting with lawyers and the case against Frankie was closer to going to court. "But a case like this will go on for quite a while, Abby, so I have to stay heavily guarded until it is all over. I miss my little girl so much. Are you doing well in classes? I know you will do your best even under the circumstances."

Abby wrote back to Dad often, assuring him that she was continuing her studies. "I even like some of the nuns a lot, Dad. Our history teacher is the coolest yet. And Sister Catherine promised to take me for a drive through the Badlands now that the snow is melted. She says they are really beautiful in their own weird way."

The last days before Easter, the 'cash cows' as Sarah had called them, returned for a long weekend. These young and middle aged nuns had Easter break at the schools where they were teachers. It was a lot more fun when they were around. The ones from Sioux Falls gossiped among themselves about problems within the Diocese. Abby overheard bits of quiet conversations about some of the priests. The nuns serving in Rapid City told stories about attending rodeos in the

Black Hills, and how the young cowboys wore big hats and sometimes long coats, which they referred to as dusters. Sister Lois asked why they called a coat a duster. "The idea originally was that when a man on a horse wore a long coat, it would protect his clothes from trail dust," explained Sister Susanna, who worked in one of the small churches on the far western side of the state. "Some coats are light tan, but others are black. Seriously, if you were a little near-sighted, you might mistake them for a group of nuns walking down the street," commented Sister Susanna. All the women within earshot burst into laughter.

"Now I have never been mistaken for a cowboy," interjected Sister Rachel.

"I really do appreciate being allowed to wear secular clothing these days," spoke up Sister Naomi. "But I know why those of you here in the Mother House have to 'keep the Habit,' " she commented. Several women exchanged knowing glances. "It must be hard for our 'guests' to conform, but of course a secret is hard to keep if all the rules aren't followed," Sister Naomi smiled sympathetically.

"Has Phoebe arrived yet?" questioned one of the Sisters. "I think she'll be dropping off her parcel in a week or two," surmised Rachel.

"How long has it been since we lost Sister Agatha?" wondered Sister Lois.

"I think it was late summer," responded Rachel. "She left quite a legacy, and I still miss her. When I was a Novice, she used to tell our class stories about when she first came here in the fifties. Of course that was several years before Vatican II. She told how the girls had their hair cut off under that cap. For some having their long hair chopped off was traumatic, even though they had chosen the life, and knew all the rules."

"Didn't they wear the veil back then too?" asked Lois.

"Oh, yes, not only the veil, but first the wimple which covered the neck and chest, the cap tied under the chin, the bandeau across the forehead, and to top it all off, over the tunic went the scapular, which was like an apron. There was even a cappa, or cape to go over all that. And don't forget the cincture."

"The what?" Abby wanted to know.

"The belt that you see Mother Marguerite wear, with her rosary attached. Sister Agatha said when she first met the Mother Superior of that time, she was scared to death when she saw that belt with what looked like a chain hanging from it. She didn't understand that was how the prayer beads were worn. I know the older nuns used to tell us how strict the rules were then. I am surprised that so many stayed after they got a glimpse of life in a convent. But they had an idealized picture of a nun in a habit, which to many at that time inspired awe and reverence. I don't think Sister Agatha or many of the other older ones really ever regretted their choices. Most of us don't have regrets either."

Abby still viewed this lifestyle as unnatural and couldn't help but wonder what her friends in Chicago would say if they knew she lived with nuns and wore one of their habits every day. If they even remembered her any more.

The observances of Holy Week began with Palm Sunday and culminated on Easter morning. The mood within the convent walls during the week was one of reverent respect of religious traditions. Abby and her new friends observed at close hand the Catholic traditions of Maundy Thursday and attended chapel with the nuns on Good Friday as they followed the Stations of the Cross.

Easter morning brought all the women out for a Sunrise service. The setting was an early morning outdoor church service. Apparently this convent owned several acres of surrounding land. They walked silently single file in the darkness from the Convent grounds down a rocky path toward the overwhelming background of the Badlands. Never had Abby imagined anything so stirring to her soul as witnessing the gospel coming alive amid the background of this ancient creation. The nuns had called this a sunrise service, and after all of the women had gathered in a group, they began singing

"Alleluia." Right on cue, the sun began to peek over the horizon and continued to show itself as the singing nuns coaxed it higher and higher. After each one had made her way back up the path to the convent, they were treated to a special breakfast of hot cross buns and chokecherry jelly, along with cups of steaming coffee. The rest of this Easter Sunday was spent in relaxation, board games, charades, and chatting. Abby almost forgot to feel sorry for herself for a brief time while she realized she could have fun learning to know these women and their lifestyle. Later in the day they were served a dinner of ham, scalloped potatoes, caramelized carrots, hot rolls, and Abby's favorite, apple pie. If only this meal could have been shared with Mom and Dad.

CHAPTER TWENTY-THREE

As the months passed, little by little, bits were revealed of the lives of a few more of the Sisters in the house. One day when Beverly was teaching Abby how to sew a new cloak for herself, she asked her just why they had to wear these garments. They were dark and hot and it was late spring. The days were getting longer and the sun heated up the walls and floors. There was no air-conditioning in this old building. She wasn't used to living without it. Trying to sleep in her little cramped "cell" was beginning to have a real stifling effect on Abby. Sometimes she felt that she had been transported back in time. They were so isolated and she was very lonely. "Abby, we need to wear these habits like the nuns used to all wear before Vatican II," she tried to explain.

"There we go again, all this talk about Vatican II," Abby retorted. "Don't you ever get tired of being a nun, Sister Beverly?" She challenged.

"Actually, Abby, I am not a nun at all."

"What do you mean?" Abby responded incredulously. She had never suspected that there might be several others here with something to hide too.

Beverly continued in her clipped New York accent, "I am actually in hiding, and I suspect you are too. It isn't a pretty story, but I may as well tell you about my life. Maybe you won't feel so alone if you can share your fears and feelings with me. Do you know anything about the mob?" probed Beverly.

There was that word again. Mob. Organized crime, Dad had explained.

"I grew up in New York City. After high school, I met a handsome man who swept me off my feet. I was shy, and he was friendly with a great smile. I was working as a seamstress in the garment district. Tony would come in often, slipping into the back room to 'conduct business' with the owner.

Each time he showed up, he would stop by my work station and make small talk. He would complement me on how pretty I looked, or how much he liked my hair, or even that he was impressed with how efficiently I did my sewing.

It didn't take long for him to ask me out. We had a wonderful courtship. He had plenty of money, and knew of great restaurants. The maître d' always gave us a good table, and knew Tony by name. When I brought him home to meet my parents, he knew all the right things to say to my mom to make her feel good too. But Dad said he thought Tony was 'too slick.' 'You better keep an eye on him, Bev. Be sure he is on the up and up before you get too involved.'

But of course by then I had fallen in love. Tony and I were married when I was nineteen. He was twenty-four, and well established in his family's business. He said he was in textiles, and that his dad and two brothers were all in this business together. It wasn't long before I noticed things about him that made me very uneasy. He had bought us a cute little house and he always drove a fancy car. But other men would show up at the house, and he would take them into his den and shut the door.

One day when I was cleaning I opened a desk drawer to drop in some pens and pencils and I found a couple of guns. Tony must have forgotten to lock that drawer. He liked guns, and had some in a gun safe in the basement. I knew a lot of men liked guns, and I had thought his were safely kept locked up. But when I realized he had two guns in a desk drawer, I got scared. He had a bad temper once in a while, and I knew better than to ask him anything about the guns. I couldn't tell anyone about my discovery. I certainly wouldn't tell my dad, as he had warned me, and I couldn't tell Mom, as she would have been terrified, and would tell my dad.

Sometimes I would hear Tony talking on the phone in his den, with the door shut. When I asked him why he had the door shut when he used the phone, he would reply, 'Babe, it's just business, and I don't want to bore you.'

Things got worse between us. He seemed to be under a lot of pressure, and started yelling some really nasty accusations at me. Then he would storm out of the house. Hours later when he came back he would smell of booze, and be all cozy and sweet, as if nothing had happened. One evening the phone rang. After he finished his conversation, he came out and told me he had a little work to do at the office. He headed toward the front door, as I headed in the other direction toward our bedroom. I turned and looked just as he reached under his jacket. I caught a glimpse of a gun tucked into his waistband.

Later that evening on the TV news, there was a story about someone having been gunned down in the garment district. The TV reporter said that the mob was suspected.

That's when I was sure Tony was involved. I was scared to death. I wanted out of this mess. I did go to my parents and tell them what I suspected. Dad had a lawyer friend who was able to get me a divorce but of course Tony would never leave me alone. Although there was no reason for him to think that I knew what he had done, we all knew he would pursue me and killing me wouldn't be out of the question. Revenge was always the name of the game with organized crime. I had turned my back on him and embarrassed him.

That's when the lawyer came up with an idea. He knew of this convent out in western South Dakota that was in a barren, remote spot. He had a great aunt who was a nun there. So he made the contacts and they agreed to let me hide out here for as long as I needed. You see, I am hiding much as I suspect you are." Beverly ended her narrative with a sad smile.

CHAPTER TWENTY-FOUR

Sam looked up with a quick grin at the sound of Danielle's soft tap.

"Danny, what a nice surprise. I thought maybe you were avoiding me so you wouldn't have to hear any more of my sad tales."

"Hardly, Sam. Actually I have been thinking about you a lot lately," she stated with earnestness.

"Oh, ho, can't get me off your mind, huh?" he flirted.

"Okay, take it easy. I only meant that I have been thinking about some of the things you told me and I realized that you never explained why you have been visiting your brother in the penitentiary if he was only given juvenile detention until he turned eighteen. Did I miss something there?" Danielle raised her eyebrows.

"Oh, that. I didn't intentionally leave it out, but Eddie's story just keeps on getting more and more complicated. He is one of those men who just can't leave his past behind and make a new life. He went straight for a few years in his twenties. Then he got mixed up in drugs and started stealing to support his habit. He got picked up a few times for minor things and served some jail time. For a while he cleaned up again. I tried and tried to help him but there is only so much you can do for someone who is intent on destroying himself. While he was on probation he held up a convenience store while armed. Of course that time he was sentenced to the state penitentiary."

"Oh, Sam, I am truly sorry. It must be terribly hard on you too," Danielle frowned.

Sam continued, "He is close to completing his time now and I am trying to get him into a rehab program that will actually work. Every time I make a trip west, I stop by to see him. He has no one else. He doesn't think anyone cares what happens to him. He is a poor Indian kid who grew up in poverty, was abused by those in authority, and when he saved me from that priest, he was rewarded with three years in a juvenile detention center.

There aren't many people I'm comfortable sharing this with either. This time I am going to try to get him to move to a different part of the state so he doesn't fall in with his local pals right away."

CHAPTER TWENTY-FIVE

Catherine tapped on her mother's cell door early one evening. "Come in, Catherine," invited the older woman. "How are things going with you?"

"Mother, I have come to get some information from you. It's private information, just between us. Please hear me out. You have never really told me about my father, much less who he is."

"Catherine, you know that I was one of the unwed mothers who came here to conceal my pregnancy, and give birth secretly. What more do you want to know? I haven't had any contact with him and don't know where he is," was the reply.

"But mother, I'd like to find him, to meet him, to know him," Catherine said.

"He has never cared about my well-being since he broke up with me over forty years ago. What makes you think he would care about you now?"

Catherine tried again, "Is it so wrong for me to want to know my own father? Maybe I have half-siblings. Maybe I look like him. Maybe I have his characteristics."

"Why, at your age, do you suddenly want to know?"

"Mother, I've wanted to know for a long, long time, but you never seemed willing to discuss it. Now that you are over sixty, I think it is past time to tell me." Catherine's mother sighed.

"You probably will still wonder if I am telling you the truth, so if you are that determined, go to our archive department. Your birth certificate is there. I've told you before what my family name was before I took my religious name. I just hope you won't be hurt or disappointed."

"Thank you. This won't change our relationship any, you know that. Good-night, Mother."

The next morning, Catherine slipped down to the archives office.

"Good Morning, Chloe," she greeted the Director of Archives.

"Why, hello Catherine. You don't make a visit to my office very often. Is there something I can help you find?"

"Oh, I don't want to bother you. I'm sure I can find it myself. Where do you keep old birth records?" asked Catherine.

"We have the last twenty years in the file cabinets in this room. We are in the process of computerizing them, but that is a big job. What year was the baby born? They are alphabetical by last name."

Catherine hesitated, then said, "I'm doing some research on our birth and adoption history. I need much older records than that."

"The older ones are in file boxes stored down in the records room. I think they go back to the seventies, or maybe even the sixties. I have been told that we started helping young unwed mothers as early as that when the homes for unwed mothers began to close. I'm sure you have a key to the records room, don't you?" Catherine nodded. "They are in boxes by year, then alphabetical. The baby's birth certificate is filed under the mother's name. Good luck," Chloe smiled.

Catherine hurried down to the basement where the old records were kept. This lowest level was dimly lit and seldom visited. Doors had old padlocks hanging from rusty locks. Convent records had been kept dating from 1885, sketchy as some of the hand written notebooks were. At least in this climate the oldest papers weren't likely to mildew. Catherine hadn't been down here in a long time. She flipped through the stash of keys she carried with her, finally finding one that was an old master key. Only the general council of women were allowed possession of master keys. As Director of Finance, she was part of the controlling core. Catherine stopped in front of the door labeled Births. Fitting the large key into the lock, she turned it and shoved the door open.

Inside, the air carried a dusty sour odor. File cabinets lined the walls, each labeled with the proper year, ranging from 1975 through 1989. Looking around, she noticed boxes shoved haphazardly up onto a metal shelf, marked 1974, 1973, 1972, 1971, 1970. The last box was hand printed 1966-1969. Hands shaking, she reached up and gently tugged it down. Surprisingly, the carton wasn't heavy. Pulling open a file cabinet drawer, she balanced the carton on top. Each box was sealed with packing tape, although some of the adhesive was loosening from the cardboard on the older boxes. Pulling the flaps up, Catherine reached inside and began thumbing through the papers. She didn't have to go far before she saw her mother's family name at the top of the page. Carefully lifting it out, she began to read. Date of birth: March 29, 1966 Sex: Female Father: Unknown. Catherine stared at the document. Father: Unknown. Disappointment and anger suddenly welled up inside. Shoving the carton's flaps back down, she didn't bother to affix the less than sticky tape back in place. Instead, she jammed the box back onto the shelf, slammed the file drawer shut, turned and ran out the door. Fumbling with the master key, tears blurring her eyes, she managed to lock up the records door marked Births, and raced up the stairs to confront her mother.

"You don't know for sure who my father is, do you, Mother?"

"Catherine! I can't believe you would imply that I had been with more than one boy. Of course I know who your father is."

"Did you love him?"

"Yes, yes. I loved him like any seventeen year old girl can love. Is that real love? I don't know. I have learned a lot about love in the succeeding years. There are many kinds of love."

"If you loved him, why didn't you list him on my birth certificate?" an indignant Catherine demanded. The astonished older woman could only gape at Catherine.

"But I did give his name as the father, when asked. The Mother General at the time must have chosen to leave his identity as unknown. In those days, the Catholic convents were much more secretive than now. They probably thought it best left this way. I'm sorry, Catherine. Your father's name is James Jackson. He never knew about you. We broke up before I knew that I was pregnant. My parents brought me here to hide their pregnant teenager from society, typical of the sixties. You are free to search for him, but I don't know any more than what I have told you. I had to close that chapter of my life, and it's too painful to reopen it."

Catherine put her arms around her mother. "I'm sorry, I didn't think about how difficult this would be for you. I was only thinking about myself. It must have been devastating to you for your boyfriend to break up with you and then find out you were pregnant. But you have been happy here, being a nun, haven't you?"

"Yes I have. Thanks be to God. My life has been very full. But a lot of that fulfillment has to do with being able to have you stay here where I can follow your life. I love you deeply, Catherine."

"And I love you to the moon, Mother. We have had good times when we could slip away together on our little sightseeing trips. Thank you for giving me this information. I needed it."

As soon as Catherine got settled into her office, she turned on her computer and pulled up Facebook. Although none of the Sisters were allowed to have personal accounts, the convent did maintain a business account, which was useful to promote their adoption agency and school. To the outside world they maintained an old fashioned persona of wearing habits, following strict rules, and not revealing too much about themselves. However, it was the twenty-first century. Younger nuns clamored for contact through social media. Part of the vow of obedience included a strict adherence to how much was revealed about life within.

Catherine sat tapping her pencil on her desk, sipping her coffee, wondering how she could use Facebook to search for her dad.

Picking up her cell phone, she punched in the contact number of her old college friend Julie. "You have reached Julie McCall," said her friend's voicemail. "I am not able to take your call at this time. Please leave a detailed message and I will get back to you."

"Hey, Julie, it's Catherine. Give me a call as soon as you get this. Oh, and don't worry, everything is OK. I just need some information. Thanks a bunch."

Now that Catherine had finally found out her dad's name, the search was on. The rest of the morning dragged on as she plowed through financial details while waiting for Julie's call. Leah stopped by for a quick chat.

"Catherine, I sort of mentioned to some of the history class girls that maybe I could twist an arm or two to take them out to see the Buffalo Roundup. Remember when we went out together with Lydia and took one of the other women hiding here at the time? It's a fun little trip and a great diversion."

"Leah, you don't have to try so hard to convince me. I'm all for it. I think the convincing needs to be done with the Prioress. It will depend on her mood. I'll leave that one up to you."

"Oh, Catherine, I was hoping you would ask her. She seems to always give you what you want. You have more pull than I do."

"No, not true. I am just a financial manager, pushing the money around. You on the other hand are a school teacher. The girls love you and look up to you. I'm sure the Prioress does too! Good luck!" Leah turned and gave Catherine a playful scowl as she went through the door.

When Catherine's cell phone jiggled, she grabbed it. "Hi, Cath, what's up?" she heard Julie ask.

"Oh, Julie, thanks for getting back to me so soon. I'm just wound up about something. You know how I have always wanted to know who my dad is, but my mother would not discuss it. She has finally caved under my pressure. Though not willingly. She gave me his name, but says she doesn't know anything more. Not even where he might be. I was wondering if we could use Facebook to put up a notice like those people you showed me on your account. You know, the ones who stand there holding a sign detailing where and when they were born, hoping someone will connect with some information?"

"I guess we could try that. But do you really want to post a picture of yourself in a Catholic nun's habit? A lot of people still feel that a nun should keep a low profile, excuse the pun! Maybe we could photograph you without the habit. You could wear some of my clothes. That way someone glancing at it wouldn't be distracted by the habit. Of course, we will have to post it through my account."

"Would that be OK with you, Julie? I really would appreciate your help."

"Yeah, sure. I'm fine with that. Can you drive out here this weekend? We'll catch up, make a sign, take a photo, and post it."

"All right! Thanks ever so much, Julie. See you on Saturday," said a grateful Catherine.

Later that evening Catherine found her mother quietly reading in a corner of the common room.

"I'm going to be gone for the weekend. I've decided to drive out to Rapid City to see Julie. We haven't caught up with each other for months."

"That sounds like a good idea, Catherine. Thanks be to God. Maybe it will help take your mind off this obsession with finding your father. Have a good time, and give my love to Julie."

After tossing a few weekend things into a bag, including a pair of jeans and a tee shirt that she kept shoved in the bottom of a drawer, Catherine jumped into her car and headed west on Saturday morning. She always loved this drive across the open spaces of South Dakota. After arriving in Rapid City, she drove on out to Nemo Road and pulled up in front of Julie's home. Still wearing her habit, Catherine grabbed her overnight bag and dashed to the front door. Just as she was about to ring the bell, the door flew open and an excited Julie opened her arms wide.

"Oh, oh, what have you done now, Julie, that requires you to confess to a nun?" Julie's husband, Rick reached for Catherine and wrapped her in a bear hug.

"Rick, if she needed to confess, I would have brought a priest along with me," chuckled Catherine. "It's just so great to see both of you."

"Come in and tell us about this crazy plan you have for finding your dad, Catherine," invited a more serious Rick.

"Oh, Rick, you know how I have always wanted to know more about my father. I finally got some information out of my mother, so I am enlisting Julie's help."

"If anybody can play detective, it is probably my wife," he laughed. After a few minutes, Rick excused himself and left the two women to their scheming.

"I'll go light the grill. I imagine you two will need protein to keep those devious brains focused on the issue at hand," laughed Rick.

"Julie, I'd really like to change out of my habit and be as comfortable as you look."

"Sure. Do you need to borrow a pair of jeans?"

"No, I keep one pair and a tee shirt hidden in the bottom of a drawer in my sleeping room. Although my mother would be mortified if she ever found out I did this," giggled Catherine.

Julie served a wonderful lunch of grilled trout and roasted vegetables over quinoa.

"I certainly didn't expect you to serve fish. I thought Rick would have wanted you to serve beef, having grown up on a cattle ranch."

"Oh, he usually does, but I try to get him to vary his diet with fish and fowl. And he did actually catch this trout himself up in Spearfish Canyon. He wanted you to see that I married a man with varied talents," smiled Julie.

"OK, I can take a hint. I'll clean up the lunch dishes so you girls can get to work on your, ah, project," conceded Rick.

"Come into my office, and we'll figure out what to put on the sign," suggested Julie. "I have poster board and markers in there." The two women settled down and drafted their notice.

> I am searching for my birth father.
> I was born on March 29, 1966 in South Dakota.
> My father's name is James Jackson.
> If you have any information on his whereabouts,
> please contact me through Facebook Message.

"Now for the photo. Catherine, why don't you put on a pretty blouse instead of that tee shirt? A teeny bit of makeup wouldn't hurt either, since you already are being disobedient to your dress code," smirked Julie with a giggle.

"Ok, ok, friend. I'll put on your blouse and a little lipstick," Catherine replied. "But no more trying to lead me astray, OK?"

After brushing her hair to a luster, she tossed her head, picked up the sign, and mugged for Julie's camera.

"Hey, that's really cute. This picture will probably bring a few replies from some lonely men, too."

"Stop it, Julie, you are making me nervous now. This is already difficult enough. What if I do find my father? I haven't thought about what I'd say."

"Now is a fine time to consider that!" retorted Julie. "OK, I am posting it right now. Too late to back out! Let's enjoy the rest of the weekend and give Facebook viewers time to find your photo."

"I'm glad we didn't use a phone number for response or I'd jump out of my skin every time it rang," Catherine commented.

After a relaxed weekend of catching up on each other's lives, Catherine changed back into her habit, packed up her overnight bag and got ready to get on the road.

"Just a minute. Let's at least check Facebook once before you leave. You know how fast social media travels." Julie pulled up her news feed with Catherine hanging over her shoulder. There were three comments from strangers wishing her luck, but nothing else.

As Rick gave her a hug goodbye he said, “You know I want you to find him if that’s really what you want, but I hope you won’t be disappointed. What if he turned out to be a guy like me?”

Julie and Catherine both burst out laughing, and Julie added, “You know Rick has a point there!”

CHAPTER TWENTY-SIX

Hannah joined Abby and Emily each day as they wound their way through the corridors from their cells over to the classrooms in the west wing. Sister Leah was teaching Native American history this term. Abby and Hannah didn't know much about South Dakota history but Emily had a better understanding of the lives the Native Americans had lived here on the prairie. Her ancestors had settled in the state back when the homesteading act was passed, and the Native Americans as a result were driven from their lands.

Sister Leah began by reminding the class how the Native Americans were the first inhabitants of the Americas. They had been hunters and fishermen long before they began to cultivate plants and harvest the edible portions for food. The girls were not very familiar with the history of the 1800's in the United States, but Abby volunteered, "I thought the Pilgrims and the Indians were friends back when they celebrated their Thanksgiving at Plymouth. What happened?"

"That's a good observation, Abby," Sister continued. "Back in the 1600's, the Indians, as they were then called, taught the settlers how to plant corn, or maize, pumpkins, and beans. The Pilgrims also learned where to hunt and fish from these native people. They actually even had a treaty with the local tribe which was honored during their lifetimes. Eventually, white people tried to force their ways of life on the Indians. For instance, the Native Americans believed in a spirit world, which permeated everything in their lives. They had no understanding of the earth being divided up and owned by individuals or groups. To them the land was their Mother, a nurturing force for everyone."

"Wow," said Emily, "I never thought of it that way before. That is kind of a nice thought. A little like 'Mother' Marguerite being a nurturing force for us, right?"

"That's very perceptive of you, Emily," responded Sister Leah.

"Didn't there used to be a lot more Native Americans in this country?" questioned Abby.

"Yes there were," responded Sister Leah. "But they had never been exposed to dreaded diseases like smallpox, measles, and typhus. The European settlers brought these diseases with them, and because the Indians had no resistance, it wasn't long before up to ninety percent of them had died from diseases, according to some estimates. And if that wasn't bad enough, the white settlers now wanted to get the natives off the land so that they could claim it as their property, and begin raising crops and pasturing livestock."

Hannah had attended school such a short time in her life that she was fascinated to quietly listen to stories of both the Native Americans and the Pioneers. She said little, but followed the conversations with interest.

"I thought there were treaties between the white man and the Indian that made it fair for both sides," ventured Emily.

"That's where we don't usually understand what really happened. Sometimes the Indian leaders were plied with alcohol before being asked to sign a treaty, and fraud was committed to take the land from them. Have you ever heard of Andrew Jackson's Indian Removal Act of 1830?" questioned Sister Leah.

"No, but it sounds unfair," said Abby.

"The removal act allowed the federal government to force the Native Americans to move from the southeastern part of the United States to west of the Mississippi River. The settlers wanted the land for raising their crops. Do you know what the Trail of Tears was?" questioned Sister Leah.

"I know I have heard of it but I don't really know what it was," answered Emily.

"I am going to give you reading assignments about this part of history. Next week I want reports from each of you on some aspect of the lives of Native Americans that you found interesting."

CHAPTER TWENTY-SEVEN

Sister Catherine knocked on Abby's door late one afternoon. "Would you like to help in the nursery for a couple of hours today, Abby?" she asked. "One of the Sisters who usually helps care for the preschoolers is sick today, and a little extra help is needed."

"Sure, I'd like that," Abby quickly answered. "I always liked playing with my little cousin, Vickie, back home. She is so cute and loved for me to read books to her."

"You certainly can do that here," assured Catherine. The two of them wound their way from third floor down to first, and then across to the west wing of the massive building. This was not far from the classrooms where Abby had heard children's voices.

Catherine introduced Abby to Sister Deborah, a woman Abby remembered seeing in the common room. Catherine made her way back to her office in the main part of the structure, leaving Abby to help with the little ones.

Two of the small girls shyly eyed this new person. Abby had an engaging smile when it came to children, and soon the preschoolers were eager to have her share in their pretend tea parties. "Would you like me to read you a story?" asked Abby. The girls climbed up beside her and snuggled one on each side, patiently waiting for Abby to begin. There was a stack of books on the low circular table in front of the sofa. Abby picked up the top one.

"Mary's New Baby Sister" was the name of the book. She opened it and began to read out loud.

"Mary's grandma told her that Mommy would be bringing a new little baby home today. Mary was so excited. She had waited and waited for this day. Mommy said that the baby would be very small and would not be able to do anything for herself. 'Just like you couldn't do anything alone when you were a tiny baby, Mary,' Mommy had said. Soon a car stopped outside the house, the front door opened, and in walked Mommy, carrying a very little bundle. 'Here is your new baby sister, Mary. Would you like to take a peek at her? She is sleeping, so be very quiet.' Mary tiptoed over to Mommy and looked at the baby. 'I will put her in her bed and then you and I can play, OK, sweetie?' Mommy came back and sat down and pulled Mary onto her lap. 'I love our new baby, but I will always love you. Now we are a family of three.' "

"Another Mary book, read another," begged one of the little girls.

"Which one would you like?" asked Abby. The girls both reached for a book and pulled a couple from the stack.

"This one, this one," said Clare.

"This one is called 'Mary Goes to School.' " Abby began reading, "It was the first day of school and Mary was excited. She had new shoes, a new dress, and her very own backpack. Mommy told her to eat her breakfast and then they would go to school. Mommy walked Mary to her classroom door, met the teacher, and hugged Mary good-bye. Mary was given a desk beside a little girl named Heather. There were other little girls in the classroom, but Mary couldn't remember their names. Mary loved the things she was allowed to do in school. The teacher read books and the girls learned to share crayons and coloring books. That night Mommy asked Mary if she had any new friends. 'Heather is my best friend, Mommy.' "

As Abby thumbed through the other books in front of her she noticed that they seemed to be a series of "Mary" books. Sister Deborah saw Abby glancing at the books. "Did you know these 'Mary' books are all written by one of our Sisters right here in the convent?" asked Deborah.

"There don't seem to be any men or boys in the stories," mentioned Abby.

"No, there aren't. They are special books for our little girls. We want the children to be comfortable with the idea that they live in a totally female world," Deborah told her.

CHAPTER TWENTY-EIGHT

Sister Leah had given her students a choice of Native American topics to write about. Abby sat in her cell in the evenings reading old history stories of how the Native Americans had been driven by the United States government from their homes. First she was going to write about "The Trail of Tears," but then ran across stories of the buffalo that had roamed this part of the country many years ago. Emily tapped on her cell door one evening. "How are you coming along on your report?" she asked.

"I am tired of reading about the sadness that the white people caused the Native Americans, so I wrote about the Crazy Horse Memorial," continued Emily.

"Oh, I know," said Abby, "but I have learned so much about this part of the United States, particularly the Dakotas, and also the Native Americans. I am actually glad that Sister Leah gave us a hard assignment. I just wish I could share it all with my dad."

"Why don't you send him a copy of your report along with your next letter?" suggested Emily.

"Hey, that's a great idea. He will really be proud of me, and maybe it will help take his mind off what is happening to him, too."

"Abby, you have never told me much about why you are here. You just said that you were being safely hidden here. Is your dad in big trouble? Is he going to prison?"

Abby could only respond with, "I have told you as much as I am allowed. And I really don't fully understand it all either. I think he doesn't tell me too much, so that I can't accidentally reveal something that might endanger either one of us."

"I hope I don't have to go first tomorrow when Sister asks for our reports," Emily pouted.

The next afternoon the girls slid into their desks in Sister Leah's classroom.

"Okay, who would like to give their report first? I want you to tell the story, rather than read it to us. You can refer to your report if you need to," pointed out Sister Leah. "Abby, would you like to go first?"

Glancing around her at the other girls, Abby raised her eyebrow at Emily and half grinned as she made her way to the front of the class.

"My report is on the Buffalo herds. I couldn't believe it when I read that there used to be between thirty and fifty million buffalo roaming the western United States before the Europeans came. One man said he had shot about five thousand eight hundred buffalo in a two month time frame. The hunting season was about three months long each year. Another bragged that he had killed twenty thousand buffalo, or bison, as they were properly called, within nine years.

The Native Americans had used all parts of a buffalo, wasting nothing. Really, it was amazing. Besides the meat, they used the horns, hair, bladder, skin, bones, tails, teeth, and even manure. When the white people came, along with guns and railroads, the buffalo were hunted mostly for their hides, tongues, and bones. The tongues were actually considered a delicacy. Hides were transported to market by the train car load. The carcasses were usually left to rot. A new kind of gun manufactured in the 1860's was called the "Big Fifty." It could shoot up to 600 yards, and the Native Americans said it "shoots today and kills tomorrow."

Finally, the government tried to stop the killing. But by the time South Dakota enacted a law, the population of buffalo was practically extinct. And of course, the well-being of the Native Americans was destroyed as a result.

The good news is that the American Bison Society was created in 1905, and slowly the population began to increase. Some of the ranchers out here even realized that they could raise buffalo for profit.

Now there are many large buffalo herds again, and there is even one in Custer State Park, in the Black Hills.

"Thank you, Abby. That was a very interesting report. Does anyone have any questions?" asked Sister Leah.

"What did the Indians do with the bladders?" asked one of the girls.

"Bladders were used for medicine bags," answered Abby.

"What about the hair?" asked Hannah.

"Hair was braided into ropes, used to fill pillows, and even to line their moccasins," responded Abby.

"I can't believe they could use the tails," commented another student.

"Actually, they made good whips," Abby replied.

Sister Leah moved to the front of the classroom. "Do you girls know about the Buffalo Roundup held every fall at Custer? I think there is a possibility that we can convince Sister Catherine to take a road trip and let you all see the big shaggy beasts close up. I'll try twisting her arm," grinned Sister Leah.

The next morning Leah stopped by Catherine's office. "Hi Catherine. I sort of told the girls in my classroom yesterday that I might be able to let them take a trip out to the Black Hills in the fall to see the Buffalo Roundup. Have you thought any more about it?"

"Leah, that is months away. We don't even know who will still be with us then. But you just gave me an idea. And yes, I will consider that Black Hills trip later," she laughed.

CHAPTER TWENTY-NINE

For long moments Catherine sat very still alone in her office thinking how much the girls must miss their families and the excitement of new adventures. She had grown up on the convent grounds and remembered how much she had loved the little trips into the Badlands and Black Hills with her mother. Even though she loved the older nuns who were a family to her, the desire to have a real family still tugged at her heart.

Catherine stopped by Abby's cell Friday evening and asked, "How would you like to go for a drive into the Badlands tomorrow?"

"Oh, Catherine, I would love to get out of here and see where we are," exclaimed Abby.

"Okay, you can ask a couple of your friends to come along too. Be ready in the morning and we'll take a drive around the Badlands loop."

"Can we wear jeans, Catherine?" begged Abby.

"Absolutely not! You will stay dressed in your habits as usual. We are to look like a car load of nuns out for a little drive. You cannot raise any suspicions. You should know by now how important our persona is to the safety of some of our residents, you included."

"Oh, all right, I just thought it would be nice to forget for a little while that we are cooped up here," complained Abby.

"I know that it is hard for you young girls who have not chosen our lifestyle, but it won't be forever," consoled Catherine.

"That's exactly what Sam said to me," Abby replied. A shadow flickered across Catherine's face.

"Don't forget; be ready to leave right after breakfast. Meet me at the front gate."

Abby quickly found both Emily and Hannah and told them the exciting news. The three girls were ecstatic to be allowed off the convent grounds. Abby still wanted desperately to be allowed to return to her dad in Chicago, but Hannah by now had come to discover what safety was. Here she had a warm place to sleep, plenty of food, a chance to go to school, and best of all, real friends. She sometimes missed her mom, but even she hadn't stopped Hannah's dad from trafficking Hannah for drug money.

The next morning Catherine pulled her Dodge Minivan up to the front gate and the three girls quickly slid into the car. "Buckle up," she instructed, as each of them began turning their heads, looking over their shoulders, and taking in the landscape outside of the convent walls. A big smile crossed Hannah's face as she realized there was no street activity. She had never felt this way before, and didn't recognize her feeling as one of freedom.

"Our convent land is situated right on the edge of the Badlands," explained Catherine, as she pulled out from the gravel road and headed onto Highway forty-four.

"But first we will drive east across the Buffalo Gap National Grasslands. Do you remember when Sister Sapphira was telling about her ancestors homesteading near here? This is where so many families tried to ranch and later discovered how very dry the climate was and many were unable to produce crops. Also the Depression added to the miseries of those decades. But now this area has been restored to original native prairie grasses. Now this grassland covers more than a half million acres." The girls were silent as they stared out the car windows at the desolate beauty.

Soon they reached the Badlands Visitor Center. "You can read some of the history and learn about the wildlife found here," suggested Catherine.

As she pulled into a visitor's parking space, Hannah looked around her and quickly asked, "Is it safe for me to get out of the car here?"

"Hannah, you are a long, long way from Chicago and the people there who hurt you. There isn't crime here like there is back there. This part of the country is full of good hard working people and lots of tourists who want to see our great United States. Besides, we have you pretty well camouflaged in your habit. You look like a young postulate out for a drive. You may notice tourists staring at you, but that is only going to be because they are curious about the lifestyle of nuns. Don't engage in conversation that might cause you to reveal where you are from. Just smile and they will leave you alone. And most of all, girls, stick together, and don't get out of my sight," Catherine instructed.

The foursome piled out of the minivan and made their way to the visitor center. Once inside they relaxed and began to look at the exhibits, read the history, and study the geology information. "All right, Sisters," Catherine grinned conspiratorially, "back into the car and we'll head around the Scenic Loop." Once settled back in their seats, the three girls were in for quite a surprise as they began the drive through the panoramic terrain.

"It looks like we are on the moon," burst out Hannah.

"I think it looks like fairyland, with castles everywhere," added Abby. Emily had seen the Badlands before with her family, but she readily agreed that this was breathtaking.

"Some of the castles like formations are called Buttes," interjected Catherine, "and the canyons were formed by millions of years of wind and rain erosion on the volcanic ash."

Catherine turned off onto Sage Creek Rim Road and drove on until Abby shouted, "Look at those little creatures! What are they?" Catherine began to chuckle.

"I'll bet you have never seen Prairie dogs before, right?"

"Prairie Dogs?" exclaimed Hannah.

Catherine pulled the car off the road onto a viewing spot as she continued, "Yes, these little rodents live in their own villages. Do you notice how they stand on their hind legs and watch us? They live underground in burrows and build a complex tunnel system. They are really fun to watch. They live in families and actually have their own towns."

Finally Catherine told her passengers that they needed to continue on if they were going to have their picnic. "Picnic?" exclaimed an excited Hannah. "I never had a picnic before." Abby and Emily exchanged glances and both turned their eyes toward Catherine, who tried to cover her compassion by concentrating on her driving.

Continuing on around the loop, Catherine caught sight of the place she was searching for as it came into view. She slowed the car and turned into an overlook area. "Be careful out here, girls," she admonished. "It is a little hard to walk in habits, and I don't want any of you tripping and falling." She opened the lift gate of the little van to reveal a basket full of picnic food. "We do have a short hike to my favorite picnic spot," she declared. All three girls were giddy with excitement at the prospect of being out of the convent, and sharing a surprise picnic was more than they had dreamed.

Catherine and the girls managed to perch on flat rock formations and relax with a lunch prepared by the kitchen staff. "How did you get them to fix this for us, Catherine?" asked Emily.

"Oh, I have friends in high places," laughed Catherine.

The girls hungrily devoured the pasta salad, egg sandwiches and pickles. This was followed by cookies and homemade lemonade. "What kind of cookies are these?" asked Abby.

"These are our kitchen's famous peppernut cookies. They are actually called *pfeffernuse* in German, and there really is a little bit of black pepper in them. It does give them a unique flavor, doesn't it?" replied Catherine. Abby decided she would ask for the recipe and send it to Dad. "I bet Antonio has never heard of these," she thought.

After they had packed up their picnic remains and stowed the basket back in the car, Catherine led the girls down a trail overlooking spires and buttes. "The French fur traders called this area *les mauvais terres pour traverse*, or 'bad lands to travel through.' But the Native

Americans call this place *mako sica*, or 'land bad.' " One by one the four managed to find perches to accommodate them so they could enjoy this landscape together.

"Listen with your heart. Can't you almost hear the canyons singing? There is an ethereal, primeval feeling," Catherine mused aloud.

"I like to think of ethereal as whispery," Emily said softly. A hush fell over the girls as they submerged themselves in this sensation.

"Abby, do you remember when I told you this was considered to be a holy site by the Native Americans?" quietly asked Catherine.

"Yes, I do, and you said that is why the convent was built on its particular location," Abby recalled.

"The badlands are especially breathtaking at dawn and dusk," reminisced Catherine.

"It sounds like you have come here often," Emily said dreamily. "This seems so romantic. I would like to come here with my boyfriend. That is if I had a boyfriend."

"Did you ever have a boyfriend, Catherine?" asked Abby. After a thoughtful silence, Catherine looked at Abby.

"Yes, I did. There was a boy I met at college. We spent a lot of time together for a couple of years."

"What was he like?" prodded Emily.

"He was quiet, gentle, thoughtful and funny."

"What did he look like?" wondered Hannah.

"The first thing you noticed about him was his height. And I can't really put it into words, but there was strength in his features. His eyes were dark and brooding. When he looked at me it sent a shiver through me. He had beautiful black hair. He wore it a little long. Sometimes I teased him that he might just tie it up in a ponytail."

"Did you bring him out here?" asked Emily.

"Oh, yes, we spent a lot of time hiking the trails through the badlands together," replied Catherine.

"Were you in love with him?" Abby asked.

"Yes, we were in love, but it just couldn't work out. We both knew it. Our families and backgrounds were so different. Neither of us would ever have been able to live in the other's world."

"But why would you have to? Couldn't you just compromise? My mom and dad were different from each other, but we were a very happy family," Abby quietly said, as her heart nearly burst with sadness at the memories.

"It was pretty complicated. Ty grew up in a very different environment from my life in the convent. There were many beliefs and feelings that neither of us could understand about the other," Catherine cautiously volunteered.

"Was that his name, Ty?" asked Emily.

"Yes it was a nickname. I always called him Ty."

"What happened to him? Did he ever get married?" Abby wanted to know.

"No, he has never married."

"Did he think it was weird that you lived in a convent?" asked Hannah.

Catherine thought back to the day that Ty had asked her where she lived. She had shrugged and casually said, "Oh, out west, in west river country." "That's where I grew up too," he had replied. They had for the time dropped the topic. Later when they realized they were falling in love, he had asked more about her family. That was when it got very complicated.

"Did he think it was weird that I lived in a convent? Oh, yes! I tried to avoid explaining for weeks. Finally I had to tell him that I had never met my dad, and that I lived in a convent. When I told him that my mother was a nun, he nearly flipped his lid. It took a lot of talking to explain that one!"

"Catherine, is your mother really a nun?" asked an incredulous Hannah. The girls all stared at Catherine. Abby frowned, Emily's mouth fell open, and Hannah's eyes got as big as the moon. "The answer to that is yes."

"Does she live in our convent?" Hannah wanted to know. "Yes, she does." Catherine was not quick to divulge any more information than needed to satisfy the girls' curiosity.

"When you told me that she is with you all the time, I thought you meant that she had died, like my mom, and that only your memory of her was with you," Abby choked out with a catch in her voice.

"I'm sorry if you misunderstood, Abby. My mother is one of the nuns in the convent, but we do not openly acknowledge that relationship. A number of the older ones do know, but it might cause difficult relationships for me with some of the others, so we try to keep it from being obvious. It's just never mentioned."

"I want to hear more about your boyfriend. Did he ever meet your mother?" questioned Abby.

"Oh yes, I brought Ty to the convent and introduced him to her."

"What did she think? Did she like him?" Abby had joined the other two girls in grilling Catherine.

"She liked him very much. Everyone did, ah, or does. She would have been happy for me to marry him. He actually came to the convent several times. The three of us would secretly have dinner together. He liked her a lot too. My mother really wanted for me to leave the convent and have the kind of life that most girls have. I think she sometimes wished that could have been her destiny, but it didn't work out that way for her."

"Didn't you want to marry him?" asked Emily.

"I thought I did. We dated for a couple of years, but near the end I loved someone else more." Catherine stood up and walked toward the parking area.

CHAPTER THIRTY

When Catherine delivered the girls back to the convent, Abby discovered that she had received another letter from Dad. She tore it open and dropped down on her bed to read it.

Dearest daughter, I miss you every day. How are you getting along there? I only hope that you aren't too sad. The time is getting shorter for us to be apart. My lawyer tells me that we are getting closer to our court date. There will be a trial, but with the evidence against Frankie he assures me that it cannot last too long.

As long as I remain in hiding until the trial begins, there should be no danger to you or me. I will be under heavy guard all during the trial. We are pretty positive that Frankie will be convicted and sentenced to prison for murder. Then our new life can begin. We will have to be put into the Witness Protection Program. It will be hard at first, but we will get used to it. You can then attend college and go on to have a good life. We will put all this behind us. The government will take care of all the arrangements and we just have to obey the rules.

I want you to know this is what we are facing, so that you can get used to the idea, and start imagining what it might be like. The more mentally prepared you and I both are, the easier it will be when the time comes. I am eager to forget this terrible chapter of our lives, and I am looking forward to being with my little girl again.

Love as always, Dad

P.S. Remember you can't tell anyone about Witness Protection!

Abby sat without moving for a long time. The tears trickled onto her nose and down her cheeks. Trying to wipe them away with her sleeve, she slid down onto her pillow and continued sobbing.

A gentle knock on her door from Sarah woke her from a fitful sleep. "Are you feeling okay, Abby? You look kind of sick. It's time for dinner. Are you coming?" Abby climbed off the bed, ran a comb through her hair, and followed Sarah to the cafeteria.

CHAPTER THIRTY-ONE

Megan and Chelsea were not only college roommates, but had become best friends during their first two years at the University. As soon as Megan walked into their dorm room after classes, she snapped open her laptop.

When Chelsea arrived shortly after, she tossed her books on her bed and flopped down to put on her running shoes.

"Megan, are you going to sit there looking at Facebook all afternoon, or are you coming jogging with me?"

"Hey, Chels, look at this! Oh gosh! There is a photo of a woman who is searching for her father and she looks so much like your mom!"

"Let me have a look. You know I'm much more rational than you," Chelsea teased. Peering over Megan's shoulder, her jaw dropped.

"Yeah, I'd say this woman sure does resemble Mom. But they say everybody had a doppelganger somewhere. Get your shoes on and let's go. Forget about it Megan."

Later that evening Chelsea opened Facebook and pulled up the photo that Megan had been staring at earlier. She began reading the short message on the poster that the woman was holding.

"Yikes! Meg, you didn't tell me that the father's name is James Jackson," shouted an excited Chelsea.

"So, who is James Jackson?" frowned Megan.

"James Jackson happens to be my grandfather!"

"You've got to be kidding! Chels, you better call your mom. Now. Before someone else does," cautioned an excited Megan.

Chelsea speed dialed her Mom and impatiently waited for an answer.

“Hello?” Chelsea heard the soft familiar voice.

“Mom, are you sitting down? I’ve got news for you. I think you have a sister.”

“What on earth are you talking about, Chels?”

“Go to your Facebook feed. I shared a pic of a woman to your timeline who is searching for her father, and she looks just like you.” All the words came in such a rush that Chelsea’s mother had to ask her to slow down and repeat.

“Oh, that can’t be. Lots of people look similar, honey.”

“Quick, look it up, Mom. She says her father’s name is James Jackson. Now what would be the chances of someone looking like you AND her father having the same name?”

“Oh, my, she does look like me. A little older though, don’t you think?”

“Mom, do you think Gramps and Gram could have had a baby when they were young, and put her up for adoption? Maybe before they were married?”

“Oh, honey, I don’t think so. Your gram would never have done that.”

“You don’t know that for sure. Maybe her parents forced her to give the baby up. It happens. You’ve got to answer this woman.”

“I don’t think I could do that. I wouldn’t know what to say.” Chelsea’s mother rolled this idea around in her head while chewing her lip.

“Come on, Mom. I’ll help you. Just message back and tell her your father’s name and that she looks a lot like you. Maybe send a photo of yourself to her. See what she says then,” urged a determined Chelsea.

CHAPTER THIRTY-TWO

Emily was now working in Food Service. She loaded the labeled items for the infirmary onto a food cart and headed toward the ramp, pushing it down to the infirmary floor. When she rolled the cart through the swinging doors into the ante room, she saw Catherine talking to Leah in a small office. Catherine's back was to the window, but Leah sat at the desk looking down at ledger papers. Leah looked up at the sound of the clamoring cart wheels, and Emily grinned and waved. There was no reaction from Leah.

Emily heard Catherine ask, "Have we had enough deposits to guarantee success? We are running a little behind on the numbers lately." Emily slowed her cart down and tried to hear what else was being said.

"Why don't you make a call to a few donors and see if we can get the donations up a bit."

"All right, I can do that. I'll try to get a hold of some of our reliable donors this afternoon. If they are willing, they can go directly to the bank and make their deposits," Leah agreed. "Then we'll know what we have to work with next week."

Emily continued on her way into the infirmary kitchen.

"Oh, there you are," exclaimed one of the kitchen staff. "We were just ready for the labeled foods. How many 'B' jars did you bring?"

"Mary Ann put three on the cart," answered Emily.

"Yes, that's all we'll need today. And how many 'E' jars do we have here?"

"I think six," counted Emily. "Good. And I see only one 'RE,' but that too is enough for now. Thanks for getting them here on time."

Emily glanced around, still wondering exactly what these were for, but Mary Ann had said they were special blends for those who needed them. She wheeled her empty cart back out of the kitchen, down the hall, and past the little office door. Catherine was now gone and Leah again glanced up but said nothing.

Later that day Marguerite summoned Catherine to her office. "How are our assets holding out?" the older woman asked. "I haven't had a financial report this month."

"We're doing fine. With the donation of 160 acres of grazing land, plus the investments and all the monthly income, we're actually doing very well," Catherine assured her. "Not to worry."

"That's good to hear. You do an exemplary job of handling our money, Catherine. I am very thankful for that." Catherine was always glad to get words of praise from the Prioress.

CHAPTER THIRTY-THREE

When Emily had finished her work shift in food service, she hurried into the exercise yard, looking for Abby.

"What do you think is wrong with Leah?" asked Emily. "I took the food cart down to the infirmary, and Catherine was in an office talking to Leah. They both looked so serious, but the weird thing about it is that when I passed the door, I smiled and waved, and Leah clearly saw me, but didn't acknowledge me in any way. That's so unlike her. She is my favorite teacher, and usually so much fun. And there was something else weird. I don't know what, but she just looked different. Mostly something about the way she was sitting. Her papers were turned at an angle, and her head was tilted."

"Maybe something is wrong with her neck and she was just so preoccupied that she didn't really notice that it was you," suggested Abby.

"I don't know. I'm afraid she must be angry with me for something."

"Oh Emily, I doubt that. Do you know what they were talking about?" probed Abby.

"Actually, I did hear some of it. I'll admit I even slowed my cart down to try to listen," Emily confessed. "They were talking about money. Catherine asked if there had been any deposits lately, and she told Leah to make some phone calls to donors to see if they could get some deposits before next week. Do you think the convent is in trouble? What if there isn't enough money and they have to close it up? I want to finish high school here. I don't want to go back home while my brother is still living there. And where would you go, Abby? You really need the convent for a hiding place."

Abby shrugged the conversation off, telling Emily that what she heard was probably normal financial talk. But the thing that puzzled her was that Leah was the history teacher. Why would Catherine confide in her, or ask her to help with financial matters?

CHAPTER THIRTY-FOUR

Did you hear that Sister Miriam died last night?" Sarah mentioned this bit of news to Abby as they walked together to breakfast.

"Oh, I thought she was such a dear old lady. That's sad." remarked Abby.

"Not really, Abby. Our goal on this earth is to go to heaven when we die and live forever with Jesus. Yes she will be missed, but you will realize soon that there is often not much real mourning when a nun passes on, at least not one of the really old ones."

"How do you have so much faith, Sarah?" asked the teenager.

"I have been raised in the faith, and so have believed in eternal life ever since I can remember."

"I hope someday I can feel the same way," said Abby thoughtfully. "It's just that I'm sad about my circumstances, and find it hard to be as cheerful as you. I miss my mom and dad so much. I hope I can be back with Dad pretty soon."

"Oh, Abby, I do hope that for you too, but you know I would really miss you if you left. And so would Emily and Hannah. But I suppose it will happen soon enough," said Sarah, with thick emotion in her voice. "Anyhow, you will get to see first-hand how a death is handled in a convent. Other Sisters have been taking turns sitting vigil with Miriam day and night, to be with her when she meets her Lord. Then the mortuary is called and they take the body to be prepared. Out here, there isn't a mortuary very near, so a hearse has to be driven from a neighboring town. Next is the 'Reception of the Body' when the mortuary brings the prepared body back here. All the nuns stand in two lines and the morticians process between the lines, carrying the casket. It is then placed in our chapel for a couple days. The next evening is the 'Remembering Service.'

I really like to attend those services. Different women get up and tell things about the deceased Sister. A lot of the time they tell funny stories about their lives. All of their lives are not somber by any means." Sarah glanced at Abby. "You should come with me to this one. I think you would get a different picture of the life of a nun. Right now you think of all nuns as being disciplinarians."

"No I don't," quickly interjected Abby. "I really like Leah, and of course Catherine is always nice to everyone."

The evening of the Remembering Service Emily decided that she would join Abby and Sarah. Hannah wanted no part of it. The three girls found seats near the back of the chapel. There were a couple of hymns sung, and then one by one different Sisters went up to the front to tell a little of their favorite memories of Miriam. Abby was surprised at how much laughter there was. Some of the stories of her life were told by some of the oldest nuns. Eunice had been her roommate when they had been young women on their first teaching mission in 1935. The two of them had gone by train to a distant town and discovered that there was no place to live near the school, so they boarded with parishioners and rode horseback to school each day. Of course, this was South Dakota, so that wasn't so unusual, except that Miriam had never been on a horse in her life. Eunice told how Miriam had hung on screaming the whole way when she couldn't slow her horse down. Eunice had ridden up beside her and grabbed her reins. That evening Miriam got a lesson in horseback riding from the rancher with whom she was lodging.

The girls were amazed at some of the events these older nuns had experienced. It was hard to imagine ninety year old women as having been young like themselves.

"Where are the nuns buried?" asked Emily.

"Oh, we have our own cemetery behind the convent," explained Sarah. "Actually it isn't very close. Tomorrow there will be a long procession out there. There isn't a road and the path isn't really wide enough for cars. To keep our location private, the funeral home uses a lane from the neighboring rancher's property to deliver the casket to the grave. If you want to, you may accompany me out there too. I can ask Mother for special permission for you to leave your jobs for an hour. Actually, I think I could just ask Catherine for permission. You can meet me out back right after the funeral service is completed, and you can walk with me to the cemetery."

The next morning the girls heard a large number of nuns exiting the building. Abby and Emily quickly slipped out the door and joined Sarah. The girls were overwhelmed by the beautiful voices singing old favorite hymns as they walked together. When they approached the old cemetery, they saw that it was very well taken care of and the stones were all in good repair, even though many of them were over one-hundred years old.

"The local ranchers are very good to the convent," explained Sarah. "They come over here and keep the weeds out and make sure there are no rattlesnakes around when the Sisters will be coming."

"Rattlesnakes!" exclaimed Abby.

"Yes, Abby, South Dakota does have rattlesnakes," grinned Emily, "but you just have to be aware of your surroundings."

On the way back up the path to the convent, Abby overheard one of the out of town nuns saying to her companion, "I haven't been asked to make the trip to Sioux Falls yet, but I think this may be my time. Mother hinted at it this morning. I wonder who will be picked to go with me."

"Abby, I went downstairs to return a book to the library before breakfast this morning, and I saw Ruth going out the door with a small suitcase, and she was crying," confided Emily. "What do you think happened?"

"I don't know. Maybe someone in her family is sick and she had to go home to help," suggested Abby.

"I watched her through that little window in the door, and when she went through the fence gate, I saw Catherine's car parked right outside, waiting for her."

"Emily, your imagination is running away with you. Catherine is probably taking her to the airport," answered Abby.

"I suppose you're right. I hope everything is okay."

Emily turned to Sarah. "Do you know where Ruth was going early this morning with Catherine?"

"Ah, no, not really. I suppose they might have been going for an early morning walk," suggested Sarah.

"No, they got into Catherine's car and drove off. Before breakfast even," insisted Emily.

"Oh. Well don't worry about it. I'm sure everything is okay." Sarah again tried to dismiss the topic.

"Do Sisters ever leave here?" asked Abby.

"Sure, look at those who work outside in parishes," answered Sarah.

"That's not what I mean. Do Sisters ever decide they don't like this life, or get homesick and leave the convent for good?" Abby persisted.

"Yes, once in a while. It doesn't happen very often though. I've never known of anyone leaving. Except those like you, who are not planning to stay at all," smiled Sarah.

When Abby got to class that afternoon, she brought up the topic again. This time she asked Leah if she knew any nuns who had left the convent for good.

"No, I don't but why do you ask?"

"Emily saw Ruth leaving early this morning with Catherine. We wondered if something was wrong. Emily said Ruth was crying."

"If something happened, I'm sure they will tell us later. But the older women have told stories about what it was like before Vatican II, in the sixties. In those days, religious communities usually didn't discuss the departure. There even used to be a rule asking the members to never discuss the situation in community again. It was common for a woman who was leaving either by her own will, or by the will of the superiors, to be escorted out during the night, preferably after midnight when others were asleep. She would be driven to a temporary women's shelter, or perhaps the train depot or airport. She wasn't allowed to tell her classmates ahead of time, and no one was to speak of it after. A lot of things have changed over the years since Vatican II. We are not nearly as secretive and autocratic as before. If I had been here in those days, I don't think I could have stayed."

CHAPTER THIRTY-FIVE

"Ow, ow! Oh, no. I cut myself. I'm bleeding!"

"Hannah, what have you done?" MaryAnn rushed over to grab Hannah's bleeding hand.

"It does look pretty deep. I think you had better get to the infirmary and have a nurse take a look at it. Anna, will you take Hannah down there, please? I'll finish up this chopping for her," said Mary Ann as she wrapped a kitchen towel around Hannah's hand. Anna pulled Hannah out the door and the two hurried along the hallway toward the infirmary. Hannah held back her tears as she allowed Anna to propel her toward the elevator.

Once inside the infirmary doors, Hannah calmed down and took a seat while Anna sought help. Hannah was relieved when she saw a familiar face in her history teacher, Sister Leah, who gently examined the laceration.

"I don't think it needs stitches, but I will disinfect it and bandage it up for you."

"Leah, are you a nurse too?" questioned Hannah. Both the nurse and Anna laughed as Anna explained, "This isn't Leah. Lydia is Leah's twin sister."

"Twin sister? You and Leah are twins?" a puzzled Hannah frowned.

"Actually we are mirror twins. Didn't you notice that Leah is right handed and I am left handed? I know most people can't tell us apart. "Of course, I am the smarter prettier one," joked Lydia.

Hannah couldn't wait to find Emily and Abby and share her news.

"So that explains why she didn't recognize me when I saw her talking to Catherine last week. And I thought she must be mad at me," exclaimed a relieved Emily. "She didn't know who I was."

CHAPTER THIRTY-SIX

Abby, I know you enjoyed helping out in the nursery a couple weeks ago. Would you like to come down again and help out? We have several children and are a little under staffed right now."

"Sure, I really like playing with the little girls in the nursery," responded Abby.

"Great. They can use you about seven o'clock tonight. You can go down alone and Deborah will give you instructions when you get there. Just be back in your cell by nine o'clock. And thanks, Abby," said a grateful Catherine.

When Abby arrived in the nursery, Deborah greeted her with a heartfelt "Oh, Abby, I am so glad you could come help out. The little girls really liked you. They have asked about you. However, they will be put to bed soon. I really need you to help with a newborn baby."

"A newborn baby? I really haven't babysat tiny babies much. I don't know what to do."

"It's pretty easy, really. When they are this tiny, they mostly eat and sleep. You just need to give him a bottle when he is hungry, and hold him and rock him until he falls asleep. Oh, of course he will need a diaper change too. He is ready to eat now, and he probably won't stay awake more than an hour or two. That's your only assignment tonight. I just couldn't manage him with my short staff, until the other little ones are all in bed," said a relieved Deborah, as she placed a tiny bundle into Abby's arms.

"So this is a boy?" Abby asked.

"Yes, this is a boy." As she stared at the little baby who was wrapped up in a blanket like a burrito, Abby wondered why the convent had a newborn baby here.

"Deborah, I thought we just had nursery school age children in our day care and school. Do all these little children live here?"

A hesitant Deborah cleared her throat and replied, "Some of them are unwanted by their mothers. Young unwed mothers come here and stay until their babies are born. Then they leave and Mother Superior puts some of the babies up for adoption."

"Are they actually born here, in the convent?" an incredulous Abby asked.

"Yes. In the infirmary. Sister Lydia is a trained midwife. She delivers the babies. I think it is very nice of the convent to act as an adoption agency. Some of these unwed mothers have no idea where to turn. When they are here, they wear the robes just as you and I do and their pregnancy can be camouflaged for quite a while. I think it helps the pregnant girls to feel a little like they fit in. They don't have classmates or family looking at them with disapproval. Here, no one really knows anyone else's story unless they want to share it. So no questions asked," Deborah gave Abby a penetrating look.

The next morning when Abby saw Emily she excitedly told her about the visit to the nursery.

"Do you remember when we worked in the laundry together and we saw blood stains on the sheets sometimes? I think I know what was going on. Did you know babies are actually born here, and that Lydia is a midwife?"

CHAPTER THIRTY-SEVEN

Before Father Gregory left after he had heard weekly confessions, he paid a visit to Sister Marguerite.

"Are you keeping up with the rumors of a possible Apostolic Visitation? Rome is making noise about sending Vatican priests to the United States to nose around and ask questions." Marguerite shot him a look.

"And exactly why are you bringing this to my attention, Father? Out here on the Dakota plains, where those priests from Rome would think they had landed on another planet, do you actually think they would worry that we have gone astray? They would be so distracted by the cowboys, Indians, Badlands, and eternal wind that they would most likely not only think they were on another planet, but also that they had traveled back in time," she threw her head back and laughed.

"You know Marguerite, you can be very descriptive when it comes to painting a picture of South Dakota," Father Gregory chuckled. "You're right. They most likely would concentrate on convents in large cities, where they would expect the most disobedience, among headstrong American nuns with their own ideas. And you, of course follow all the rules."

"Father, why do you think we still wear the black habits, insist upon the Grand Silence, and expect the young novices to show total obedience? Whether we follow all the rules or not, we certainly look that way to outsiders," Marguerite gave Father Gregory a hard long look. "And do you have any reason to suspect otherwise, Father?"

"No, Sister, no reason. I only wanted to make you aware. I had better be taking my leave. I have another convent to visit today, although certainly not as remote as this one. Have a good day, Marguerite."

"Father."

"Yes Marguerite?"

"Just remember that I know plenty about what has gone on with priests before you try to suggest anything is irregular here at our convent."

Father pushed himself out of his chair and retreated through the door. As he stepped into the hallway, he nearly collided with Catherine. "Oh, excuse me Catherine, I didn't see you there."

"Good morning Father," exclaimed Catherine. "Have you been giving Marguerite a hard time?" she joked. "Or was she giving you a hard time? You seem in a hurry to get away. She can be a bit determined at times."

"No, no, we just had a nice little chat. Good to see you as always. I really must be on my way now," Father Gregory said over his shoulder as he hurried out into the bright sunlight.

"Good morning, Mother. Father Gregory nearly plowed me down in his haste to leave. Is there a problem?" Catherine raised the question.

"Ha, he should run. He knows who is in charge around here," Marguerite smiled at Catherine. "He is trying to warn me that there might be an Apostolic Visitation from Rome in the future. It seems they are worried the American nuns have ideas of their own. And with the pond between, they evidently don't feel they are keeping us in line over here," remarked Marguerite. "Did you stop by for a reason, Catherine?"

"Yes, I did. Since some of our young guests are homesick for their real lives, I thought maybe I could take them on an outing into the Black Hills. It's only about an hour and a half drive from here. We can spend the day touring the Hills and be back in plenty of time. With your permission, of course."

"You may go on one condition."

"And that condition is?"

"Pick chokecherries in Spearfish Canyon. Then get the kitchen staff to make chokecherry jelly. I used to love to eat chokecherry jelly on fry bread years ago," reminisced Marguerite.

"I'm sure they will make the fry bread, since they will also have to make the chokecherry jelly for us," laughed Catherine.

Catherine asked Sarah to accompany Abby, Emily and Hannah on their outing into the Black Hills. The girls were so excited to escape for a day that they could hardly sleep. After breakfast, Catherine pulled the minivan up to the front gate and the girls tried to unobtrusively slip out without drawing attention. Neither Abby nor Hannah had ever been west of Scenic.

"There sure ain't much to see out here," a disappointed Hannah pouted.

"Isn't, Hannah. And you just wait," replied Sarah.

"Yea, my family took a couple of vacations out to the Black Hills," chimed in Emily. "You will be amazed at what you'll see. I especially remember the smell. The pine trees smell so good. We stayed overnight in a log cabin right in the woods, and there was a little stream right behind our cabin. We went to the Mount Rushmore lighting service at night."

"What's that?" asked Hannah.

"I'm sure you know what Mount Rushmore is. The faces of four presidents carved into a granite mountain. Every night they have a patriotic ceremony and turn spot lights on the faces. It is really cool," added Emily. Catherine cruised through Rapid City and on to Keystone. The scenery certainly did change, as Hannah gazed out the window at the pine trees of the Black Hills National Forest.

"Did you know that dinosaurs roamed this area? A lot of dinosaur bones have been excavated near here," smiled Catherine.

"For real?"

Catherine had Hannah's attention now. She continued, "And the Black Hills were formed by a movement deep in the earth after the dinosaurs became extinct."

Abby asked, "About how long ago was that?"

Catherine felt a giggle gurgling up as she replied, "Oh, about sixty million years ago!" She was enjoying immensely her chance to give the girls a history lesson along with a day of sightseeing.

"No way!" an astonished Hannah blurted.

"I think I better let Leah know that you need a little tutoring in history," Catherine smiled. "I know, it is a little hard to comprehend." They drove past the little town of Keystone. Suddenly there, through the trees, loomed Mount Rushmore. As the girls stared, the four presidents stared back at the girls. Catherine pulled into a tourist sightseeing parking area, and they all piled out of the car to get a better look. They hurried to the viewing terrace. There the awe struck girls were told that the men in stone measured sixty feet from their eyebrows to their chins.

"I never thought I'd get to really see them," said Abby, with a catch in her throat. She remembered how Dad had been planning their family trip out here before Mom's accident.

"We better get on our way," urged Catherine. "I have a lot more to show you." They drove through tunnels, over bridges, and around curves as they ascended. Catherine took them on the Wildlife Loop through Custer State Park. "Didn't one of you write a report on the buffalo in Leah's history class?" asked Catherine.

"Yes, I did," answered Abby.

"Now you can see for yourself," she commented, as the huge beasts came into view. "This is one of the largest public buffalo herds in the United States."

"Oh, wow, they are real buffalo, ain't they?" exclaimed an excited Hannah.

"Aren't they, Hannah. We'll stop for buffalo burgers at the Custer State Game Lodge," suggested Catherine.

"I am getting hungry," admitted Abby.

"Me too," chorused the other girls.

"Did you say buffalo burgers?" Hannah had never heard of eating buffalo.

"Why yes, I did," laughed Catherine. "You need to experience as much as you can now that you have escaped from the confines of the convent, don't you think?" Hannah still didn't know just what to make of Catherine's humor.

"And then we can stop at the Purple Pie Place and have a piece of pie for dessert."

"Is that really the name of a restaurant? The Purple Pie Place?" asked Emily.

"Yes and you'll see why when we get there," answered Catherine.

"How do you know so much about everything in the Black Hills, Catherine?" pressed Abby.

After a quiet moment, Catherine answered, "You know I grew up in the convent and you see how it isn't really very far from there into the Black Hills. When I was a child my mother and I would sometimes go for a drive out here."

"Did your boyfriend from college ever bring you out here?" asked Abby.

"Yes, sometimes. We did take drives through the Hills. That's actually how I know about the Purple Pie Place," laughed Catherine. "His favorite pie was raspberry rhubarb jalapeno."

"Buffalo burgers taste just like beef to me," said Emily, as they slid back into Catherine's Chevy and headed toward the promised pie.

The Purple Pie Place appeared ahead. It was a little pink and purple building, painted more like a child's play house than a serious restaurant, but it had a reputation for baking quite a variety of pies, some of which the girls had never heard. Catherine's favorite was sour cream raisin, while Abby ordered blackberry, Emily wanted chocolate, and Sarah tried bumbleberry. Hannah couldn't decide between chocolate and peanut butter, but finally settled on peanut butter.

It was a beautiful sunny afternoon and the girls were in no hurry for it to end.

"The Lakota called August *Capa Sapa Wi*," mentioned Catherine.

"What does that mean?" asked Abby.

"Cherry black moon," replied Catherine. "We still have a drive to get up to Spearfish Canyon," she prodded them into her car and settled down for another leg of their sightseeing day. The drive was gorgeous with its canyons, ridges, bridges and tunnels. "Did you know the Native Americans called the Black Hills *Paha Sapa*?" asked Catherine.

"What are we going to see at Spearfish?" interrupted Abby.

"We are going to pick chokecherries!" announced Catherine. The girls looked at each other.

"What are chokecherries?" ventured Hannah.

"They are a popular berry that grows on trees," explained Catherine.

"Oh, my mom makes jelly from chokecherries," volunteered Emily. "It's really good too."

"And that is exactly why we are going to pick chokecherries. We'll take them back and ask the kitchen staff to make jelly. But we'll also beg them to make Indian fry bread. Chokecherry jelly on warm fry bread. I love it. Ty loved it too," Catherine said quietly.

Catherine turned onto Spearfish Canyon Scenic Byway heading toward Roughlock Falls. The girls were silent as they looked in awe at the towering limestone walls and the deep canyon. Pulling the car into a parking area, Catherine urged the girls to each grab a bucket from the van and start their chokecherry picking. The bushes were heavy with the ripe berries. Picking their way along in their long black robes, the quartet of women caught the eye of no small number of tourists. They stared as the girls laughed and joked while reaching across each other for the biggest berries.

"Spread out," instructed Catherine. "There are plenty of ripe berries for everyone!" Abby and Hannah each popped the first berry they picked into their mouths.

"Ugh," Hannah quickly spat out the cherry. "Why are we picking these? They taste terrible."

"Oh, gross," agreed Abby. "Now I see why they are called chokecherries."

"Sorry, girls. I forgot to tell you that they are very sour. You don't want to eat them this way, pretty as they are," laughed Catherine. "That's why we are going to ask the kitchen staff to cook them into jelly. With plenty of sugar added, you'll change your minds," she smiled. When the buckets were full Catherine dumped them all into the cooler in the car as the girls stared at their purple fingers.

"It will wash off eventually," Catherine teased, "but I don't know how you will explain your purple fingers to the others at the convent tonight," she grinned.

Back in the car, the girls were quiet on their drive back. It had been the best day of Hannah's life and she was unable to express her feelings in words. A couple of tears trickled down her cheeks. Abby put her arm around Hannah's shoulders and gave her a little hug. It was one of the best days for Abby too.

When they arrived back at the convent, Catherine pulled her car to the back door and the girls piled out. Opening the van door, they lugged the cooler of chokecherries to the kitchen door.

"What do you have there?" exclaimed a surprised Mary Ann. "I thought your cooler would be empty. Didn't you like your picnic food?"

"Oh, it's not picnic food, Mary Ann. Your sandwiches and cookies were the best, as usual. But we went chokecherry picking."

"Oh, my, chokecherries," sighed MaryAnn. "We haven't had chokecherry jelly for quite a while." Looking into the cooler, she mumbled to herself, "And who gets to do all the work?"

“And don’t forget, we have to have warm fry bread with the jelly,” winked Catherine.

CHAPTER THIRTY-EIGHT

Julie dialed Catherine's number.

"Tell me, Julie. I can't stand this waiting. I forced myself to wait until you called me. Have you heard anything?"

"I have. I heard from a lonely old man who was sure you must be his daughter, but he is eighty-nine years old. Although I suppose he could be the one! And then there was a message from a woman who was sure her husband had fooled around, and that you must be his daughter. I guess James Jackson is a pretty common name. And then there was a woman who thought you might be her twin, although her mother had said the twin died at birth. But there was one message that sounded fairly legitimate. It is from a woman in Sioux Falls who says her father's name is James Jackson. And get this… her college age daughter's roommate saw your picture on Facebook and showed it to the daughter, who in turn called her mother and had her take a look. They all agreed that you look just like the mother. So rather than finding your father, you may have found a sister!"

"Julie, do you really think this might be the right one?"

"I'll give you the woman's phone number and you can give her a call. Her name is Lisa Connor."

When Catherine hung up the phone from talking to Julie, she sat with trembling hands, her heart pounding in her ears, thinking to herself. Do I tell mother? No, no, I can't do that. Not yet. She tapped her pencil on the desk, her leg jiggling nervously. She took a deep breath, blowing it out through her mouth. Then another deep breath. She prayed for courage. Why was this call so difficult to make? Hadn't she wanted for years to find her father? There was a good chance that she had found him. Or at least someone who could tell her more. Lisa. She rolled the name around in her mouth. My sister? Lisa, my sister. It had a nice sound. Okay. She'd do it. Catherine punched in the number that Julie had given her. It rang. And rang. And rang.

"Hello?" A breathless woman's voice answered. "Is that you Chelsea? I was upstairs without my cell phone, as usual."

"Hello. Is this Lisa Connor?" Catherine cautiously questioned.

"Oh, Hello. Yes this is she." The woman quietly waited for a response from the caller.

"You don't know me. My name is Catherine. Are you the Lisa who responded to my Facebook search for my father?" There was a long silence. Catherine tried again. "Mrs. Connor, are you there?"

"Oh, yes, I'm here. I am just so stunned. I guess I didn't really expect to hear anymore from you," she continued with a nervous little laugh. "Did you receive the photo of myself that I e-mailed back to you?" Catherine assured her that she had.

"Yes, and I do think we look a lot alike. But I need information from you about your father. Do you think it is possible that he could be my father too?" Lisa took a deep breath.

"Frankly, I don't see how that could be. My parents were married after college and I have no reason to believe that he ever had an affair during their long marriage. They have been very happily married for over forty years."

"But, Lisa, I am forty-five. I would have been born before they ever met."

"Oh, right." Lisa drew out the words very slowly. "Oh, I see. What does your mother say about this?"

Catherine was hesitant to speak about her mother. A couple answers might lead to too many questions. She felt she had to protect her mother's privacy.

"She acknowledges that I was born out of wedlock. She hadn't finished high school at the time. Her boyfriend was a James Jackson who attended Jefferson High." Now it was Lisa's turn to acknowledge a truth about her dad.

"I see. Yes, he did attend Jefferson High school. He graduated in 1966.But are you saying that he has known all these years that he had another daughter?"

"No, no. I have tried for years to get my mother to tell me who he was. She had only referred to him as Jim. She had never told him she was pregnant. He was a year older, and they broke up when he left for college. I suppose he never knew she had a baby girl the next spring."

"I agree it is possible that we are half-sisters. The dates all fit, and we do have a striking resemblance to each other. I don't know how he will take this, and I really don't know how my Mom will feel. But we do need to get to the truth. Where do you live, Catherine?"

"I am out in the western part of the state, not too far from Rapid City." Catherine wasn't ready to explain that she was a Catholic Sister, and that she lived in a convent in a rural area. Enough shocks for poor Lisa for one day.

Lisa continued, "Why don't you make a trip here to Sioux Falls and we can sit down and talk more. I confess my daughter and her college roommate think this is just the coolest thing, and are both dying to meet you. Of course they are convinced we are sisters. You know the romantic notions of the young." The women ended their conversation with plans to meet on a weekend when Chelsea would be home from college. Catherine sat back down in her chair. She hadn't realized how tense she had been, pacing around her office during the entire conversation.

CHAPTER THIRTY-NINE

Sam strode into Danielle's office late one morning. She looked up from her notes and grinned, "Why hello Sam. To what do I owe this honor?" He held her eyes in suspense, a slow quirky smile spreading across his face.

"I came to ask you if you'd like to accompany me on a little get-away trip. Just the two of us."

"Ah, so you must have another delivery to make out west, and you need a chaperone again, is that it?"

"Not this time, Danny, not this time. Out west, yes, a delivery no, and a chaperone, no."

"Are we going to a tropical island then?" she smirked.

"Not exactly, although the heat will be close to tropical, and it is a sort of island in the midst of society as you know it."

"Now I am intrigued, Sam, as I usually am by your stories. Just where is this island?"

"Do you remember my ribbon dance regalia that you were just chomping at the bit to see me wear? I am going to a powwow in South Dakota next week and I am proud to say I will be a featured dancer," he explained.

"And just how does that affect me?" wondered Danielle. She waited patiently for him to continue, a common occurrence in their conversations.

"I can't take off too much time, so I plan to fly into Rapid City and drive over to Pine Ridge. How would you like to come along? Maybe you could carry my ribbons," he teased as he wiggled his eyebrows and waited. "I think you would enjoy being an observer of a real powwow. We can watch the whole dance event, feast on some cool

Indian tacos, fry bread, wojapi, and lots of beans. We will have to fly back later that night, because I have an important meeting the next afternoon back here at the salt mines. What do you say?"

Glancing at her on line calendar notes, Danielle slowly looked back up into his intense brown eyes, as a warm blush spread across her face.

"All I can say is this will be a first time for me," she laughed.

Five days later Danielle was riding with Sam from Rapid City east to the Pine Ridge Indian Reservation.

"I don't think I can prepare you for the poverty you will see out here on the Res, but today I just want you to see some of our heritage." As they approached the entrance to the powwow grounds, she was surprised to see how many observers she was joining.

"I thought this was an Indian thing. I was afraid I'd feel out of place, intruding on your culture."

"And you thought maybe you'd be kidnapped and scalped, is that it?" Sam ventured.

"Please, Sam, sarcasm aside. I just didn't know what to expect, that's all." They made their way to the observation area as Sam greeted a few older men and grinned at some of the young boys already dressed in their regalia. "Those little boys are so adorable in their costumes," she commented.

"No, no they aren't. Never use the word costume. This is our regalia."

"Oh, I'm really sorry, Sam. I forgot."

After Sam had made sure Danielle was comfortably settled among the other visitors, he excused himself and made his way among the throngs of family members and old friends. This powwow was a social event consisting of Dakota and Lakota tribal nations, coming together to reconnect.

At the opening ceremonies, young and old Native Americans rode into the arena on horseback, some carrying various flags. The drum beat began and the spirited drumming saturated the air as singers and dancers began entering the field. There were to be competitions in special categories of traditional, fancy and jingle-dress dancing. Sam's specialty was ribbon dancing, something he had learned as a young boy. Performers began moving in a clockwise direction, to represent the circle of unity. Singing and chanting became intense, as the South Dakota sun beat down on the assembly. Danielle was surprised at the variety of music being performed. The singing varied from songs of war and conquest to songs of joy, humor, and even mourning.

Eventually it was dance competition time. Men and women began to circle around in an unbelievable mixture of regalia. The traditional, fancy, and jingle-dress dancers took their places. Danielle glanced around to see if she could find Sam. Her eyes squinted and surveyed the spectacle until she spotted him advancing with the ribbon competitors. Visitors were clapping and excitement was mounting. The colors were mesmerizing, and the jingles jangled while the ribbons fluttered gaily. The speakers blasted out the next competition. Danielle was captivated by the entire extravaganza. The singers and the beating of the drums provided a bewitching background for the rhythm of the dancers.

Glancing around, she noticed that many spectators were clapping along with the beat. She was too intent on watching Sam to keep up with the clapping. Pulling out a pair of binoculars Sam had brought along, she kept her sights on him as he began his routine. He circled with the rest with a look of intense concentration across his face. The pace of the frenzied dancing and beauty of the colorful fluttering ribbons was indeed something Danielle had never imagined. At the end of the dance she cheered and clapped as wildly as any of the spectators. When Sam had changed out of his regalia and found Danielle, she saw a wide smile glued to his face, and he saw a respectfully teasing look on hers.

"There are no words, Sam, there just are no words."

Sam suddenly reached for Danielle, put his hands around her waist, lifted her off the ground, and swung her around in the air. Setting her back on her feet, he planted a quick kiss on her lips. They both were surprised. On the flight home, he quickly fell asleep, while Danielle closed her eyes and relived the day.

CHAPTER FORTY

Danielle entered Sam's office with a shy tap on the open door. "I want to thank you again for allowing me to share in the nuances of your culture."

"Oh, I think you really want to tell me how great my legs look in my ribbon skirt."

Blushing, Danielle continued, "I've been thinking about some of the things you told me about Enapay and the abuses you described while you were at the boarding school. Why haven't there been lawsuits on the part of the Native Americans against the boarding school? Surely you would have a legal case against them." Sam folded his hands behind his head, leaned back and stared at the ceiling. Danielle began to think she had trod where she wasn't allowed, when he slowly straightened up in his chair and looked into her eyes.

"Believe me, there have been lawsuits. When I got to college, I started learning about legal rights. Later I contacted a pro bono lawyer who was handling other Native American legal cases involving the abuses of Indian kids at the hands of the boarding school employees, and the Catholic Church, actually." Danielle raised her eyebrows.

"You sued the Catholic church?"

Sam continued, "One of the Catholic Dioceses, to be more specific. Eventually more and more Native Americans got the courage to come forward. There was a lot of heartache in the telling of their stories. Enapay had prevented me from actually being a sexual abuse victim, although Father Tobias' attempt was also an abuse. But many of our race had horrible stories to tell, including rape, sodomy, and other molestations. There were specific priests who were moved from position to position to hide their crimes. The detailing of abuses and transfers is now a part of public court documents as a result of lawsuits filed. There were also many girls who were abused by not only the priests, but by nuns as well. Coming forward to expose these abuses was extremely difficult and heartbreaking for most of the Native Americans. Of course some came forward with open anger."

"Thankfully there were lawsuits to seek justice," interjected Danielle.

"Not so fast. You can't jump to that conclusion," corrected Sam. "There had been a state law passed that did not allow childhood sexual abuse lawsuits to be brought forward by victims who had reached the age of forty. Most of these victims had tried for years to forget what had happened to them, and were very hesitant to talk about their experiences. The result of course was that they were by now over forty years old." Sam's face took on a sullen demeanor. "Case dismissed." With a slight edge in his voice, he remarked, "However, it is ironic that these so called Hail Mary lawsuits were brought against the Catholic Church!"

CHAPTER FORTY-ONE

Leah popped into Catherine's office.

"Catherine, the girls are getting excited about their trip to see the buffalo roundup. It is coming up soon now. The last Friday of September is only a couple weeks away. I have been making the plans. Have you cleared your calendar?"

"Leah, I'm not coming along."

"You're not coming? But I thought you and I were taking the girls. I can't do it alone. Can't you clear your schedule?"

"No, Leah, I can't. I have some important business in Sioux Falls, and my meeting is all set up. Why don't you take your sister again? You two have always had so much fun together, and the girls will get a kick out of going with identical twins. They rarely get to see the two of you together. Imagine the fun you two will have tricking them." Leah grinned.

"I suppose you're right. I'll see if Lydia is free. She would like a get-away too, I'm sure." With that settled, Leah headed to find Lydia while Catherine stared at the photo of Lisa on her computer for the umpteenth time.

Lydia was more than anxious to accompany Leah and the girls to the roundup at Custer State Park. When the girls piled into the car, they all erupted into giggles to see Leah and Lydia side by side.

"Which one of you is driving?" asked Abby.

"Which one do you think?" shot back Lydia.

"Too bad for you that you can't tell us apart by our clothes, either," grinned Leah as she glanced at Lydia's black and white habit, identical to her own.

"And too bad all three of us had to wear the same outfit too. I still don't see why we couldn't wear jeans and tee shirts when we leave the grounds," complained Hannah.

"You know why, Hannah. We are keeping you in a safe place. You never know when someone will recognize one of you. Abby is especially in danger, since her dad is still in protective hiding."

Hannah turned and looked out the window, aware that she had better obey the rules. The girls again enjoyed the drive to Custer.

"I don't get what this buffalo roundup is all about," commented Hannah. "Where have the buffalos been, and why do they need to be rounded up?"

"Didn't you listen when I gave my report in Sister Leah's history class, Hannah?" asked a perplexed Abby.

"Oh, yeah, I remember now. You said a big herd lives in Custer State Park. So why do they need to be rounded up then?" Hannah repeated.

Sister Leah stepped into the conversation. "Once a year the buffalo are all herded together, or rounded up, and about two hundred of the thirteen hundred are sold at auction. The new calves are also vaccinated and branded. Depending upon how good the grasslands are in any given year, the park can only maintain a certain number of animals, so an excessive number must be sold. This is all done to keep the herd healthy from year to year."

"Just exactly what are we going to see, Leah?" asked Emily.

Lydia replied, "Cowboys and cowgirls will be on horseback herding the buffalo from a large area into corrals."

"Wait a minute. I thought I asked Leah," challenged Emily. "Aren't you Lydia?"

"Am I?" responded the nun.

Hannah jumped into the confusion. "When I got cut working in the kitchen, which hand did you bandage for me?"

Now Leah answered, "If I remember correctly it was your left."

"No, right," Lydia interjected.

"Oh, yes, right, that's right," laughed Leah.

When the car was parked in the visitor's lot, the young women all piled out and headed for the viewing areas.

"Catherine told me to warn you again to not answer too many questions if strangers try to find out where you are from. Our convent location cannot be disclosed."

Spectators got quite a treat in addition to watching the buffalo being rounded up, when they saw five women in full habits parading toward the viewing area, two of whom looked exactly alike. Abby overheard a woman say to her companion, "I think they all look just alike in those clothes. I don't know how they even tell themselves apart."

The excitement was palpable in the crowd when in the distance could be seen hundreds of buffalo lumbering along, chased by cowboys and cowgirls on horseback, as well as several pickup trucks following. The noise became deafening and the dust flew. The ground shook and rumbled as the huge animals picked up speed. The observers stood with cell phones and cameras raised above their heads, trying to capture the thundering spectacle. When the buffalo began filling the corrals, the onlookers began to cheer.

Leah, Lydia, and the three girls in their charge joined in, caught up in the frenzy. Several bystanders were enjoying watching the excitement of the nuns almost as much as the roundup itself. When the buffalo had all been corralled the crowd began to break up.

Abby asked, "Can we get something to eat before we leave?"

Leah and Lydia steered the girls to the food vendors for a quick meal before heading back to the convent. On the drive home, the girls chattered on, reliving the excitement of the powerful animals charging across the grasslands. Lydia reminded them of how the buffalo herds had roamed the plains for centuries in the past.

Leah said, "You do know your American history, don't you?"

Emily tried to untangle the web the twins were weaving. "OK, which one of you is our history teacher?"

Leah laughed, “I think we both have taught you some history today.”

CHAPTER FORTY-TWO

Catherine and Lisa had agreed on the weekend for Catherine to make the trip to Sioux Falls to meet each other. As the day approached, she felt she had to tell her mother something about what she was going to do. Stopping by her mother's room one evening, she took a deep breath as she tapped on the door.

"Hi, Catherine. I'm so glad to see you. I know you have been busy. Sometimes I feel we just don't get to see enough of each other. Have you made any progress on your search for your father?"

"That's exactly why I wanted to talk to you, Mother. Yes, I have. It may be a totally false lead, but through Facebook I have located a woman whose father has the same name, and guess what? She sent a photo of herself. She looks enough like me that she could be my sister!"

Her mother's mouth fell open. "But you haven't received any kind of reply from him, have you?"

"No, but do you really think he would have a Facebook account? Actually, it wasn't even this woman who looks like me who saw my search. It was her daughter's college roommate who noticed how much my picture looked like this girl's mother. So the girl, Chelsea, called her mom and eventually she, Lisa, e-mailed me. I did call her and we chatted a little. We decided that I should go there and at least meet her. How to approach him is another matter."

"Catherine, I don't know if this is wise, but I do know that you are determined. I only hope that you will not be disappointed."

"Mother, I know how you feel. But either way, I will finally meet him, if this one is really my father."

"By the way, did you expose yourself as a nun by putting your picture on the internet? I don't know if that was wise."

"No, I didn't wear my habit. Lisa loaned me some of her clothes for the picture."

"Really, Catherine! You pasted your photo out there for the world to see and you didn't even stay true to your family of Sisters?"

"Mother, which family are you talking about? And what should I have done? I couldn't do it both ways. And by the way, it's called posting."

"What's called posting?"

Catherine rolled her eyes. "I posted the picture. Internet talk."

"At any rate, I do wish peace and happiness for you. Have a safe trip and I'll be in prayer for you. I will actually be anxious to hear all about it when you return."

"Thanks Mother. I'll only be gone a couple days."

As she rolled through the peaceful ranch land, Catherine began to get a real case of the jitters. What if she didn't feel any connection to this woman? What if Lisa didn't feel comfortable with Catherine? What if she decided to not let her even meet her father? And then there was the issue of Catherine's lifestyle. She had decided it would be deceitful for her to wear street clothes and try to conceal the fact she was a nun. Might as well be totally honest and let the chips fall where they may.

When Catherine reached Sioux Falls, she found a motel and settled in for the night. She spent plenty of time tossing and turning, but in the morning the sun was shining and she determined to accept whatever the day might bring. After a leisurely breakfast and two cups of strong black coffee, Catherine punched into the GPS the address Lisa had given her. She pulled up in front of a lovely two story house on a street lined with old oak trees. Sioux Falls was a pretty town filled with parks and hiking trails. Catherine had made numerous trips here on convent business, usually bringing one or two of the younger

Sisters along shortly after the death of an older nun. But she couldn't think about that business now.

Parking the car, she said a quick prayer, glanced at her nervous reflection in the rear view mirror, and opened the door. As soon as she stepped out of the car, the front door of the house opened and the woman whose photo so resembled her own stepped forward. Over her shoulder a teen aged girl, whom Catherine supposed was Chelsea, whispered,

"Oh, that can't be her, Mom. Looks like a nun who got lost. Must need directions." The woman hesitated as Catherine took a deep breath and advanced up the walk.

"Are you Lisa?"

"Yes I am. And you are…."

"Catherine." Lisa stood and stared as her daughter recovered and stepped forward, extending her hand.

"Oh, this is just so cool! Mom, you have a sister who is a Sister!" At that, the two older women burst into laughter at the same time.

"Please, come in, come in," Lisa invited, ushering Catherine into a bright room, filled with green plants, a trickling fountain, and plush pillows strewn onto sunny yellow sofas. "Do sit down. May I get you a drink? Perhaps iced tea or lemonade?" Catherine stared at the woman, who so strongly resembled herself, but who had the softest sweetest voice.

"Yes, that would be nice. Tea please." Lisa turned to her daughter.

"And of course this is my daughter, Chelsea. Chels, would you be a sweetheart and get both of us an iced tea please?"

"Sure, Mom," this lovely girl replied with a smile as she headed for what Catherine assumed must be the kitchen.

"Did you have a good drive, Catherine?"

"Oh, the usual. Not a lot to see but still I always love crossing the state," replied Catherine.

"So you come here often?" questioned Lisa.

"I do have some convent business to tend to in Sioux Falls periodically, yes. I do apologize for not having prepared you for the fact that I am a nun, but somehow I felt that we both had already had enough surprises, and this one could wait until we met," smiled Catherine. Lisa nodded.

"I understand. This will give Chels a good story to tell when she goes back to school. Her roommate wanted so badly to be here today, but I told them we were all under a lot of pressure, and I could only handle so much. In retrospect, perhaps having both of them here would have lightened the mood, as you know how these young girls are. Nothing is too serious for them. These two have a way of seeing the best side of most situations." Chelsea returned with the tea and the three sat and tried to get acquainted, sharing bits and pieces of themselves. When Chelsea discovered that Catherine had attended the same University at which she now studied, the ice was broken, and they tossed impressions and stories back and forth.

Lisa watched with fascination at how comfortable her daughter appeared to be with this stranger, who of course might turn out to be Chelsea's aunt. Eventually Catherine decided it was time to turn the conversation to the matter at hand.

"Lisa, do you have photos of your father that you would allow me to see?" Chelsea jumped up, left the room, pulled a framed photo off a table in another room, and quickly reentered, thrusting it into Catherine's hand.

"This is Gramps and Gram at Mom's birthday party last year," beamed Chelsea. Lisa watched the emotions of interest, tenderness, curiosity, and awe chase each other across Catherine's face. Catherine slowly raised her eyes and wiped at tears sneaking down her cheeks.

"He's very handsome," she spoke with hoarseness. Mother and daughter exchanged glances.

"Yes, even in his sixties he remains a striking man. I've been sorting through old photos since we first talked by phone," offered Lisa. "Would you like to see those too?"

"Of course I would," smiled Catherine. Lisa left the room and returned with a box of assorted photos. Several were recent pictures of Lisa's family that included her parents. Eventually she got to the bottom of the box and found photos of Lisa's father as a young man. There was his college graduation, one of his beaming face in front of a red 1972 Mercury Comet, and one pouring over a stack of books in a public library. Then she picked up a photo of his wedding picture, with his beautiful new bride. Catherine sat staring at the photo as she fantasized, pictures floating before her eyes, conjuring up her own album of imaginary memories. Lisa remained silent, uncomfortably watching Catherine and knowing the emotions she must have been feeling. Lisa finally broke the silence.

"Catherine, I know how you must be anxious to meet my father, but I truly don't think the time is right just now. I need to prepare him for the shock of discovering that he very well may have another daughter. If it is alright with you, I think I need a little time to broach the topic, and suggest the possibility to him before we rush into introductions. I do hope you understand."

"Oh, Lisa, certainly I agree. Having taken this first gigantic step is a weight lifted from my shoulders. I was so afraid you might not really be open to the possibility that I could be your half-sister. I realize that this is a huge shock for you, as well as it will be for your father, hopefully, our father. I have some brief business in the city again in two weeks. Will that be enough time for you to try to talk to him?"

Lisa acknowledged with a smile, "Why of course. I see my parents quite often. I have always been close to them. I can easily arrange a private lunch with him and see where this leads. I will stay in touch with you. By the way, are you willing to take a DNA test, if he agrees that his paternity is a possibility?" she added apologetically.

"Absolutely," reciprocated Catherine. "I too would insist upon testing. I'll head back home for now, and look forward to hearing from you."

Both women felt a need to comfort the other with a hug. Chelsea had been quietly listening to this conversation. She now stepped forward and gave Catherine a big hug and whispered, "I really do hope you are my aunt."

"Thanks, Chelsea. It has been great meeting both of you. From my standpoint, I hope there will be many more such opportunities."

CHAPTER FORTY-THREE

Catherine called Abby to her office.

"I think it is time for a change of work assignments. You haven't assisted in the Archive department yet, have you?"

"Archives? I don't even know what that is," replied a baffled Abby.

"Archives encompass all of our historical documents. It is a complete record of all activity that has happened here since the convent was founded.

We have records of births, deaths, adoptions, finances, school records, priests who have served here, and of course the dates of each Sister's professions."

"But what would I know about that? How can I help there?"

Catherine smiled her easy relaxed smile. "You don't have to know anything about our archives. I'm sure you are very proficient on a computer, however, aren't you?" Now Abby relaxed.

"Oh, sure. I can use most programs."

"There you go," grinned Catherine. "We are trying to update the department and record all documents digitally. Up to now, everything has been stored on paper. Some of the oldest records are getting very hard to read, so we need to make this a priority. I think I will ask Emily to help also. The two of you should be able to accomplish a fair amount each day, after you finish with your classes. Hannah can help you on a part time basis as well."

"Okay. Thanks Catherine. I think I'll like this assignment a lot better than laundry or even the foods department."

Catherine gave a hearty chuckle. "I thought maybe you would," she laughed. "And tell me, what do you hear from your dad?"

"Nothing good. I guess when the government is bringing a lawsuit against the mobsters, it takes a lot of investigation and documentation in preparation."

"Yes, I know, Abby. I just want you to know how much we have learned to care about you, and how sorry I am that you have to be separated from him," Catherine said quietly. "A yearning for your father can be a heavy burden to carry."

"Yeah, it sure can."

The next day after classes, Emily and Abby walked down to the Archive department together. Chloe greeted them with a friendly smile.

"You must be Abby and Emily. I sure am glad to see you two. Catherine tells me you are going to have this department shaped up in no time. She says you both are very computer savvy, which of course I would expect from teenagers these days."

"We're just here to do whatever computer entry you need done," commented Abby.

"I believe you will have a job here as long as you want, based on the amount of archival material we have stored. This will be a better job than laundry or housekeeping, don't you think?" Chloe asked with raised eyebrows.

"For sure," giggled both teenagers.

"Alright, first I'll explain a little about the types of documents we have filed away. In this office we keep approximately the last twenty years of records. That's why you see so many file cabinets in here. There are also a couple other rooms down the hall. Records prior to that are stored in the basement. There is hardly ever a need to go down there, and it is kind of a dingy place. But rarely a query is made about something in the past, and we do have a good history of the convent stored down there. For now, I think we'll begin up here, in this room. I'd like to get all current records stored digitally first so as new records come in to be archived, they will follow in a timely sequence.

Then eventually we will decide how to tackle the really old stuff, which will take a lot more time to decipher."

Chloe took the girls on a quick tour, indicating from which file cabinets they would each begin pulling paperwork. She pointed out cabinets labeled Births, Deaths, Adoptions, Novices, Postulants, First Profession, Final Profession, Exclaustration, Finances, School Records, Land Acquisitions, Priests, and Mother Generals. Emily glanced at Abby and raised an eyebrow as she tilted her head toward the cabinet labeled Exclaustration. Abby caught the look, and shrugged her shoulders as she returned a look of bafflement. They would have to look that one up later. Chloe led them to computers and assigned each of them a password.

"I think I'll start one of you on Deaths, and the other on Novices. I have already finished entering Birth records, and adoptions."

"Why do you have births and adoptions here?" asked a very curious Abby.

"Oh, we still get unwed mothers who come here to have their babies. And then we subsequently handle their adoptions. We have a reputation for the utmost privacy. The young mothers and their parents can be assured that their private information will never be exposed. And that brings me to a most serious aspect of this job." Chloe grew stern and continued.

"You must realize that any and all information that you become aware of must be held in strictest confidence. I'm sure that Catherine chose the two of you for that very reason. She knows that your own situations are confidential, and that you will therefore hold other's information in confidence. Do I have your word on that?"

Both girls nodded in unison.

CHAPTER FORTY-FOUR

Hey, Will, come in here a minute," Sam beckoned with a wave of his hand.

"Oh, morning, Sam." Will sauntered into Sam's office back in Chicago, and plopped into the closest chair. "What's up? Did you take another young girl across state lines?"

"Not recently, Will, not recently. Do you own a gun?"

"Do I own a gun? Don't I carry one every day?"

"I mean do you own a shotgun," continued Sam.

"Just what are you getting at? Are you trying to accuse me of something?" Will shot back.

"Will, how many years have we worked together? Twelve, maybe fifteen? And how well do we really know each other? You seem to regard me as 'that Indian guy' in the next office.

I'm going hunting out to South Dakota and I thought maybe you would like to come along. See what you are made of," grinned Sam. "And maybe you will see what I am made of too," he continued on a more serious note.

"You and me, on a hunting trip together?" Will questioned.

"That's the idea. Take a few days off, drive out where the tall grass grows, and you won't see any armed police where we are going. Stomp through the fields, maybe shoot a few birds."

"Birds? What kind of birds?"

"It's pheasant season out there in a few weeks. You'd be privileged to get to hunt pheasants alongside men from probably every state in the union and a few foreign countries too," Sam replied in his slow easy way.

"Oh, yeah, I have heard about the pheasant hunting in South Dakota." Will remarked. "So do you sleep in a teepee when you're out there?" he needled.

"Actually, I have an old friend from years ago who invites me to stay on his land when I hunt. He owns a few acres and lives in the old farmhouse. We can bunk there." Will sat back and stretched his legs. He crossed his arms behind his head and looked at Sam.

"Is this some kind of a joke, Sam?"

"No, I'm perfectly serious. I think it would do you good to get out of the city and hang out with some real cowboys and Indians for a while. The offer stands."

"Let me think about it and see how my work schedule looks. I did already take some vacation time when I took the family to Disney World in the summer."

Sam spoke up, "You can bet this will be no Disney trip, Will." Will was silent a minute. Then he laughed and pushed himself out of the chair.

"I'll let you know." When he reached the doorway he turned and said, "Thanks, Sam."

CHAPTER FORTY-FIVE

Late in the afternoon on a sunny day in Omaha, a young man picked up his cell phone and punched in a familiar number.

"Aunt Laura, can I stop by and talk to you about something on my way home from work today?" Laura heard wistfulness in her nephew's voice.

"You know you can talk to me about anything, anytime, Mike. Can you make it around 5:30? Then you may as well stay for dinner too."

"Thanks. See you then," replied Mike in his brief manner.

After the dinner dishes were cleared, and Mike's uncle had retired to his den, Laura sat back down at the table and motioned for Mike to join her.

"What's on your mind, Mike?" Aunt Laura had been like a second mother to him, growing up as he had, with just his mom. His cousins had also been like his brothers.

"You know I have always felt like a part of this whole family, even as an adopted kid, but now I have been thinking about who my birth parents might have been. Mom never seemed comfortable talking much about my adoption. And now that I have started wondering, and she is gone, you are the only one who can help me, Aunt Laura."

"Mike, I wish you had asked more questions when your mother was still alive. I don't know how much she wanted you to know. There may have been a reason why she didn't feel good about talking to you about it."

"But what's done is done. I think I have the right to know about my heritage," responded Mike. With a big sigh, Laura began.

"I suppose you do. My sister was divorced and had no children. She was in her mid-thirties, and felt she never would have the opportunity to have children of her own. By then I had the three boys, and I knew she was jealous of how happy our family was. Sharon started looking into adoption. Someone told her about a convent in western South Dakota where unmarried girls could go to have their babies, and the convent would then help them find adoptive homes for the babies. After a little more research, Sharon felt that this was the answer for her. She wrote to the Mother Superior, or whatever you call the head honcho in a convent. You might think a single woman would want to adopt a baby girl, but Sharon wanted a boy for sure. I guess she thought our rough and tumble little boys would be good for her little boy too.

The convent didn't usually allow a single person to adopt, but Sharon made a preliminary visit out there and she was as impressed with them as I imagine they must have been with her. Your mother was, as you know, a wonderful person, and that personality shined through as soon as anyone met her. She was given an approximate time for when she might expect the baby to be born. They were doing ultra sounds by then, so they would know which expectant mother was due to deliver a boy."

Mike interrupted, "Did Mom get to meet my birth mother?"

"I'm sorry, Mike, but no. They had very strict rules about that. You know how secretive you've always heard convents used to be. This one was no exception. Sharon had to agree to never try to make contact with the birth mother. Of course, that doesn't prevent you from seeking information now that you are twenty-five years old. I think your mom probably felt that as long as she didn't tell you too much, you wouldn't start digging into it, and therefore she would be holding up her end of the promise of secrecy. Anyhow, she got the call, and was absolutely ecstatic. I went out with her. She was so excited I didn't think she should try to bring a baby back here alone. I remember meeting with that Mother Superior. Her name was something like Ellen, or Helen. No, that doesn't sound quite right. It was more complicated, more Catholic, probably," laughed Laura. "Ah, Helena, I think.

She sat us down in her office and had Sharon sign papers and made it very clear that there was to be no contact at least until the child was eighteen. But, Mike, there is something I know I should tell you, but I hesitate to do so."

"Aunt Laura, You have to tell me everything you know. Is there something bad in my DNA? Do I carry a gene for a disease? What is it?"

"No, nothing like that. Helena asked to speak to Sharon privately, so I got up and left the office. While I was out, Sharon later told me that she had been told that the baby actually had a twin sister. The Mother Superior wanted to know if there was a chance that Sharon would consider taking both babies."

"What?! I have a twin?" Mike practically shouted. "Aunt Laura! Where is she? What happened to her?"

"Mike, you have to understand that your mother was only prepared for one baby and remember she was a single woman. She really couldn't have afforded more than one child."

"But didn't you try to convince her that we should be raised together?" Mike's voice shook.

"Mike, your mom didn't tell me about the twin girl until a few years later. She knew I would have tried to convince her to take both of them. You know I would have helped her any way I could. I think it probably always bothered her that she didn't take the other baby too, and that may have been why she never wanted to tell you much about your adoption. It has always bothered me too, but I decided to wait until you showed an interest in your adoption history before laying that one on you. I'm sorry, Mike." Mike sat quietly for several minutes.

"Thanks for being honest, Aunt Laura."

"What are you going to do with this information, Mike?"

"I don't know. I just don't know."

CHAPTER FORTY-SIX

"I have to be honest with you, Sam. I'm kinda looking forward to this trip, and kinda not," confided Will as he climbed into Sam's Crown Victoria and stretched the seat belt to fit around his bulk. "I think I'm mostly going along to satisfy my curiosity about you."

"There's nothing wrong with that, Will. At least you're being honest. And you might actually enjoy yourself, or at the very least, learn something new." Sam pulled the car into hectic Chicago traffic. "Once we get out of the city, I think you'll see why I love driving west every chance I get."

As they crossed into Iowa, the tension lines eased in Sam's face, and were replaced with contentment. Will, in all his years, had never taken a road trip west. Having grown up in Chicago, he usually flew whenever he left the state, both for business, and for pleasure trips. He remained quiet as they drove past harvested corn fields. Sam purposely pulled into small towns when he needed to stop for gas, instead of exiting into the mega truck stops along the freeway. He was aware that Will was dumbfounded by the huge machines for sale in implement dealer lots, and the hundreds of thousands of dollars this equipment cost. Sam had a sense of satisfaction knowing that Will was becoming aware of how sophisticated a career farming had become.

But as of yet, Will couldn't drop his condescending language. When they rolled into South Dakota, Will asked, "Okay, where are the teepees?"

"You won't see any here, Will, and actually you won't see many Native Americans, either."

"So then where did you grow up, Sam? I thought you were all kept on reservations." Sam clenched his jaws, trying to swallow the screaming retort that he held back.

"I'm going to assume you meant that as a joke. And remember I've heard quite a few Polish jokes, Mr. William Jachimowski."

"Okay, okay, Sam. Truce time. I'm sorry, just nervous, I guess. When I am nervous, my sarcasm kicks in." Sam glanced at Will, and laughed.

"Yeah, I've noticed. What are you nervous about? This is supposed to be an enjoyable relaxing experience. Now, Will, it's time for you to learn the South Dakota wave."

"The what?"

"The South Dakota wave. Most people in rural South Dakota wave at each other when they meet on the road."

The driver of the next pickup truck that they met kept his hand on the wheel, raised two fingers and did a slow wag of his hand. Sam in turn acknowledged the gesture with an identical wave of his own. "Like that, Will."

"Sam, you know I don't know the first thing about South Dakota, or hunting, and I've never known anybody who hunts pheasants. I have been reading a little about the terms I have heard you throw out. Like flush out, fence row, marshes, and CRP."

"Good for you," Sam laughed. "At least you're trying."

As they drove farther into South Dakota Sam noticed the change in the scenery.

"How far west are we going? All the way to the other side of the state?"

"No," Sam replied. "Pheasant hunting is best in the middle and northern part. Like I told you, we will be staying with an old friend of mine, and we will hunt on his land only. And another thing I should prepare you for, Will. Out here we don't eat breakfast, lunch, and dinner."

Will shot a stricken look at Sam. "Huh?"

Sam grinned. "We eat breakfast, dinner and supper. And probably a couple of lunches in between meals."

"Oh, well, now you're talking my language, Sam," replied a relieved Will. "But why do you call lunch, dinner, and dinner, supper?"

"Actually, dinner just means the largest meal of the day, so farmers traditionally need more food in the middle of the day because they are using a lot of energy during the working hours. Supper is usually considered to be a meal eaten later in the day. Sometimes the evening meal is another hot meal, but often a lighter supper is okay too."

Will had heard too many stories about the poverty on South Dakota Reservations, and was preparing himself mentally for meeting an Indian who probably worked too little and spent his money on too much alcohol. Sam turned off the interstate and headed north on a county road until he came to a gravel road. After a couple miles he turned onto another long road that looked more like a path to Will. *Oh boy, here we go, out into the great beyond,* thought Will.

"What kind of a road is this?"

"This isn't exactly a road, Will, this is the driveway." Will then saw an old farmhouse set back with a white fence all around the property, and a couple of horses pastured beside the house. There was a wrap-around porch on the three sides that were visible to Will, and colorfully painted rockers and lounge chairs scattered along its length. As the gravel crunched beneath the car tires, Sam eased to a stop in front of the yard, pulling up under a pair of large trees which had lost their fall leaves into a colorful carpet.

The front door opened, and out stepped an older man, tall, with a thick head of wavy silver hair. His weathered face crinkled into a big grin as he strode toward the car. Sam jumped out and the two embraced in a bear hug. Will watched through the window of the car. This must be Sam's friend's father, he was too old to have been Sam's classmate. Actually, he didn't even look like a Native American.

"Get out here, Will, I want you to meet Dr. David Porter, one of the best political science professors a guy could ever know."

Baffled, Will climbed out and covered the space between himself and this pair. "Dave, I want you to meet a colleague of mine, Will Jachimowski." Dr. Porter extended his arm and clasped Will's hand in a powerful grip.

"Mighty pleased to meet you, Will, and please, call me Dave. Sam here was one of my star students, and has remained one of the best friends a fellow could ever have. We've hunted birds together for a lot of years, now, haven't we, Sam? Grab your gear and come on inside. You can get settled and we'll have a cup of coffee." As the three men entered the house, a short slender woman probably in her mid-seventies wearing stylish jeans and cowboy boots came toward Sam with both arms outstretched. She wore her salt and pepper hair pulled back and tied at the nape of her neck.

"Oh, it is so good to see you, Sam. We miss you when you don't come around for so long." Sam gave her a warm hug and turned to Will.

"Peggy, this is Will. Will, Mrs. Porter."

"We are happy to meet you Will, and please call me Peggy. Mrs. Porter sounds like an old lady," she chuckled. "Now, how would you like a little lunch to hold you over until supper?" She asked. While the men enjoyed cups of coffee, Peggy placed thick slices of her lemon loaf drizzled with a lemon glaze in front of each one. After supper in the big dining room with its décor of western art, the men meandered into Dave's den, where the bookshelves were filled, both with textbooks and also western biographies. Sam and Will each found a comfortable leather chair, while Dave settled into his favorite old recliner, pulling the footrest up.

"Will, are you a Federal Marshall too?" probed Dave.

"Yes, sir, I am, though I have different duties from Sam. He somehow has managed to land the plumb position of depositing special clients to their destinations, while I mostly stay in the office and deal with the criminals." Dave raised an eyebrow.

"So most people on witness protection are criminals, then? I thought you were protecting the innocent from the criminals." Sam jumped in, explaining that some are intentional criminals, but others are people who think of themselves as innocent while doing business with criminals.

"And," added Will, "we protect plenty of criminals who have testified against their mob enemies." Dave changed positions in his chair, crossing his ankles and leaning back.

"I know enough to not ask too many questions. All these years since Sam became a Marshall, he has kept his work pretty close to the chest. I respect him for his integrity, just another reason Peggy and I think so highly of him."

Peggy entered the room, asking, "Is there anything I can get you gentlemen before I go upstairs? How about a little lunch before you turn in?"

Will coughed to hide his grin, while Sam raised an eyebrow in his direction.

"No, sugar, we can take care of ourselves," Dave smiled at her as she gave him a goodnight kiss on the cheek.

"Good night, Peggy, and thanks again for your generous hospitality," said Sam.

"Yes, ma'am, and thanks for that great meal too," added Will.

"Boys, we probably should all get some sleep tonight. We will have a full day tomorrow."

Will questioned, "Is this one of those ventures where we have to get up before dawn?"

"No, Peggy will cook us a big hot breakfast before we set out. You're going to need it to stomp the fields."

The next morning dawned cold. After a breakfast of eggs, sausage, pancakes, and hash browns, plus several cups of steaming coffee, the men donned their layers of clothing, topping all with their bright orange hunting vests.

"I think we went over all my tips last night. A couple neighbors will be joining us this morning. A few extra men always help to flush out the birds. Will, we will be walking in a linear fashion, in other words, crossing a field in a line, much like policemen do when searching for evidence. That way if there are birds in the grass, there is a better chance that one hunter will get a good shot. Pheasants tend to run when startled, instead of flying, and sometimes can run circles around the hunters."

"How many pheasants does a hunter usually get in a day?" asked Will.

"The limit is only three a day per hunter, but getting one will be an accomplishment this year. Like I told you last night, our bird population has gone way down, since we've had several harsh winters, plus a lot of farmers have taken their acres out of the Conservation Reserve Program, and started farming marginal land," explained Dave.

"And you say that is partly due to the use of ethanol fuel, right, Dave?" added Sam.

"That's right. Since Ethanol is made from corn, more acres planted to corn yields more money in the farmer's pocket. Okay, let's get out there." Just as the trio headed out the door, a pickup truck drove into the yard, and out climbed a slightly stooped older fellow and a younger man whose resemblance to the older man left no doubt that this was a father and son pair.

Will leaned close to Sam and quietly said, "Now they look like a pair of cowboys!"

Both men were wearing western boots, denim jeans, deerskin gloves, and of course the typical cowboy hat with its high crown and wide brim.

After introductions were made all around, the younger man, introduced as Pete, let the tailgate of the truck down, and out jumped a hunting dog, immediately running to Dave wagging his tail.

"Ah, an English springer spaniel," exclaimed Will. "And a beauty too."

"Do you have a spaniel of your own, Will?" asked Pete.

"No but my uncle does. His is liver and white, instead of black and white like this fellow. They're great dogs, all right." The men collected their gear and headed out for the day. That evening Peggy asked Will what he thought of his first day of pheasant hunting. Dave stepped in and declared,

"For a greenhorn, I'd say he did pretty well, wouldn't you, Sam?"

"Yeah, he surprised me. I've always used a Winchester Model 12, but I just may have to switch to a Browning A5.That twenty gauge has a lighter recoil, and maybe Will won't be as stiff and sore tomorrow as I will," he laughed. "Oh, and Peggy, he shot one of the four birds we got today."

"Then who was the unlucky fellow who didn't shoot a bird?" she tilted her head to the side and gave a teasing look to Dave and Sam.

Dave gave her a wink and replied with a grin, "We'll never tell."

After a couple more days of hunting, it was time to head back to Chicago.

Peggy took Will's hand in both of hers and said, "I sincerely hope you will come back out here with Sam another time. We have enjoyed getting to know you, and I always like to have a few extra men to cook for every chance I get."

Will's farewell to the Porters was heartfelt.

Dave gave Sam another of his famous bear hugs and whispered, "We are praying that Eddie will find a good job this time, and stay on the outside."

"Thanks, Dave, thanks for everything, as always," Sam responded.

Will had a curious look on his face at overhearing this conversation.

On the drive back east, Sam asked, “I thought you hadn’t ever hunted before. So how did you learn to shoot a shotgun?”

Will laughed and said, “My uncle, the one with the Springer Spaniel, had me come out to his place and he let me shoot at a few clay birds.”

“Just how many is a few, Will?” Sam coaxed.

“Oh, you know, a few.” Both men laughed. Will had dropped his sardonic demeanor and dared to broach a question to Sam.

“I overheard you and Dave talking earlier about Eddie. Who is he, anyway?” Sam glanced at Will and weighed the consequences of whether to confide in this man who had so often in the past made jokes about Sam’s Native American heritage. After a few minutes of consideration, he began his tale of two brothers.

CHAPTER FORTY-SEVEN

Abby tore open her newest letter from Dad.

Dearest daughter,

I have good news for us. My lawyers assure me that the trial is nearing a close. The evidence is pretty clear cut, showing motive of mob rivalry. It had been really hard being on the witness stand. They tell you to not look at the defendant, but that is pretty hard to do. He sits there with half a smile; half smirk on his face, as if to taunt me. His lawyers are arguing that it is all circumstantial, and it is true that I didn't see him actually pull the trigger. But I did see him tucking the pistol back in, and sauntering up the street as if nothing had happened, while Tommy lay on the sidewalk in a pool of blood. Because he turned and saw me, I know for sure it was Frankie.

Pretty soon it will be up to the jury to decide his fate. And in a way, our fate will be decided too. But I suppose they too are scared to death to be involved in sending a mobster to prison. Either way, it will end soon. And either way we may have to go into hiding. We sure can't live under their noses here in Chicago. I worry so much about you, Abby. To think something like this would happen after we just survived the loss of your mother.

Abby's tears began to flow as she read the words, 'your mother'. So many nights since she had been in this place of hiding, Abby had dreamed about her mom. Only children were often close to their mothers, and Diane had been not only a mom, but a fun pal for Abby during the long evening hours when Dad was still at the restaurant. Sometimes Mom would come home from the dress shop with new outfits for both of them, and they would put on a fashion show for each other, parading around the room, pirouetting in their best imitations of fashion models. After collapsing into gales of giggles, they would have a favorite dinner together. Of course Abby's favorites were tacos, burgers, fries, hotdogs, mac and cheese, spaghetti, chicken Alfredo, and ice cream. Mom managed to sneak in vegetables, either raw or steamed, and usually fruit. "What would your dad and Antonio think if they knew we were eating mac and cheese and hotdogs?" she'd ask with a conspiratorial grin. She hid the hotdogs behind a package of liver in the freezer, explaining that it was safe there, as Abby's dad hated liver, and would never touch it to look behind it.

Once in a while he would say, "Diane, that package of liver has been in there a long time. When are you going to eat it?"

Her reply was always, "And what makes you think that is not a new package?" After dinner she always reviewed Abby's homework assignments and if there was time they would challenge each other to a board game or get on the floor and see who could do the most pushups and leg lifts. Abby couldn't imagine what her friends must be wondering now. She had been whisked away from everything familiar and driven to this faraway place without any explanations. She had been wary of the man who picked her up to drive her out here, but Sam carried U.S. Marshall's identification and Dad assured her he would take care of her. On the long drive, Sam had tried to ease her fear with stories about his childhood riding horses and learning to dance. He tried to get her to sing along with him to the radio, but she was in no mood for singing or conversation.

CHAPTER FORTY-EIGHT

Catherine grabbed her phone, noticing the caller was Lisa. "Hi, Lisa, I've been waiting for your call," she said with breathless excitement. "Have you had a chance to speak with your father?"

"Hi, Catherine. Yes, I have. I told him I had to speak to him privately so I know he was worried that maybe I was sick and that I wanted to keep it from Mom. So actually, when we had lunch together, and I assured him that I was fine, he breathed a sigh of relief and seemed ready to hear what I had to say."

"Yes, yes, and..."

"As you know, I had to take it pretty slowly. I tried to get him to tell me a little about when he was in high school, whether he had a girlfriend, and that sort of thing. At first he barely scratched the surface, all the time wondering, I'm sure, what I wanted to talk about. He did tell me that there was a special girl his senior year.

I asked him, 'Dad, how close were you? I mean was it a once a week Saturday night date for a movie, or something more?'

He looked at me intently and asked, 'Is this about Chelsea? Has she gotten too involved with a boy?' I assured him that it had nothing to do with her. Then he asked whether my marriage was in trouble! Imagine that! Always worried about the rest of us, and having no idea that I was about to drop a bombshell!

'No, no, Dad,' I said. I asked him to tell me more about his girlfriend. He said she was a junior when he was a senior. They started dating the summer before, and all through that year. Then when he was leaving for college, she agreed they should not try to continue a close relationship when they would be so far apart. They wouldn't 'go steady' anymore, was how he worded it. I guess that's what they used to call it.

'Dad, whose idea was that?' I asked.

'Oh, I guess it was my idea. You know I was going off to college, and wanted to taste freedom. And anyhow, I had plans to go on to law school, so I had years ahead of me before I could consider settling down.' I asked him what she thought.

He continued, 'She was sad, of course. We both were. She acted kind of wistful, and there were plenty of tears, but in the end we both knew it would be for the best. You know, Lisa, high school breakups are never easy. When kids are so young, they think they'll never find love again.' I asked him if he thought they were in love.

'That's a good question. Don't most teenagers think they are in love? At that age who knows what real love is?' was his reply.

'Lisa, just what are you getting at? What's with all these questions? Are you writing my biography, or what?' Dad laughed.

I figured I had chased my tail long enough so I asked, 'Dad, is there any possibility that you could have fathered a child with this girl? Were you intimate?'

'Geez, Lisa, is that any kind of question to ask your father? What's gotten into you?' He leaned forward, put his face close to mine, and asked, 'Why?' I told him that a woman had contacted me and thought she might be his daughter. First the blood drained from his face. He sat there staring at me.

Then he got his steam back and replied, 'What kind of nut would try to say a thing like that after forty-five years? Is somebody trying to blackmail you? Or me? Of course I don't have another daughter. I don't have any skeletons in my closet. Thank goodness you didn't bring this up in front of your mother, Lisa. And why would Judy have kept a thing like that from me? None of it makes any sense.'

I tried to tell him to calm down. That we were going to investigate the story. I'm sorry, Catherine, but I had to take that approach."

"Oh, I fully understand your predicament, Lisa," Catherine's voice dropped to a whisper.

"Then he said 'Did Judy have a baby by some other guy and now they are trying to say it was me? Isn't forty-five years a little long? Or does this woman think she deserves to be written into my will? I'll bet that's it.'

'No, Dad,' I told him. 'She just found out the name of her father. Her mother would never tell her before. It just happens to be the same as your name. And the dates coincide. She did a search on Facebook.'

'Are you telling me my name has been plastered on Facebook for the world to see? Does she realize that I am a lawyer? Wait till I have a talk with her!'

'Dad, Dad,' I continued. 'There's more. She just happens to resemble me enough to really be my half-sister.' After that soaked in, I ventured, 'And she also happens to be a Catholic nun.'

You should have seen the look on his face. It was priceless. I don't mean to laugh about it, but for him to be told that he may have a daughter who is a Sister was just too much," Lisa giggled. "Bottom line is that he did agree reluctantly to meet you. I think he plans to prove you are a hoax. How do you feel about that?"

Catherine was shaken, but managed to finish the conversation. "We do owe each other that much, I guess."

"I'm so sorry, Catherine. I hoped he would take it better. But you never know. When he meets you he may have an entirely different attitude after he thinks it through. You know how men are."

"Actually, I don't," said Catherine softly.

CHAPTER FORTY-NINE

Laura remembered that after her sister Sharon had died, Mike had wanted her to keep some old papers that were stuck in a box, thinking maybe there was something he would want to look through someday. Mike had been in college when his mother had gone through her long illness, and by the time she died, he wanted nothing to remind him of the last few months. Laura now opened the box and saw the death certificate on top, where she had placed it after they had disposed of Sharon's personal items. She slowly pulled out her sister's birth certificate, graduation diploma, passport, a prom photo, a photo of Laura and Sharon as kids, the letter Sharon had received from the Mother Superior, and there, folded with it were the adoption papers. She carefully unfolded them, and found the name of the convent, along with Mike's birth certificate.

Of course, the birth certificate was an amended certificate, showing all original information, except the names of the birth parents. Upon adoption, the amended birth certificate had the birth parents names changed to the names of the adoptive parents.

Mike picked up his ringing phone, "Hi Aunt Laura. What's up?"

"Some good news for you. I dug out that box of old papers belonging to your mother that you gave me to keep. And what do you think I found?"

"My birth certificate, I hope."

"Yes, it is there with other papers, but you know that when a child is adopted, the adoptive parents receive an amended certificate. So this one shows your mom as the parent, and there is no information on the birth parents."

Mike groaned into the phone.

"But wait, I also found something that might help you. Folded up with it I found information on the name and location of the convent from which you were adopted, and also a letter on their letterhead from the Mother Superior."

"All right!" exclaimed Mike. "I'll stop by and pick it up later today. Gee, thanks, Aunt Laura."

When Mike arrived at his aunt's home, she had the box of papers already set out for him to see. Together they slowly examined each photo and document.

"Now how should I proceed?" Mike wanted to know. "Shall I call out there and see what they can tell me?"

Laura thought a minute and replied, "If it were me, I think I'd take a trip out to the convent and do this face–to-face. I'm afraid that if you call, you will get a curt, 'We can't disclose that information,' sort of reply. But if you are standing there, you might be able to speak to a sympathetic person who will go the extra mile. And actually, their records might not be sealed. I think this was kind of a secretive situation, but probably not legally sealed."

The next day Mike arranged for a few days off work and booked a flight to Rapid City, South Dakota. He packed an overnight bag, including the documents he thought necessary to prove his identity, his mother's identity, the amended birth certificate, and carefully added the letter his mom had received from the Mother Superior all those years ago. The following Saturday he landed in Rapid City and rented a car for his drive to this place that was supposed to be near Scenic.

His GPS told him to start going northwest on Terminal Rd, get onto Kitty Hawk Rd, turn left onto Airport Road, and then left onto Highway 44 East toward Scenic. When he had driven less than an hour, he turned off into the driveway of a nearby ranch, and stopped the Chevy Impala in front of the house. Two dogs began furiously barking. A young woman came to the door.

"I am looking for an old Catholic convent around here. Can you give me directions?" Mike politely asked.

"I'm sorry, I don't know exactly where it is, but I do know there is one. Just a minute and I'll call my husband." She picked up a cell phone and punched in a number. "Hi, honey, it's me. There is a man here who is looking for the old convent. Can you tell him exactly where it is?" She listened to his reply, grinned, and handed the phone to Mike.

The rancher's wife listened as Mike commented, "Ok, then turn right at the two mailboxes, yes, about how far? A stockade fence? Hey, thanks a lot." He jumped back into the rental car, waved a good-bye, and headed back toward the road. He was within five and a half miles of the convent. Mike's breathing came fast as his heart began a rapid dance. And there to his right was the tall fence the rancher had described. He pulled the Impala off the road, crossed the clearing, and came to a stop. Taking a deep breath, he tried to relax the tension in his shoulders.

CHAPTER FIFTY

Catherine finally received the call she had been waiting for so impatiently. Lisa's father had agreed to meet with her. She cleared her calendar, let her mother know that the big day was approaching, and packed a bag. She would leave early and drive to Lisa's house first. Together they would meet with Mr. Jackson. As she travelled across the state again, she worried this might very well be the last time she would visit Lisa. Or, maybe, just maybe, this would be the first time of many that she would feel part of a larger family.

When she arrived, Lisa suggested they have lunch together downtown. "I think a little glass of wine might calm your nerves, and mine too," she laughed. Over lunch the women bonded a friendship that hopefully wouldn't be broken, regardless of what happened at this meeting.

Lisa glanced at the time on her cell phone, and announced, "Dad suggested two o'clock and he likes people to be prompt. Even though he is semi-retired, he goes into the office most days, so that is where we will meet him."

They were only a few blocks from the office, so Lisa suggested they walk over, hoping to get rid of some of the nervous energy they both felt. They exited the office elevator and checked in with the law firm's receptionist, who pressed the intercom and announced,

"Your favorite daughter is here to see you." She noticed the sudden look that was exchanged between Lisa and Catherine. A handsome man with a thick head of white hair, bushy eyebrows, and an easy gait opened his office door, glancing from Lisa to Catherine.

"Come in, come in please," he spoke to his daughter as he gave her a quick hug. "And this is Catherine?" he added, as he carefully closed the door behind them. There was no mistaking the look of curiosity that passed across his face as he eyed the nun's habit that Catherine wore. He reached for her hand, holding it a moment in his.

"Sit down, please," Mr. Jackson invited, always the proper professional, regardless of his true feelings. "What shall I call you? Is it Sister Catherine?"

"Yes sir that would be proper, but not necessary. Please just call me Catherine. Lisa is already comfortable with that."

Lisa jumped in, "Daddy, doesn't she look a lot like me?" Jim quietly weighed out the situation before answering.

"Yes, Lisa, she does, but that doesn't prove anything. You know they say we all have a double somewhere." Jim was beginning to be uncomfortable as he began to notice the similarities between the two women seated in front of him. Catherine had that awkward grin that crinkled her face more on the right side than the left, just like Lisa. This was something about Lisa that he had always found to be endearing, and here was a stranger with the very same characteristic. Their voices had a similar softness, too. There was already an easy camaraderie between the two that added to his angst.

"Tell me about yourself, Catherine," he continued politely. Catherine took a deep breath and plunged into her story.

"I was born and raised in a Catholic convent in the western part of the state, near the tiny town of Scenic. It is little known around there, much less in this part of the state. I know you must wonder how I could have been born in a convent. My mother attended high school here in Sioux Falls, and discovered that she was pregnant the summer before her senior year. She said her boyfriend and she had agreed to break up before he left for college, even though she thought she was in love with him. It was very emotional for her to talk about it with me. Even after all these years, I guess the split had left a scar on her heart. Her parents were mortified that their daughter was pregnant, so they whisked her away to this convent where they knew an unwed girl could stay until her baby was born. Then the convent was supposed to help them with an adoption."

Jim sat as if in a trance, staring across the room seemingly paralyzed by this unfolding tale. "Her dad had a sister in Rapid City, and they pretended that my mother was going there to help out with her little cousins, and finish her senior year there. I was born on March twenty-ninth, nineteen sixty-six. My mother finished her classes at the convent and I was cared for in a nursery there. When her parents, my grandparents, came to pick her up, she refused to go home. She told them that she could not leave me. She would not let me be adopted."

"That must have been a very difficult situation for everyone," interjected Lisa.

"Oh, yes. As it ended up, my grandparents finally drove back to Sioux Falls while Mother cried and pleaded with God and the Mother Superior to allow her to stay with her baby. She said she had quite a talk with the Mother Superior, begging to let her stay and become a nun! Apparently the Mother Superior had a soft spot for her, and did allow her to stay, along with the baby, me. She then had to study the Catholic doctrines, and eventually went through all the hoops, becoming a postulant, novice, and then making her professions."

Jim finally focused his eyes on Catherine. "I don't know much about all that mumbo jumbo, but that is quite a story, Catherine. And what is your mother's name?"

"Her name was Judy Bjorg. She said her family and her boyfriend's family also attended the same Lutheran church here in Sioux Falls."

"He still does attend a Lutheran church, don't you, Daddy?" Lisa got a 'Don't help her out here' look from her father. The women sat quietly, glancing at one another occasionally as Mr. Jackson looked at the ceiling and steepled his fingers.

"Judy Bjorg was my Judy, all right. March of nineteen sixty-six, you say. I was a freshman in college. If this story were true, why would Judy not have told me about the pregnancy? I find it hard to believe that she would have gone through all that alone without even letting me know."

Catherine tried to answer his question. "I know how you feel. I really can't yet understand that myself. She not only deprived me of having a father, but chose to face this really without any family help. She said her parents didn't want your parents to know about it either. They were ashamed to have an out-of-wedlock grandchild. Remember, it was the sixties. I guess things were quite a bit different then. They thought their standing in the community would be tarnished."

Lisa's mouth turned down in a frown as she heard the sorrow in Catherine's voice. She was barely speaking above a whisper as she related this part of the story.

"And she also knew that you would have married her whether you wanted to or not. That would have most likely ended your pursuit of a law degree. She cared about you enough to not allow that to happen to you."

Jim now was filled with unspoken emotion as he dropped his head and stared at the floor. He reached in his pocket and pulled out a handkerchief, wiping tears from his eyes. "Catherine, I don't know what to say to you. All the pieces seem to fit, unless there was another boyfriend."

Lisa interjected, "Daddy, her mother was already pregnant before you left for college. If she was in love with you, I doubt that she would have had another boyfriend."

"I suppose you are right," Jim agreed as he took a deep breath and slowly blew it out. "Catherine, will you agree to a DNA test? I need to feel sure about this before I break the news to Lisa's mother."

"I think she will be okay with it, since it was such a long time ago, and before she ever met you. And besides, when she sees how crazy

Chels is about you, she'll make you a welcome member of our family," Lisa added.

Jim looked at Catherine. "By the way, where is your mother now?"

"As I told you, she became a nun. Actually, she is in the same convent where I live," explained Catherine.

"Sister Judy," Jim slowly rolled the sound of it around on his tongue.

"Well...ah…not exactly. We all get a name change when we take our final profession. She is now Sister Marguerite. Actually, she is the Prioress of the convent," Catherine related with a smile.

"And what is a Prioress?" asked Lisa.

"Four women are elected for a six year term; then become the governing body. Among these four, one is elected Prioress. You may be more familiar with the older term Mother Superior."

"In other words, she is the top dog there?" asked Jim.

"I guess you could call her that!" laughed Catherine.

"I'll be damned!"

"Daddy!" exclaimed Lisa, looking with shock from her father to Catherine.

"Oh, it's all right," said Catherine. "We are not a group of sheltered women. We are in the world too, just not of the world."

Mr. Jackson sat very still, looking from Lisa to Catherine, while noticing more and more similarities in not only their appearance but also in mannerisms. He asked Catherine more about convent life, not so much to know what her life was like, but to satisfy his curiosity about Judy's life.

After Jim suggested that he set up DNA testing for both himself and Catherine, the women rose to leave. Catherine mentioned that she had a stop to make at a medical facility while in Sioux Falls, and therefore could have her testing done there. Jim agreed, but insisted that the bill be sent to him. His attitude toward Catherine had evolved from one of stiff politeness to one of cautious fondness, as he took one of her hands in both of his and held it a few seconds while he smiled into her eyes.

"I was not expecting this, Catherine, but if it turns out that I indeed have a daughter, I will be proud that it is you."

As the women walked back to her car, Lisa asked Catherine, "Do you have a medical concern that you would like to share with me?"

"Oh, no," Catherine hastily replied. "I have periodic business there that I tend to for the convent. That's all."

The two women bid one another a fond good-bye at Lisa's house, and Catherine drove directly to the medical facility, where she had an afternoon appointment. While there, she had her swab completed for the DNA testing. The afternoon was waning, as she pulled into the motel parking lot where she had made a reservation. Complete exhaustion overcame her. A good night's sleep was welcome. The next morning Catherine eagerly headed back to the convent, bursting with the news she wanted to carry to her mother, but equally apprehensive as to how it would be received.

As soon as she had parked her car and dropped her overnight bag in her room, Catherine hurried to her mother's office.

"Well, well, well, the prodigal daughter has returned."

"Mother, I am not sorry for what I have done," began Catherine.

"And this James Jackson, did he deny that he could be your father?"

"On the contrary, after I told him your story, he softened and suggested we have DNA testing done."

"When pigs fly!" exclaimed Marguerite.

"Mother, I am serous. I already had my swab taken when I stopped at the lab. He will have his done, and he insisted that he pay for my testing too. Now we wait."

"Yes, Catherine, now we wait."

CHAPTER FIFTY-ONE

Marguerite continued, "By the way, a young man just arrived, who came to search our records regarding his adoption. Seems to be a day for searching, doesn't it?"

"Yes, I guess so, and I have sympathy for him too if no one would tell him the truth. What did you do with him?" asked Catherine.

"I have him waiting in the library. I was undecided as to who should handle this case. But now that you are here, maybe you'd like to deal with him?"

Catherine gave her mother a long look and said, "Yes, maybe I would," as she headed for the door.

Entering the library, Catherine saw a young man seated on one of the sofa chairs, glancing around the room uneasily. He raised deep brown eyes to stare at her, obviously ill at ease to be meeting yet another nun. Catherine extended a hand and approached him as he stood to meet her.

"Hello, Mike?"

"Yes, that's right, Mike Pearson," replied the young man.

"I am Sister Catherine. I understand you are searching for your birth mother. Please follow me and we will sit down in my office and have a little chat." After Mike had repeated his story to Catherine, she invited him to follow her down to Archives. It was now mid-afternoon and Abby and Emily were at their computers, inputting data from the file cabinets.

"Hi, girls." Looking around, Catherine asked, "Isn't Chloe here today?" Explaining to Mike, she continued, "Chloe is in charge of the Archive Department. Abby and Emily are students in our high school, and have been helping to catalogue old records into a digital format."

Both girls grinned at Mike, and Emily said, "Hi, Mike." Abby smiled and returned to her data entry.

"Oh, there you are, Chloe," Catherine greeted the woman with warmth. "This is Mike Pearson. He is looking for his adoption records. He has documents that indicate he was born here in nineteen eighty-five."

"I'm sorry, Catherine, but I am just swamped today. I have a meeting in ten minutes. But I'll tell you what. I think Abby here could find the birth certificate for him." Chloe went to her computer screen. "I entered the recent births myself, and devised a system where I entered the adoptive parent's name, cross referencing it with the birth mother's name." She pulled up her spreadsheet. "Mike, what is your adoptive last name again, please?"

Mike answered, "Pearson." Chloe typed in the name, wrote down the birth mother's name on a piece of paper, and handed it to Catherine. "Do you have time to show her where the records are?"

"Sure, I can do that," answered Catherine. "Come along, Abby. Hannah, why don't you come too? It can be a little scary down there alone on your first trip. I'll run down with you girls so I can show you where to look. Mike, you can make yourself comfortable here. This shouldn't take too long. Oh, I guess we had better take a second key so you can lock up. I'll open it for you, Abby, but I also have another appointment in about fifteen minutes." Catherine opened Chloe's desk drawer and pulled out a ring of keys, handing them to Abby. Abby caught Emily's look as she walked past her desk. Abby raised her eyebrows and tried to hide her grin.

Abby and Hannah trailed Catherine down into the lowest level of the building. Catherine hurried past the locked doors, including the one labeled "Births" where Catherine had so recently found her own birth certificate. Abby's eyes darted from door to door, reading labels as they walked down the corridor. Novices, Postulants, Diaries, School Records, Priests. She couldn't read them all quickly enough.

She knew Emily would later grill her on what she had seen. Catherine stopped at the door marked "Adoptions."

She unlocked the old lock with one of the keys she always carried and switched on a light. Inside were file cabinets and on shelves were stacked boxes. "The cabinets are labeled by birth year, so it shouldn't be too hard to find Mike's records. He was born in nineteen eighty-five, so I am hoping his record is filed accordingly. We can only assume at this time that his birth mother used the name on this slip of paper, which is Meyer. I really do need to get to my meeting. You can pull the record and stick this check out sheet in its place. You also have a key to lock up. Each key on that ring has a room label, so you won't have any trouble finding the correct one. Just remember to make a copy for Mike, and then return the original here. Good luck," she said over her shoulder as she exited the musty room and closed the door.

Abby and Hannah were left standing alone in the lowest level of this massive building, in a dusty old record room, stuffed with archival material dating back decades. Abby looked around, feeling the ghosts of nuns long deceased, as she wondered what it must feel like in the room labeled "Deaths." All of the nineteen eighties cabinets were nearest the door, and locating eighty-five was not difficult. She gave it a tug and out rolled a drawer stuffed with papers. Whoever had filed these hadn't bothered to insert alphabet dividers so Abby thumbed through until she came to Manning. She slowed down and carefully pulled each sheet forward until she saw Meyer. Date of birth July 11! This was it. Glancing over the information, she read Mother, Donna Meyer.

Anxious to get out of this stuffy airless room, Abby stuck a checkout sheet in place of the record that she had pulled. Noticing that the used sheets had a nun's name, followed by a date, she realized that she should log the date that she pulled the birth certificate. Luckily there was a box of used pencils on a shelf. She jotted down her name, the birth certificate that she pulled, and today's date. She gave the drawer a shove and it rattled closed.

"That wasn't really so hard," she said to Hannah. "But I am glad you came along. It is a little spooky down here."

Quickly retracing her steps to the door, she pulled it open, stepped into the corridor, found the correct key, and locked up the room, with Hannah at her heels. They rushed along the corridor, up the flights of stairs, and into the Archives office. Mike was talking to Emily, who seemed to be more engrossed in the conversation than in her data entry. "Oh, hi, Abby," she greeted.

"Did you find my original birth certificate?" Mike eyed the paper in her hand.

"Yes, I did. Just a minute while I make a copy for you." Abby turned and went into the next room, ran a copy, and returned, handing the copy to Mike.

He looked it over slowly. "So my birth mother's name must be Donna Meyer. But this doesn't say anything about their having been a twin sister. My Aunt Laura said that my mother had reluctantly told her that the Mother Superior tried to get her to take a twin sister also."

"Geez, really?" exclaimed Emily.

"Catherine didn't tell me that. She just said to find your birth certificate," Abby responded. "I'm sorry that you didn't find what you had hoped to find. I can ask Chloe about it later. She may know if there is some other filing system. You know, similar to her cross referencing." Mike thanked the girls and Emily offered to walk him back to the main door.

CHAPTER FIFTY-TWO

Sam picked up his phone on the first ring when he saw that it was his brother calling. "Hi, Eddie, is there something wrong?"

"Heck, no, Sam. Good news this time. I'm getting out of this hole next week."

Sam sighed. "That's good news all right, brother. Do you have a plan?"

Eddie said with a hint of sarcasm, "Do you mean do I have a grand plan for my life? Not exactly. But I have a buddy who will let me stay with him until I get my head on straight."

"Eddie, I know you don't like to take advice from me, but this time you need to. I'd rather you got out of town, away from your old pals. Make a new life. An honest life. Get a decent job."

"Sam, Sam. Just how can I do that? I've done this before, you know, so they aren't going to be generous with gate money this time."

"Listen to me, Eddie. Okay, so you stay with your buddy for a few days, but then I am coming out there next weekend. I'll help you if I can be assured you won't commit any petty theft before that. I have an idea. I think you should relocate to Rapid City. You can find some kind of an honest job. I'll help you find a place to live."

"Rapid City? I don't know anybody out there," complained Eddie.

"That's just the point, Eddie, that's just the point."

CHAPTER FIFTY-THREE

Mike picked up his phone and punched in his aunt's number.

"Aunt Laura, I have the original birth certificate. Her name was Donna Meyer."

"Oh, Mike, I'm so glad you got this far. Is there any indication of where she lives, or at least where she was from?"

Mike sounded dejected as he said, "No, none at all. How can I possibly find her?"

"Why don't you bring the certificate over here and let me take a look? Maybe together we can figure out how to start a search, if that is really what you want to do."

That evening Mike and his aunt sat with their heads together at the kitchen table, staring at the birth certificate. Mother: Donna Meyer. Father: Unknown. Date of birth: July eleven, nineteen eighty-five. Sex: male.

"Mike, what is this written in the corner? It looks like the number five followed by g slash c."

"Who knows? Probably some filing system they used twenty-five years ago," answered Mike.

"Like fifth file cabinet, green, in the corner?" laughed his aunt.

"Sure, something like that," Mike responded. "Their system didn't look too sophisticated. They sent a couple of teen-aged girls down to the basement to find it, and by the looks on their faces, I doubt if they'd ever been down there before."

Laura got up to find a magnifying glass. "I'm going to take a better look. Looks like it was written in pencil, and maybe even had an erasure." She returned with a large hand lens, settled back into her chair, adjusted her bifocals, and pulled the document closer. "There is a smudge, which I think was an erased mark. It is on the number five. Looks like it is really a two. I think someone had a little mark above the two, making it look like a five, and it was erased for clarity. There appears to also be another letter ahead of the two, but I can't make it out."

At that, Mike leaned forward, showing interest. "Then the notation is really two g slash c? Maybe the two means twins?"

"Or maybe it means second file cabinet, green, in the corner," chuckled Laura. "I don't think we can get too excited yet. Unless we can get more information out of the nuns, which is unlikely, our best bet now is to try to find your birth mother. Do you have a Facebook account?"

"Doesn't everybody?" Mike grinned at his aunt.

"Well, I don't. But I have heard of searches on Facebook for missing family members. Could you try that?"

"I guess so," Mike answered with skepticism. "But I have one more idea. I'm going to call that Archives department and ask them to take a closer look at the original. Maybe there is something else we can't see on this copy." He picked up the document, gave his aunt a good-bye hug, and headed out the door.

The next morning Mike tapped the convent number into his cell phone, and waited impatiently for someone to answer. When he got a response, he asked for the Archives department. When Chloe answered, he briefly explained his request. With a little convincing, she agreed to take another look at the certificate.

"I'll have Abby run down to records when she gets here after classes." Mike thanked her and completed the call with reserved enthusiasm.

When Abby and Emily arrived, Chloe told them about the call from Mike.

Emily immediately piped up, "Do you mean the Mike who came down here for his birth certificate?" Abby sneaked a grin at Emily.

Chloe replied, "Yes, Mike Pearson. Abby, will you run down to records and pull that original again, please. The keys are in my top drawer."

After she had retrieved the document for the second time, Abby sat down and looked at it carefully. Chloe was out of the office again, so Emily left her desk and stood looking over Abby's shoulder.

"What is he talking about, extra notes?" wondered Emily.

In the upper right hand corner Abby spied the number 2 followed by g slash c. "What is that other mark in front of the two?"

Just then Chloe walked in and Emily scurried back to her desk.

"Here is the birth certificate, Chloe," Abby offered. "It does look like something handwritten in the corner, just like you said Mike mentioned."

Chloe took a look and agreed. "But I have no idea what that might mean. We don't put any notations or codes on birth certificates or adoption papers. Maybe twenty-five years ago it meant something. However, Sister Judith has been here a long, long time. She worked in Archives for many years. Maybe you girls would like to pay her a visit and see if she remembers anything about additional information being written on official documents."

Abby quickly spoke up, "Sure I would. Em, come with me, okay?"

The girls, though apprehensive to approach old Sister Judith on their own, were at the same time excited to play detective.

"Isn't Judith the old nun who told the story about the blizzard of 1888?" asked Emily.

"I think you are right. And she did have a great memory, that's for sure," agreed Abby.

"What if she is so deaf she can't understand us?" wondered Emily.

"I guess we better remember to talk as loud as we can, then," giggled Abby. Judith's room was empty, but they found her working on a puzzle in the game room. As they approached the old nun, she glanced up, smiled, and invited the girls to help her with the puzzle.

"You are those girls who are hiding here, aren't you?" questioned Judith, in a shaky voice. Abby cast a fearful look at Emily. "It's okay, dear, I know everything that goes on here, and I won't tell. Now did you come to help with my puzzle, or not?"

Abby was now uncertain whether to try to question Judith. "Sister Chloe in archives suggested that we might ask you for some information."

"In archives? You know I was director of archives for many years. Of course that was a long time ago, even before you girls were born."

Emily tried to help Abby steer the conversation. "We are helping in archives for our current work assignment. We were looking at an old adoption certificate, and saw some handwritten notes on it."

Judith gave the girls a long hard look. "Adoption certificate, eh? We did send a lot of little babies out to new homes over the years. Those poor unfortunate teenage girls. My mother warned me about boys. 'Always keep the hem of your dress below your knees,' my mother said, 'and your drawers up.' " Emily coughed to cover a giggle, while Abby sat down beside the old lady.

"I brought a birth certificate along for you to take a look."

"Oh, my, let me clean my glasses then," Judith suggested, as she pulled out a hankie and wiped the lenses.

Abby began to recite the details found on the old paper. "It says, Mother, Donna Meyer, Father, Unknown, DOB July eleven, nineteen eighty-five, Sex Male. But there is something written in pencil in the upper corner. Do you see it?"

Judith adjusted her trifocals, leaned closer, took the paper in her wrinkled hands, and scrutinized it carefully.

After what seemed like a long wait, she looked up at Abby and said, "Of course. It says M 2g/c. We used to mark the birth certificate with a code only we knew. You know how secretive the church was in those days. We always kept the Grand Silence, wore our full habits, and followed all the rules. These days the young ones in some convents don't even wear habits. Can you imagine?"

Abby's own long black robe hid her impatience as she began to jiggle her leg and tap her heel. Trying to guide the conversation back to the adoption certificate, she asked, "Do you remember what the code means?"

"Do you think I'd forget something like that?" Judith turned her head and gazed at Abby.

"Sometimes more than one baby was born. The M stands for Multiple. The 2 means there were two more babies. And the g indicates a girl. The c means she was kept in the convent."

"Holey Smoley!" exclaimed Emily.

"I don't like to hear that kind of language, miss," admonished Judith with a look in Emily's direction.

Abby pushed for clarification. "Don't you mean that the 2 means two babies, total, not 2 more babies? That would mean Mike was or is a twin, like his aunt told him."

"I was director of archives for nineteen years. I devised that code. I think I know what it means better than you do, young lady. We didn't have many triplets, but when it was twins, the code was just M g slash c, without a number ahead of the g, because the M made it obvious that it was a multiple birth."

"I'm sorry, Sister Judith. I just am surprised. Were there any other codes?"

"Of course! We had to distinguish the birth certificates of the girls in another way. Theirs were marked, 'M t ampersand b slash a,' if it was a triplet birth. Otherwise twin girls were indicated by M g/c."

"What is an ampersand?" asked Emily.

"Oh, you young people don't use the English language properly any more. It simply means the 'and' sign. So M t ampersand b slash a meant multiple birth of a twin girl plus a boy to be adopted."

"Why were the boys all adopted?" asked Abby.

"What would we do with boys in a convent, dear?" replied Judith.

"What happened to Mike's sisters? Were they adopted by another family?"

"Oh, goodness no! The girls weren't adopted!" Judith pushed back her chair, grasped the edge of the table, and stood up. "It's time for lunch. I'm hungry. That's all I know." She shuffled off toward the cafeteria, as the two girls stared after her.

Abby and Emily practically flew down the halls back to Archives, with their robes flapping around their feet.

They nearly plowed Chloe over as she stepped from her desk. "What is going on, girls?"

"You won't believe what we found out from Sister Judith! She remembered the codes. The little letter in front is an M. It stands for multiple," Abby explained in a rush of words.

"Multiple births!" added Emily.

Abby raced on with her information. "And the 2 means two more babies. The g is for girl, and the c is for convent."

Chloe mulled this earful. "Don't you mean a total of two babies, twins?" she asked.

Abby quickly replied, "That's exactly what I asked. But she snapped at me and told us that she had devised the codes and knew what they meant."

"There certainly haven't been any triplets to my knowledge since I have been working in here. But if Mike is in his mid-twenties, that would explain why I have never heard of this code. They must have stopped documenting this way many years ago. I'll let you, Abby, call Mike back and explain it to him. You can also file that original certificate back where it belongs."

After Chloe left later that afternoon for another meeting, Abby nearly jumped off her chair, in her haste to get back downstairs.

"Don't you see what this means, Em? There must be a record of twin girls born on that date in the basement archives. If they file birth certificates of adopted babies in the Adoption room, they must file the rest in the Birth Certificate room. If they are also filed by the mother's last name, I should be able to find their certificates under Donna Meyer too. You'll have to stay here in case anybody comes in. When I am filing this one back, I'll slip into the other room and search," Abby explained, as she reached for the basement archives key ring.

"Wait a minute, Abby. Maybe Mike's twin sisters are Leah and Lydia!" Emily's words raced over each other. "Oh my gosh! You might be right. Wouldn't that be too cool? I'm going to find the birth certificates of those twin babies."

When she got the lock opened on the Births door, Abby realized how large this room was. There was a distinct separation between the oldest cabinets, going back as far as the late eighteen hundreds, and those dated after nineteen sixty. She quickly found cabinets marked with dates in the eighties, and stopped in front of one labeled nineteen eighty-five.

Thumbing through the papers, she found the section of last names beginning with M. It didn't take her long to locate Meyer, Donna. Sure enough, there were two birth certificates filed under the name. Both indicated female babies born on July eleventh, nineteen eighty five. Abby's hands were shaking as she scanned them and allowed her eyes to settle on the upper right hand corner. There were the codes, identical on each certificate. M, t, the ampersand sign, followed by b slash a. She quickly pulled check out cards down from the top of the cabinet, jotted down her name and the date, and stuffed them in to replace the original certificates. Abby gave the drawer a shove, letting its own weight cause it to latch, rushed out the door, turned the key in the lock, and fled up the stairs.

CHAPTER FIFTY-FOUR

"The time has come," announced Marguerite as Catherine settled herself into her favorite chair in the Prioress' office.

"Time for what, Mother?" questioned Catherine. Uncomfortable that Marguerite might be bringing up Catherine's recent meeting with James Jackson, she sighed and braced herself for more questions.

"I had a visit from Father Gregory this morning. Do you remember when he was here some time ago and warned me that Rome was rumbling about conducting an apostolic visitation?"

"Yes, I remember, but you didn't seem very concerned. As I recall, you had Father Gregory convinced that Rome wouldn't give a hill of beans about a little old obscure convent set out here beside an Indian Reservation," Catherine reminded her.

"I guess I was wrong, for once," Marguerite admitted, as she gave a lopsided grin.

"Mother, it's not often anyone hears that from your mouth. Please do continue."

"It seems that the powerful men of Rome think that the American nuns are getting a little too big for their britches."

Catherine laughed. "I do like your analogies. Maybe we should suggest that the food service discontinue desserts."

"Catherine, I think this is serious. However, I maintain that if we are guarded in what we say, nothing will be exposed that doesn't need to be exposed. I understand that they may send two priests. The good cop, bad cop routine, I imagine. Father Gregory says they will probably interview the council, and also pick a few random Sisters to question."

"Mother, the council certainly knows what to say and what not to say, and those that don't know anything can't tell anything, right?"

"Yes, I agree. But we do have to have a council meeting to be sure we will all be united in our answers. Here's the thing. Father Gregory has already received the official communication. He thinks they may arrive unannounced, with the intention of catching us off guard. Therefore, would you set up a council meeting as soon as you can, Catherine?"

"Sure thing," she replied as she went out the door. A week later Marguerite summoned Catherine to her office, with the message that there were two visitors waiting to ask a few questions. When Catherine entered the room, Marguerite introduced Father Timothy Kane, and Father Joseph Borgus.

"Catherine, these gentlemen are visiting some convents across the United States. They are both from a New York Diocese, and have been sent as emissaries of Rome. Gentlemen, I believe that I will ask the other members of our governing council to join us," Marguerite stated.

"No, Sister," Father Timothy interjected. "We would rather keep this on a more or less one on one discussion, or two on two, as the case may be," he said with a forced smile. Taking control, Father Joseph beckoned the women to take seats. Catherine was aware that Marguerite would not accept this condescending attitude graciously. Knowing that her Mother's hackles were up, Catherine, anxious as she was, managed to swallow a nervous giggle of her own. The two priests took seats and Father Timothy opened a briefcase.

"Relax, Sisters. We are only here to have a friendly visit to determine how things are going in your little convent. The powers that be in Rome have decided to, shall I say, get better acquainted with the American nuns. They feel that they have been neglecting their Sisters across the ocean. I have here a copy of the questionnaire that you, Sister Marguerite, so kindly and promptly filled out and returned to us. Among other things, you state that you manage an adoption agency here. Is that correct?"

Marguerite leveled her eyes at the priest, and stated, "Yes, Father. And one that we are very proud of, I might add. We don't handle many adoptions anymore, however. You know that these days the unwed mothers usually keep their babies, with no societal stigma attached. We have, however, helped countless young women find homes for their babies over the years."

"Ah, yes, I see that. And that all seems to be in order," nodded Father Timothy. Father Joseph leaned forward. "I'd like to discuss your finances in a bit more detail, Sister. You seem to do an excellent job in that area."

"You will need to direct your inquiries to Catherine, here. She handles our financial responsibilities."

"Very well," Father Joseph continued, with a glance in her direction. "Now this so called adoption agency, does it bring in any income?"

Catherine quickly responded. "Only if the unwed mother has means, or a friend or relative is able to donate an amount. We don't charge the birth mother a fee. Quite often there will be a substantial gift, however. You can understand, I'm sure, how grateful the parents of an unwed teenage girl would be for us to take their daughter in and help her through her situation. And we do, of course, expect payment from the adoptive parents."

"Of course, of course. I see you listed a number of sources of income. We'll begin with the obvious. You have a substantial amount of income listed here coming in from the working Sisters. Please explain a little about their occupations."

"I'd be happy to, Father," Catherine smiled. "We are, as you well know, not a contemplative order. Our women enjoy careers beyond these walls. We have Sisters teaching at the preschool, elementary, middle school, high school, and college levels. We have nurses, physician assistants, mid-wives, accountants, and even a couple lawyers. Some of our women work with the poor, and of course many serve in parishes. Obviously, some of us also serve as leaders within the convent."

Father Joseph pressed further. "And how do you maintain your vows of poverty, with such a wide range of occupations?"

Marguerite stepped in. "I realize that you are simply testing our knowledge of the rules," she interjected.

"All working contracts are between the employer and the convent, thus eliminating the sister's involvement in the income aspects."

"Yes, yes, Sister Marguerite. You do have a firm understanding of the laws, don't you?" Father Joseph didn't expect an answer. "All right, Sister Catherine. And what about this entry marked as 'land acquisitions?' "

Catherine took control of the conversation again. "Out here, where ranchers own hundreds and even thousands of acres of land, a gift of land to the convent is not unusual. Some of the families who have owned the surrounding land for generations will eventually donate several hundred acres to us, particularly if they don't have descendants who want to take over the ranching operation. We then reap the benefits of rental income when we allow other ranchers to lease the land back from us."

"Very clever, I must say," acknowledged Father Timothy with a now friendly smile. "I don't believe I have heard of any other convent acting as landlords, or shall I say landladies, to ranchers."

"And what about monies left to specific Sisters through family estates?" asked Father Joseph.

"All inherited money is turned over to the convent by the Sister who has been fortunate enough to become an heir," Marguerite assured the priests.

"Any other income upon which you'd like to elaborate?" Father Timothy raised his eyebrows. "I remember reading a line indicating donations."

"Yes, well," Marguerite began, "families of the Sisters, along with neighboring ranchers, are always more than willing to bring us furniture, clothing, and often food too. That is all in addition to sometimes generous monetary gifts."

Father nodded. "All good and well, I'm sure. Now I believe you ladies have one other source of income that you did indeed list. Father Joseph has some reservations about it and we feel we need a complete disclosure. Father Joseph, would you like to address the next questions?" Father adjusted his glasses, peered again at the papers before him, and leveled a gaze at Catherine.

"I believe you labeled this entry, WP. And I believe that on the telephone Sister Marguerite indicated that these letters referred to 'Witness Protection.' Would you care to elaborate, Sister?" Marguerite and Catherine both had suspected that this entry was the trigger that had put the target on their backs, so to speak.

"Certainly I will explain," Catherine volunteered as she took a deep breath. "Much as we take in unwed mothers and help them through their ordeals, we also open our doors to unfortunate girls and women who through no fault of their own, have found themselves in circumstances beyond their control."

"Let me stop you right there, Sister. Just what kind of circumstances are we speaking about here?" Father Timothy wanted to know. "We can't be allowing a convent to harbor fugitives!"

"No sir, nothing like that," Catherine continued.

A frustrated Father Timothy said, "I thought the witness protection program was primarily giving fugitives a new identity."

"You are correct on that assumption, Father. That is primarily the purpose of the program. But it also leaves plenty of innocent people in its wake."

"Innocent? How so?"

Catherine pressed on with her explanation. "Family members primarily. We have one teenage girl here whose father witnessed a murder. Her mother is no longer alive. The father is currently a witness for the prosecution. Another woman who discovered her husband was involved with the mob. And also some young women who aren't directly in the WP program, but are unsafe at home, for various reasons."

"And just exactly how did this marriage of government witness protection and an obscure Catholic convent in western South Dakota come about? It seems most unlikely," Father Joseph expressed his concern.

Catherine felt she was on firm ground on this one. "Actually, I majored in Criminal Justice while in college. Of course during my course of study I became acquainted with students who later pursued careers directly related to the field. Two of them eventually took positions with the Witness Protection Program. Through these friendships maintained over the years, this 'marriage' as you called it, became a reality."

"And did you initiate this union? It seems like quite a step out from the usual activities of a convent."

Catherine tilted her head and shot a determined look at Father Joseph. "In reality, one of my contacts in the Protection Program posed the possibility to me."

Father Timothy leaned forward. "Let's stop here for a moment and back up. I am most curious why a young woman like you would pursue a college major in Criminal Justice. Somehow it seems counterintuitive to the norm. Weren't you encouraged to pursue a career in accordance with the expectations of your convent?"

Marguerite at this point couldn't bite her tongue any longer.

"She certainly was encouraged to earn a degree in education. We had hoped that she would become a teacher and perhaps someday, with her exceptional abilities, to advance into administration and leadership."

Father Timothy addressed Catherine. "What happened, my dear?"

This term of endearment coming from a priest was condescending to Catherine, causing her annoyance to reach a boiling point. "What happened was that I realized that my confines in a convent had colored my world view. Being a teacher seemed all that was expected of me. When I began to study criminal justice, I knew that I could serve God by providing society with stability and control, while maintaining my commitment to the convent at the same time."

"I see," Father Timothy said with a smug sideways glance at Father Joseph. Father Joseph, always concerned with the finances, asked, "I do see how this arrangement benefits the recipients of your hospitality, but please clarify just how this benefits this convent monetarily. Harboring these women must come at a great expense. Surely you must feed and clothe them, manage their medical expenses, and perhaps even assist with their education. Am I correct?" Marguerite repositioned herself in her chair with an uneasy gaze toward Catherine, who managed to maintain her composure.

"Certainly we have a contract with the government. The convent is paid a substantial amount for the care and keeping of each person placed with us. However, we do also care for a number of young girls who come to us independent of the Witness Program. To cover their expenses, we maintain a scholarship program which is self-sustaining through donations."

At this point both priests seemed satisfied with the answers they had received. "Some of your income methods seem a bit unusual, but I can't find real fault with them. In fact, I believe I would have to commend you for your ingenuity, Sisters." These words of praise came from Father Timothy.

Father Joseph, however, added, "Just don't let your innovative methods get out of hand." Catherine stifled a giggle, thinking that he was a bit jealous of the women's creativity. Instead, she smiled and extended her hand. As Father Timothy was reaching to grasp it, Father Joseph suddenly remembered that they hadn't completed their inspection tour. "Oh, Tim, we need to have a look at records also." Turning to Marguerite, he explained that part of their visit must include not only the common rooms, but also their archived records.

This time Catherine reacted with an uncomfortable look at Marguerite. She saw in Mother's eyes a bit of fear. Both women knew that up here in the main part of the building they could maintain complete control. The lower level of record keeping could, however, be their undoing. Adopting an artificially cheerful demeanor, Catherine took charge. She realized it was up to her to jump this hurdle. "Why surely, gentlemen. Follow me. We will need to go down to our lower level, where our director of archives has her office." Catherine led the way with the priests following. Marguerite trailed behind, her marching steps not quite as confident as usual. When they entered archives, Chloe looked up surprised. "We have special visitors with us today," Catherine explained.

After introductions, she explained that the previous twenty years of record keeping was filed in the main office, with overflow of cabinets lining the walls of the adjacent rooms. She took them on a walking tour of offices, as the two men carefully glanced at cabinet labels. Births, deaths, adoptions, aspirants, postulants, novices, professions. These records all seemed to be in order.

"It appears that you are able to maintain a steady flow of novices here. Many of the American convents are losing numbers. Can you explain your successes?" Marguerite proceeded to detail facts relating to the convents' admirable reputation, its location, the lack of availability of neighboring convents, and most importantly, the fact that it was able to attract young women, while so many convents now had an average age among the nuns of approximately seventy-five years. Father Joseph appeared to become bored with this litany of attributes.

Glancing at the cabinet labeled, 'Land Acquisitions', he stopped.

"May I?"

"Of course, Father," answered Catherine.

He opened the drawer, thumbed through a few records, pulling out random deeds. "All very interesting, to be sure," was the only comment.

"Where are the older records kept?" asked Father Timothy.

"Oh, they are stored in rooms in the basement," explained Marguerite. "You know we were established as far back as eighteen eighty-five. We have a proud history and have carefully maintained records since then, albeit handwritten records. Chloe here is converting them to digital, a huge undertaking indeed."

"Could we take a look?" asked Father Timothy.

"A look at our computer system?" asked Catherine.

"Oh, no," chuckled Father Timothy. "I'd like to see your old archived records. I have a special interest in antiquities. I always enjoy reading decades old authentic documents. I won't take too much of your time, just a quick walk through with a glance into records here and there." Catherine caught Marguerite's eye.

"We'd be proud to show you some of our oldest paperwork. Marguerite knows more about that than I do. Perhaps she will lead us down there and she can steer you to some of the diaries. We actually have kept diaries from Sisters who came here as teenagers in the late eighteen hundreds."

"That would be delightful," said Father Timothy. Marguerite shot Catherine a relieved look, and proceeded to guide the visitors down into the lowest levels. As Marguerite proceeded to the locked door marked 'Diaries' with Father Timothy at her heels, Catherine noticed that Father Joseph was scrutinizing each door. They had passed School Records, Priests, Mother Superiors, and now he stopped in front of the locked door marked 'Exclaustration.'

"Tell me, Catherine, how is your record of exclaustration? Do you have many women who leave the convent for good?"

"Actually, we have very few. This room is really a catch all for miscellaneous paperwork. We probably only have a couple of file cabinets for them. In the older days, there was little opportunity for a woman to leave and do anything else, so they usually stayed, whether they liked it or not," she laughed.

Father managed a sincere smile. "I do suppose it would be pretty lonely out here," he ventured.

Catherine continued, "And in more recent times, when the girls have the opportunity to complete higher education, they realize that they can remain true to their vows, and simultaneously pursue a career of their choice."

"Much as you did, Sister?"

"Yes, much as I did," Catherine agreed.

"I think we better quicken our pace to catch up," Catherine suggested. As they walked on toward the door that Marguerite and Father Timothy had entered, Father Joseph stopped at one labeled AI.

"And what is this one? I am not familiar with anything in the church referred to as AI." Catherine had hoped to hurry past this locked door while it remained unnoticed by Father Joseph. Her mind had been reeling ever since the priests suggested this tour.

"AI? Oh one of our science teachers each year assigns her class to write a paper expanding on the pros and cons of artificial intelligence."

"Really! May I read one of these papers?" asked Father Joseph. Catherine's heart began to race.

Glancing at the time on her cell phone, Catherine suggested that the priests join the nuns in the cafeteria for lunch.

"And these essays are really not convent property. We have written permission from each student to keep a copy. The teacher enjoys comparing the advances and knowledge gained by our students regarding artificial intelligence from year to year."

"Oh, I see," Father Joseph responded. "But very interesting indeed."

After lunch, the two priests thanked the women for their time, as well as the building tour.

"I'll see you to the door," offered Catherine. As she reentered Marguerite's office, she found the older woman sagged in her chair, her head leaned back and her eyes closed. Raising her head, she glanced at Catherine.

"Am I ever glad to have that finished!"

"Yes, but I am not so sure I fared as well as you, Mother."

"Of course you did, Catherine. You answered all questions with knowledge and authority. I think you showed those two that we are perfectly capable of running this ship without interference from Rome."

"Ah, but you don't know what happened downstairs," Catherine confided.

"What? Whatever do you mean?" asked an alarmed Marguerite.

"While you were so kindly displaying old diaries to Father Timothy, and he was enjoying your company, I was deflecting probing inquiries from Father Joseph."

"What kind of inquiries could he have made that you couldn't handle?"

"As I was trying to hurry him along to catch up with you, where I knew diaries would be a safe topic, he noticed the AI door label."

"Oh heaven help us!" blurted Marguerite. "What did you say?"

Catherine explained, "As soon as they asked to see old records, my brain began to stumble over itself in its rush to find an explanation. AI, AI, AI, I repeated to myself. How can I possibly explain that door label? Then I realized that I could probably talk circles around this old priest on a topic I hoped he knew nothing about. But how to keep him out of that room? I opened my mouth and the answer just popped out. I told him that one of our teachers had students write essays on Artificial Intelligence each year, and that she wanted them filed away to make comparisons in scientific advancements."

"Thanks be to God!" murmured the Prioress.

"But then he asked to read one. I told him that they weren't really our property. That we had obtained special written permission from the students to make copies. I hurried him on to meet you and Father Timothy."

"Catherine, did you just lie to a priest?"

"Now, Mother, listen carefully. I told him that the teacher wanted to keep copies of the essays filed away. I didn't say that they were filed in that room."

"Oh, Catherine, that was brilliant! I am so proud of you in so many ways. Now if you would just drop this pursuit of your birth father, I could have some peace on this earth."

CHAPTER FIFTY-FIVE

Catherine was going through her morning mail when she noticed an envelope from the Medical Facility in Sioux Falls where the convent had some of its lab work completed. As she pulled the sheet from its envelope, she realized that the patient's name was her own. Her heart began to beat wildly. As her eyes flew down the page, she read through the medical and legal jargon until she saw confirmation that her DNA matched that of James Jackson's DNA.

She speed dialed Lisa's number. The voice that answered simply said, "Yes, Catherine. I know. Daddy just called me!"

The two women were giddy with relief to have the wait over. "What did he say?" asked Catherine.

"He will be calling you this morning. He was really excited. Can you believe it?"

Catherine's voice took on a more serious tone. "What about your mother? Does she know yet?"

"Actually, he is explaining it to her right now. But I know she will be fine. My Mom is a wonderful, caring woman. And since it all happened before she ever met Dad, she will totally understand. You will have to plan a trip back to Sioux Falls very soon, so we can all get together and celebrate," said Lisa.

"But he will be calling you as soon as Mom knows. Catherine, I am just so excited. I can't wait to tell Chelsea! Can you even imagine how elated she will be?" A huge smile crossed Catherine's face, as she thought about having a sister and a niece. "What about your mother, Catherine? Will she be upset? Will she be able to share you with us?" wondered Lisa.

"You just let me handle my mother, Lisa. She can't deny me my joy at finally having a father and a real family."

Within the hour, Catherine's phone rang. This time the voice on the other end simply said softly, "Hello, daughter."

CHAPTER FIFTY-SIX

Mike picked up his phone.

"Hello, is this Mike?" There was a young girl's voice at the other end.

"Yes," he replied curiously.

"This is Abby. You know, from the archives department at the Convent."

"Oh, sure, hi Abby."

"Mike, I have news for you. Em and I interviewed one of the really old nuns who used to be in charge of the archives department a long time ago. She knew what those letters and numbers mean," said an excited Abby. "Chloe said they don't use them anymore, but they did in the eighties."

"And what did you find out? That it really did mean the green cabinet in the corner?"

"What?" asked an impatient Abby.

Mike realized she didn't know that he was referencing his joke with Aunt Laura. "Oh, nothing. I'm sorry. Tell me what you found out, Abby."

"Sister Judith said the M means multiple birth. The 2 indicates that there were not one, but two more babies. G stands for girl and c for convent. She said the girls were not adopted, ever, I guess. She got really quiet and cut us off after she realized she had told us that." Mike had listened carefully, but now interrupted with disbelief.

"Wait a minute! Do you mean I have two sisters? That I am a triplet?"

Abby paused. "I guess so. Kinda hard to believe, isn't it? But I snuck into another storage room in the basement and searched for your birth mother's name in the Birth Certificates. Sure enough, I found Donna Meyer. There were two identical certificates. The codes on them were M, b slash a. And Judith had told us that if a girl had a twin brother, the code on her certificate would mean that there was a boy who was adopted."

Mike posed the next question. "If I am really a triplet, and the boys were always adopted, and the girls weren't, what does that mean? What happened to the girls?"

"I don't know yet, Mike, but Em and I are checking into something. I'll let you know what I find out."

"Thanks a lot, Abby, for calling me. And let me know as soon as you do figure anymore out. Oh, tell Emily hi, will you?"

When Abby had finished her call, she related to Emily that Mike said to tell her 'Hi.' Emily blushed and asked, "Is he coming here again, do you think?"

"I don't know. He just asked me to call him with any more information we find out."

Emily was silent for a few minutes. "I have an idea. Let's ask Leah if she has her birth certificate. Then we can compare all the information on hers with the ones you found."

Neither Abby nor Emily was taking a class from Leah this semester so they were eager to visit their favorite teacher. They stopped in her classroom on their way to their archives jobs the next day.

"If it isn't two of my favorite young ladies," exclaimed Leah. "And where is your sidekick, Hannah?"

"She is taking a religion class this semester, and we are both working after classes in the archives department," volunteered Abby.

"Good for you, good for you! Sit down and tell me what you two have been up to lately."

"Actually, Leah, we came to ask you a question. We know you and Lydia are identical twins. Do you have possession of your own birth certificate? The reason we are wondering is because a man named

Mike has been to the archives department searching for his original birth certificate. He knew he was adopted from here. He found a hand written code on the certificate and we are wondering if you know what it means."

"I do have mine, but it is in my locker, in my room. I can get it out and show it to you if you can stop by again tomorrow." The girls could hardly contain their eagerness to continue their sleuthing.

The next day, when they made their visit to Leah, she had her birth certificate ready on her desk.

She began, "The upper corner does have a code. It is M, t ampersand b slash a."

Emily quickly asked, "Do you know what that means, Leah?"

"Yes, I think it stands for multiple birth, twin, and born alive."

Abby's eyes grew large. "Born Alive? Really? Why would it say that?" Leah glanced from one girl to the other, noticing their disbelief.

"Birth certificates have to indicate somewhere on them whether the birth was a stillborn, or a live birth. That's perfectly normal. The certificates done here only had that information written on by hand. You know, the church does have a few secrets. I can't really tell you why."

"But Leah," Abby hurried on, "Chloe sent us to talk to Sister Judith. She used to work in archives. She told us that she invented the codes. And she said the b slash a stands for boy adopted!"

"What? That would mean that Lydia and I are really triplets? That we had a brother who was adopted? Oh, that can't be! They wouldn't do that to us, to take our brother away. Would they?"

While Abby was talking to Leah, Emily was casually looking over Leah's birth record. Suddenly her eyes got wide and she shouted, "Leah, is your birthday really July 11, 1985?"

"Sure, don't you remember that day when I brought two birthday cakes into class, and Lydia came over from the infirmary? We ate cake to celebrate our twin twenty-fifth birthdays. One chocolate and one vanilla."

Abby looked at Emily with disbelief. "Leah, the man, whose birth certificate that we have been examining, has the exact same birthday! Maybe he is your triplet!"

"Oh, that would be just too much of a coincidence, wouldn't it?" asked Leah.

Emily quickly responded, "Hey, I hear the nuns always using the phrase, 'That's a God thing.' Couldn't this be a God thing?"

"But Lydia and I are identical twins. So how could a boy be our triplet? Nice try girls, but I doubt it."

The girls sat staring at Leah, unwilling to leave. Finally she grabbed her cell phone and called Lydia. "Lydia, can you run over here to my classroom right now? It's something of an emergency."

Lydia rushed through the door with a first aid kit. She found the two young girls and her sister all sitting quietly, each with their own thoughts.

"Hey, Lydia. I'm sorry if I misled you. Our emergency isn't medical. These girls have been working in the Archives Department and have been visited by a young man who was searching for his original birth certificate. In the course of investigating, these sleuths have uncovered a code, handwritten, in the upper right hand corner," Leah began.

Abby jumped in, "And Chloe told us to talk to Judith. She told us that the code on his means multiple birth, two girls in convent."

"So we came to see Leah, wondering what code was on her birth certificate, since you are twins," said Emily in a rush.

"And hers says 'M, b slash a.' " Leah interrupted "I always thought that meant 'multiple, born alive' but Abby says that Judith told them it means multiple, boy adopted. Have you ever heard that, Lydia?" Lydia glanced from one to another of the three women staring at her.

"There haven't been any multiple births since I have worked in the infirmary, so I don't really know how they are coded, if indeed they are," replied Lydia.

Leah looked at her sister. "In addition to this craziness, Lydia, the girls have discovered that this Mike person has the exact birth date as we do. They think he might be our brother. But I told them that we are identical twins, so he couldn't be our triplet, right?"

Lydia's brow furrowed. She fidgeted. She glanced from her sister to Abby, then to Emily, and back to Leah. "Hmmm. Actually, triplets can be made up of identical twins and a fraternal triplet if two eggs were fertilized and one of them split, causing one egg to form identical twins, while the remaining egg developed into another baby. So you see the one could even be of the opposite sex."

At this revelation, everyone in the room grew silent.

"I guess we should at least meet him," ventured Leah.

"Let's take a little time to grasp this," urged Lydia. "We are twenty-five years old and the only family we have ever known in addition to each other are our convent Sisters. Now you tell me that we may have a brother out there? And not just a brother, but a triplet brother? Are you ready for this, Leah?"

Leah took a deep breath. "I surely am curious. And I think it would be exciting to find we had more family."

Emily piped up, "He is really nice too. And cute."

"Ah, that settles it!" laughed Leah. "Let's meet this nice, cute, potential brother."

"OK, Leah. You always have been the adventurous one, while I am the practical one," Lydia winked at her sister.

CHAPTER FIFTY-SEVEN

Marguerite called two of the young Sisters to her office. "I suppose you both suspect what I am about to ask you to do," she began. Rachel and Marylou looked at each other, then back to their prioress. "As you know, we have this month lost another of our dear elderly nuns. Sister Louisa was a faithful and dear servant of our Lord during her lifetime. I visited her often when she was living her last weeks in the infirmary. Even when she was sleeping most of the day, she prayed daily for her younger Sisters. I know you both have indicated a desire to take on a very special job that follows the death of a Sister." The young women glanced at one another for support. "If you are still willing to proceed, I will explain the details of what is expected of you, and then you may be excused."

The following Friday, Catherine drove both women to Sioux Falls. She had called ahead and made all necessary arrangements. Dropping them off at their destination, she let them know she would pick them up on Sunday at the host convent where they were to stay.

When Catherine arrived at Lisa's house, plans had been made for the big family reunion. Chelsea was home from college for the weekend, eagerly anticipating her first chance to say "Aunt Catherine." Lisa had made arrangements for a casual weekend where her mother could meet her new step daughter in a relaxed setting, and Catherine and her father could have privacy for a personal conversation.

As the weekend came to an end, Catherine hugged each one in turn, and whispered to her father, "This has been one of the happiest days of my life." Jim's eyes glistened with unshed tears as he held her close and nodded.

"Mine too," he managed to speak.

Catherine stopped by the convent where her passengers had spent most of the weekend as guests. When they climbed into the car, Catherine gave each a questioning look.

"I don't feel any different," volunteered Rachel.

"Not yet, you don't. But it will come. Just be patient," Catherine assured her.

The following week Catherine stopped by Marguerite's office with a piece of financial information.

"Catherine, I know you told those two investigating priests that our income came from five major sources. We do still have a sizable number of working Sisters, who do contribute substantial income to the order, and the income from our land acquisitions is holding steady. How is the adoption income coming along? I did place another baby last week."

"Yes," Catherine commented. "Those parents were very grateful that it could be done discretely. Today we received a sizable check from them in addition to our fee."

Marguerite smiled. "I'm glad to hear that. And of course with Sister Louisa's recent death I am expecting the family will be turning her inheritance over to us also. Now what about the witness protection situation? I haven't seen Sam around lately."

At this, Catherine hurried with her answer. "Our number of girls and women in hiding is down a little, and we will most likely be losing two or three soon. Abby and Emily are both finishing high school and will be going their own ways, depending upon their personal circumstances. There is another younger one, Hannah. She doesn't really have anywhere to go, but we will deal with that when the time comes. Of course there are the other women who are here in hiding also. Yes, there is still income from the government." Marguerite leaned back in her chair.

"It sounds as if you have the income under control. Now what about our expenses?" Catherine assured her mother that convent expenses were running along steady lines.

"Although we did have to make a payment on the AI account recently." Marguerite sat very still for several moments. Catherine noticed fine lines beginning on her face, and a tired look in her eyes.

"Are you still sure we are doing the right thing regarding the AI?" Marguerite questioned.

"Mother, we have been over this so many times. The entire council agrees it is the only way. You agreed to support it when you took this job of Prioress."

"Yes, I suppose I did, but you know that in the fifties the mere mention of such a thing had the Pope proposing that this would be a sin."

Catherine stood up. "Something you said reminded me. I need to run down to see Lydia. I'll let you know how that situation is going," she said as she headed for the door.

"Hi, Lydia. I was just visiting with Marguerite about income and expenses. I need to know how deposits are going. We made a couple of withdrawals recently. Are we still getting plenty of deposits to cover them?"

"Oh, that never seems to be a problem. The last time you asked me to call a few of the more frequent donors, we received a substantial number of deposits. They continue to come in pretty steadily."

Catherine sat down. "And they are secure? Earmarked only for us?"

"Absolutely," Lydia replied. "And you know there is a six month quarantine period as well. We receive only the highest quality. And certainly the product goes through a thorough 'washing.' That was one of our stipulations."

"These donors, Lydia, how are they recruited?"

"Rest assured, they are bright savvy people. I am sure they fully believe that their donations help us further our mission."

"Also, Lydia, the issue of AI is still troubling to Marguerite, although she supports it publicly. She remains a little apprehensive privately. Mostly due to the social and moral implications, I think," Catherine mentioned.

Lydia continued, "By now I would think she would have accepted the idea. You know the term was coined back in nineteen fifty-six. One of the first reports on AI was given in nineteen fifty-three. We had entered a new era in science. Labs were set up to study the possibilities. Scientists were proceeding step by step toward perfecting this science. In the sixties it was believed that within a generation AI would be in widespread use. In the seventies banking began, and then some of the assets were frozen."

"Is that still the case?" asked Catherine. "Oh, no, not all, but most. The use of AI is rather economical, without expensive infrastructure."

"Thanks, Lydia. I'm relieved to hear all is going well on your end of things."

CHAPTER FIFTY-EIGHT

Abby called Mike and explained all that she had learned from Leah and Lydia.

"It looks like your sisters might be right here in the convent, Mike. They are identical twin sisters, but Lydia says triplets can be made up of one egg that splits plus a second egg. The girls then are identical, while you are their triplet, but fraternal." Mike agreed to come as soon as he could to meet the sisters.

"But why were they not adopted too?" he asked Abby.

"I don't know, Mike. I have no idea. Maybe nobody wanted to adopt twins."

"My aunt told me that the prioress tried to get my mom to take a twin. She didn't tell my aunt that until a long time after she had adopted me. I suppose she felt guilty about separating us. She must have said 'twins', though, not twin."

When Mike arrived at the convent, he was more nervous than he had been the first time he had come. Chloe had arranged for the three to meet in the archives office. "You will have a little more privacy down here," she had told Lydia.

Abby met Mike in the upstairs waiting room and guided him along the corridors to the offices below.

When he entered the room, two young women, both wearing identical black robes, stood side by side. They were carbon copies of each other. The only differences were that one wore a skeptical look across her face, while the other couldn't suppress a grin.

Mike stopped and stared. His eyes roved from one to the other and back. When he found his voice, he whispered, "Do I really have two sisters?"

When the more serious twin reacted with a smile, Mike noticed that they each had a dimple, but on opposite sides of their faces.

Leah stepped forward and reached for his hand. “We most likely are your sisters, Mike,” she ventured. “We are actually mirror twins. I am right handed while Lydia is left handed, and our dimples mirror each other too!”

At that, Lydia too took one of Mike’s hands in hers. Realizing the three needed privacy, Abby slipped out of the room.

Later Leah found Abby and gave her a big hug. “If it weren’t for your curiosity and tenacity, Lydia and I would never have known we had a brother.”

“Are you going to have DNA testing to be sure?” asked Abby.

“I don’t really care to find out the truth. I would like to always think Mike is our brother, even if he isn’t, but Lydia insists and Mike wants to be sure too. All I can say is that he sure was a good egg!”

“But now what about the search for your birth mother? The reason Mike came here in the first place was to see if he could find her. Now you all three know her name. Are you going to search for her?”

Leah looked thoughtful. “We just don’t know. We did have a long discussion about it. Mike would like to, but Lydia isn’t too anxious. And what affects one, now affects three. I don’t want to be the tie breaker in this. I think we will have to also talk to Mike’s adoptive aunt Laura. He respects her opinions. She was in favor of Mike’s search before he discovered he was a triplet, but now she may have changed her mind. Is it fair to our birth mother to dig into this? It had to have been very difficult for her to walk away from three babies. Shouldn’t we leave well enough alone?”

CHAPTER FIFTY-NINE

Eddie had found a truck driving job the first week he was in Rapid City. "If it weren't for Sam and his insisting, I sure wouldn't be living out here in west river country," he thought as he pulled out of the wholesale foods warehouse parking lot. "He thinks my driving around out here in the sticks delivering orders to restaurants and grocery stores will keep me out of trouble. Everything has just always been easier for Sam."

Eddie had looked over the bill of lading before he climbed into the truck. This was going to be an all-day circuit, with deliveries to small mom and pop restaurants in several little towns scattered miles apart. He headed east on I-90, driving through Box Elder, New Underwood, Wasta, and finally to Wall, where the world famous Wall drug was located, making deliveries along the way. Eddie climbed back into the truck and headed toward Cactus Flat. Now he had to turn off the interstate and take highway forty four on to the little town of Interior. He wished he could turn around and take the interstate back to Rapid City, but there was one more delivery to make.

His supervisor, Bill, had told him that this last stop was a Catholic Convent at Scenic.

"A convent? Are you sure?" asked an incredulous Eddie. "I thought they grew their own food."

"Eddie, I know you have been out of touch for a while. Convents these days are usually not cloistered."

"What the heck does that mean?" asked a puzzled Eddie.

"Cloistered means the nuns in a convent or the Brothers in a monastery choose to spend their entire lives behind walls, with no interaction with the rest of society."

"Sounds like a prison to me, and I should know," shot back Eddie.

"Well at any rate, things are kept pretty quiet at this convent, but I do know some of them teach in schools in other cities and towns. Some of the locals think this one is a little too secretive but I suppose they have their reasons."

"They keep their secrets, for sure," Eddie replied. "I went to an Indian School as a kid and it was run by some pretty nasty nuns and priests. I could tell you stories, but I don't think you want to hear them." Bill took a long hard look at Eddie.

"Oh, that's right. You are that new hire who served time in the state pen in Sioux Falls. Didn't you try to murder a priest, or something?" Eddie didn't reply.

"How am I supposed to act when I get there? Do I have to bow, or something?" asked Eddie. "Is there a secret password?"

Bill threw his head back and laughed. "No, none of that. They are pretty normal women. My sister saw a car load of them touring the Black Hills last summer. She said they were laughing and talking among themselves, but I guess they didn't interact much with other tourists. And she said they were all pretty young. Not the old ones you usually see. But you should be prepared for the fact that this bunch does still wear those black habits."

Eddie looked at Bill. "Don't they all? Any nuns I ever saw did. And believe me, I have seen more than my share of them."

Bill continued, "Now days a lot of them don't wear the habits. They dress just like anybody else. So you probably have seen some of them, and didn't even know it."

Eddie carefully followed the directions Bill had given him. Evidently this convent was pretty well hidden. Saddle Pass. Sage Creek Road. There was even a sign pointing south toward Potato Creek. This sounded like something out of an old western movie. Then he saw the top of an old cupola peeking over a stockade fence. Turning down this unpaved road, he circled the building, and brought the truck to a stop in front of a small sign marked "deliveries."

Jumping out, he stretched his frame, and looked around. This was desolate all right. Jabbing the bell, he waited for someone to open the door. One of the nuns who worked in the kitchen seemed to be expecting him. He noticed a couple of other women discussing something between themselves. He opened the truck doors, pulled out the two wheeled dolly, and loaded boxes of produce onto it.

After pushing it through the open door, he was directed to stack the boxes near the sink. As the woman was signing the delivery receipt, one of the others turned to speak to her regarding the menus. Eddie glanced at the woman. Why did she look so familiar? Had he seen her somewhere before? She couldn't have been a teacher at the school. She wasn't old enough for that. She was closer to his age.

"Catherine, when I am finished here, we can go over the entire week's menus," offered the kitchen nun.

The one called Catherine smiled and replied, "Sure, finish what you are doing. There is no hurry."

Eddie stared. The voice sounded so familiar. But he had been locked up in the state penitentiary in Sioux Falls, and this was his first trip with the delivery truck. She must just resemble someone else. Who knew? Maybe she was a relative of one of the boarding school nuns who had abused so many of the Indian kids. With one more backward glance, Eddie pushed his two wheeler through the door and loaded it back onto the truck.

On the drive back to Rapid City, he ran the voice through his head. He didn't know any Catherine.

Arriving back at the warehouse, Bill asked, "How did it go? Did you find the convent?"

"Yeah, sure. It was right where you said it would be."

"Do you want to take that run again next week, or do you want to try a different route?"

Eddie considered. "It was a pretty boring drive, but I kinda would like to make a stop at that convent again. I saw somebody there that just seemed so familiar. Maybe I could get another look at her."

Bill gave Eddie a quizzical look. “Well, if that doesn’t beat all! Eddie wants a second look at a nun! I never had a driver say that before.”

“Aw, shut up, Bill. It’s not like that at all.”

The next week when Eddie pulled the truck into the convent yard, he hesitated before driving around to the delivery door. How would he find that woman? He was sure she had been called Catherine. But there could be more than one Catherine in a convent full of women. Should he go to the front door and ask? He decided to make the delivery just like last week, and maybe ask in the kitchen about a Catherine. If that didn’t work, he could still pull around to the front, and try the main entrance.

There was only one woman in the kitchen when he rang the bell. She answered the door, introduced herself as Sister Christine, and motioned for him to bring in the boxes, and deposit them beside the sink, just like last time. Eddie noticed that the last three cartons were a variety of wines. “That’s a lot of communion wine, isn’t it?”

Sister Christine grinned from ear to ear and replied, “You think?”

When she had signed the delivery receipt, and turned to open the first carton, Eddie cleared his throat.

“Excuse me, but last week there was a woman in here speaking to another nun. I thought someone called her Catherine. Would you know who I mean?” Christine looked up at Eddie in surprise.

“We do have three Catherine’s here, but one of them is very elderly, and wouldn’t have been down here. I guess it could have been either of the other two, but most likely it was our Finance Director. She often discusses the food budget, and likes to keep tabs on food waste.”

Eddie brightened. “How would I find her? I would just like to speak to her for a couple minutes, if that would be all right.”

Christine suggested, “When you drive back around to the front, go up to the main door and ring the bell. Someone will come to the door, and you can explain who you want to see.”

"Gee, thanks," Eddie quickly responded as he hurried out to the truck and drove it back around to the front of the building. As he climbed out, he began to have second thoughts. What would he say? How should he address a nun? What if she thought he was crazy? Swallowing his fears, he quickly walked up to the door and pushed the bell.

A young woman wearing a long black habit opened the door, with a questioning look. "May I help you?"

Eddie tried not to stammer. "I was wondering if there is a Catherine here. I think she is the Finance Director." The young woman motioned for Eddie to enter.

"You can have a seat here, and I will see if Sister Catherine is available," she said with a pleasant smile.

"Thank you ma'am," Eddie tried to sound confident.

After several minutes, a woman, probably in her mid-forties, entered the room. She approached Eddie and offered her hand.

"I am Sister Catherine." Eddie stared into her face.

"Excuse me, ma'am, but I saw you last week in the kitchen when I was making a delivery, and you just looked so familiar that I felt I had to see you one more time. Even your voice reminds me of someone I knew a long time ago." Catherine now stared back. She saw a middle aged Indian man, probably a few years older than herself. He had high cheekbones like many of the Native Americans, and full lips. But she was taken aback by his eyes. They were Ty's eyes. But this was not Tyee.

"Enapay?" Catherine's mouth fell open.

"Yes, I'm called Eddie now though," he replied. "You are Carrie, aren't you?"

"Yes, Enapay, I am. But what are you doing here?"

"I saw you last week. I was delivering produce to your kitchen facility and when I heard your voice, I was pretty sure it was you. But why are you called Catherine instead of Carrie?"

Catherine explained, “When we take our final vows, we take a new name. I used Carrie all through college, but when I did my vows, I chose Catherine. How is your brother?” asked Catherine.

Eddie relaxed a little. “Oh, he’s great. But he doesn’t use his native name either. He is known as Sam now. He’s got a big government job. At least one of us made a success out of our life.”

Catherine sat down. “Yes I know he is a U.S. Marshall. He does come here you know, delivering girls and women who need a safe house to hide in for a while. But I am careful to avoid him. He does speak to Marguerite, but she is very careful to never mention him to me. It just would be too painful for both of us.” Eddie sat quietly.

“He rarely mentions you either. I never understood why you turned him down. You were so good together. When you were both in college and he would bring you along to visit me once in a while, I thought you were perfect for each other. Why didn’t you marry my brother? Why did you become a nun instead?”

Catherine leaned forward. “Enapay, Eddie,” she corrected herself, “there is a lot to our story. I doubt that he ever told you that I was born and raised right here within this convent. Can’t you understand how difficult it would have been for a girl who grew up in a convent to marry a boy who was raised on an Indian Reservation? We were really from different worlds. But my mother, who is now the Prioress here, did wish for me to marry and have a family. She did really like him a lot. He used to come here when we were in college, and the three of us would have a private dinner. She learned to love Indian frybread with chokecherry jelly as much as Ty did.”

Eddie ventured, “But didn’t you want to get married?”

Catherine smiled at Eddie. “Eddie, I know you can’t understand, any more than Ty could, but I knew deep down that I had to spend my life serving God. And in the end, I chose to marry Jesus.”

“O-k-a-y,” Eddie said slowly. “But didn’t you want to have children, either?” At that, Catherine just smiled.

CHAPTER SIXTY

Girls, I'm going to be out of the office for a couple days this week. I have to go to a convention out of state. You can still come in after classes each day and continue your work. We have so many old records to enter into the computer, that I don't want to have you miss any days," Chloe told Abby, Emily and Hannah. "I'll have Catherine come down and unlock the offices for you after school. You can lock up when you are finished, and take the keys back up to her office."

The next afternoon Catherine had the Archives door unlocked when the girls arrived.

"How is your entry work coming along?" she asked.

"Really well, Catherine," answered Abby. "But there are so many old records that I can't imagine ever getting finished with this job." Catherine smiled.

"That kind of explains everything we do here. We are never finished with the Lord's work."

After Catherine left, a nun from the mail room stopped with a stack of envelopes for Chloe.

"I'll just leave her mail here on her desk," she said, as she dropped the mail and went out the door.

Emily looked over at the desk. "I wonder what kind of mail she gets?"

"It's none of your business, Em," cautioned Abby.

"I know. But I'm just going to look at the envelopes, Abby." Emily got up and walked over to Chloe's desk. She gingerly shoved the envelopes around until she could see the return addresses of each one. "This one is from Midwest Medical Labs."

"Em, leave that mail alone," Abby scolded.

"But, Abby, under the name it says, 'Specializing in Infertility and AI.' What could that mean?" At that, Abby jumped up and scurried over to take a look.

Emily continued, "Why would a convent get mail like this?" The girls looked at each other and started to giggle. "Why would they care about infertility in a convent? Seems like that is what they would want!"

Hannah stopped her data entry and listened to the girls.

"I am more curious about the AI, Emily," continued Abby. "Remember when Leah told us a little about artificial intelligence in science class? Why do you suppose they have an interest in it?"

Emily remembered, "Leah told us that the church has an interest in just how far humans can progress without God. She even told us that later in the year we would have to write a short paper on it after we did some research." Abby was quiet for several moments.

"But why would a lab that specializes in infertility also have anything to do with artificial intelligence? It almost seems a little creepy to me. But we better get to work." The girls took their places at their computers and went back to their document entry. Hannah listened to the exchange but said nothing.

Catherine stopped by later in the afternoon. "Would one of you file these birth records back into archives for me? I have been doing a study of our old records and have pulled quite a few."

Hannah quickly volunteered. "I have been down there with Abby. I know the way," she said as she pulled the keys from Chloe's desk drawer.

Hannah hurried through the underground tunnel that opened into storage rooms. She recognized the door labels that she had seen when accompanying Abby down here. This time she stopped in front of the door marked AI. She tried the key in the lock. This one didn't seem to be an old lock, like the others. It was much newer looking and must have been replaced recently. The door hinges were still old and creaky. She slid into the room and found a light switch, pulling the door closed behind her. Looking around, she saw file cabinets similar to the other storage rooms. These too were labeled with years.

Pulling open the current year's file, Hannah noticed that the documents inside were again filed in alphabetic order. She began flipping through the papers. The first name she saw was Abernathy, Ruth. The next was Dugan, Maribeth. Then she came to Goetz, Rachel. Quickly thumbing through more of the alphabet, she came to Piper, Marylou. The last one she looked at was Taber, Jeanine. Grabbing a piece of paper and a pencil from the checkout box, she jotted down as many of these names as she could. Going back to Abernathy, she pulled the document up and glanced over the information. It was on letterhead from Midwest Medical Laboratories. Under the name Ruth Abernathy, was Artificial Insemination Date. At the bottom of the page was a line stating live birth. Hannah's heart began to race. She flew through the pages, writing dates beside the names. When she pulled Goetz, Rachel, there was nothing filled in under live birth. Then she realized that the insemination date was only last month. The same for Piper, Marylou. Her insemination date was exactly the same as Ruth's. Shoving the records back into place, Hannah quietly closed the drawer, slipped into the hallway, locked up the room, and fled up the stairs.

"What took you so long, Hannah?" asked Emily.

"I got a little lost," she grinned. "It is confusing down there."

Hannah stopped by Sister Leah's classroom the next day. "Leah, what exactly is artificial insemination?"

"Hannah, why would you want to know about that?" asked a curious Leah.

"Oh, I just read something about it in a science book, but I don't really understand what it is."

"It's when a woman can't get pregnant the normal way, so a doctor does it artificially."

“What? The doctor has sex with her?” asked an incredulous Hannah.

“No, no. I said artificially. He puts sperm in a medical syringe and injects it up into her vagina so she can get pregnant.”

“Do you mean the woman doesn’t have to have sex with a man to get pregnant?” asked an astonished Hannah.

“Yes, that’s exactly right. She can get pregnant by the sperm that is in the syringe, without having sex with a man.”

“But where does the sperm come from, the doctor?”

“No, a sperm bank. Men can go there and deposit their sperm. It is frozen and then a woman without a husband can be injected with it.”

“You’ve got to be kidding, Leah,” Hannah blurted.

That night Hannah lay in bed unable to sleep. She mulled over the records she had seen, wondering what happens to the babies born to these women. Some of these records had a line filled in under Live Births, and some didn’t. But the ones that aren’t filled in, have an insemination date of just last month, she remembered. So maybe that means that there are some pregnant nuns here now. Everyone wears habits. They are made up of yards of black cloth, hanging to our ankles. What better way to camouflage a pregnancy that to hide it under a habit? Actually, that’s probably the real reason that everyone in this convent has to wear a habit. And some of them hold their arms across their chests when they walk. “How would we really know whether they were hiding a baby bump or not?” The questions kept swirling around in her head. “But why would a nun want to have a baby? I wonder what they do with the babies? Maybe they sell them. But here are always little girls in the nursery school, and middle school. Maybe they just stay here and become nuns. Catherine was born here and stayed and grew up here.”

Finally Hannah dozed off and slept fitfully.

The next morning she had an idea. She would take these dates of live births, and go back downstairs and look in the births record room. Compare them to dates that babies were born. Judith had told Abby and Em that G slash C meant girls in convent. And B slash A means boys adopted. And if there isn't a match to a girl birth record, those live births should then match baby boys in the adoption files.

Hannah was antsy all throughout the day. She could hardly sit still in her classes. Even Abby noticed.

"What is wrong with you today?" she asked.

"I just have a lot to do, working part time here in archives and part time in foods this semester," explained Hannah. "Every day I have to run a cart all the way down to the infirmary with special foods. They look disgusting. Cook purees regular food into mush for the babies, which is okay. And guess what! There was a brand new baby in there. I asked if it was a boy or girl and Mae said it was a girl. She also said the mother was happy about that. I asked if she didn't want a boy and Mae said, 'Of course not. Then it would have to be adopted.' But I thought unmarried girls came here to have their babies and that they were always adopted. Anyway, they also mush up stuff for the sick old women. I can't believe they can eat that stuff!"

That captured Abby's attention. "Hannah, have you taken any pureed food down there that was marked RE?"

"Oh, sure. That mushy mixture is for the really sick ones who aren't expected to live very long. They get a smaller amount that is thinned so it is easier for them to swallow, I guess."

"And do you know if the RE means really elderly?" asked Abby. "I don't think so. One of the nurses down there asked me if I had brought any rotation jars. I didn't know what she meant but she said when a nun is close to death and eats very little, they refer to them as the rotation nuns, so I asked her why they call them that. She said because they rotate the old ones out and make room for new ones. She kind of snickered about it, like it was a joke."

"Oh my gosh!" blurted Emily.

"What's wrong?" asked Hannah.

"Oh, nothing," Abby jumped in. "I suppose she thinks that is gross, like a lot of other things, right Em?"

"Yeah, Abby, really gross," retorted Emily.

Abby and Emily went straight to archives after classes. Catherine was again waiting for them inside. As soon as they got settled, she hurried off to an appointment and again told them to drop the keys off at her office when they were finished for the day. Hannah came in as soon as she had finished her work in foods.

"I ran into Catherine in the hallway and she asked me to file all these records back too."

She grabbed the keys from Chloe's desk and took off for the basement archives before Abby or Emily could say anything. This time she carried along her list of women who had been artificially inseminated, and the dates of their live births.

She unlocked the Births door, hurried in, closing it behind her. She had been in here before, and knew exactly where to search. Going to the current file, Hannah pulled open the top drawer and began searching alphabetically for the names that she hoped would match those on her list. Sure enough. There was the first one, Abernathy, Ruth. Pulling the record out, Hannah carefully looked it over. It was a birth certificate for a baby girl with a birth date that was an exact match to the live birth date on the insemination record! Her eyes flew to the upper right hand corner, but there was no g slash c written there. Perplexed, she pulled the next one. It too was a certificate of live birth for a baby girl whose birth date exactly matched the birth record on the insemination paper.

Next Hannah pulled the record for Taber, Jeanine. This one was the record of a live birth for a baby boy! Again she wrote as much information down as she could and put everything back in the drawer. She gave it a mighty shove and retreated into the hallway, locking the door behind her. Now all she had to do was check the adoption room. Nearly running along the hallway, she stopped in front of Adoptions, unlocked the door, and raced to the file for the year that matched the Taber baby's birth date. She had heard Chloe say that instead of current birth certificates only containing the names of the adoptive parents, they now also were recording the birth mother, due to so many young people wanting to trace their birth parents. This was a bit more tedious, as she had to flip through all the adoption records for the year so far, looking for Taber as the birth mother. These were filed by the adoptive parents' last names. But there it was, birth mother Jeanine Taber, on a certificate of adoption of a boy by a couple with the names Linda and Jeffrey Wills. Having discovered that the birth dates on the certificates exactly matched the birth records on the insemination records, Hannah closed the drawer, turned off the light switch and locked the door.

As she neared the AI door, she decided to make one more stop to count how many insemination records she could find. After searching for the key, she turned it in the lock and pushed the door open. Approaching the first file cabinet, Hannah pulled open the top drawer. She noticed a folder in the front marked Confidential. It contained an envelope. Curious, she pulled the partially sealed envelope out and carefully worked the seal open. Lifting the document from its resting place, Hannah began to read.

> July 12, 1976
>
> This document hereby details and explains the events leading up to the decision regarding Artificial Insemination, herein known as AI, made by the ruling council of this convent in July of 1976.
>
> Following the declaration of Vatican II in 1969, vowed religious sisters across the United States began leaving their convents for a secular lifestyle. One of the contributing factors was the desire of the young nuns to bear and rear children of their own. A small number of our own nuns became pregnant during these tumultuous times. A plea was made by these young women to be allowed to raise their babies within our convent walls. The response of the council was an emphatic 'no,' until it was brought to our attention

that Sister Marguerite had indeed given birth to a baby girl ten years previously. Although Marguerite was not at the time of the birth a vowed sister, she did later take her vows and the decision was made to allow her to keep her baby and raise her in the convent. Little Catherine Ann, known to us as Carrie, is at this writing ten years old, and a welcome addition to our family.

After much agonizing discussion, the current council of 1976 came to a most controversial decision. It was decided that the young nuns who so desired, would be allowed to experience pregnancy and birth only if they were able to keep their vow of chastity intact.

Thereby, the practice of Artificial Insemination, herein referred to as AI, was approved and put into usage.

We of the present council do fully acknowledge that our decision is unorthodox. We fully accept that our Diocese would not approve if this information was ever divulged.

In contrast, however, we do firmly believe that allowing AI by means of a woman being injected vaginally with donor sperm becomes a medical procedure, and is not a form of breaking celibacy vows. In addition, our convent reaps the benefit of having an above average chance of maintaining a sizable membership into the next millennium.

We do also acknowledge that each nun subjecting herself to this procedure accepts the fact that approximately fifty percent of these births will be male babies.

It was additionally decided that this convent will therefore establish itself as an adoption agency specializing in male babies.

Each young woman undergoing this procedure must sign an agreement that she accepts the outcome of adoption in the event of giving birth to a boy.

Signed this twelfth day of July, 1976,

Sister Judith	Sister Sapphira
Sister Helena	Sister Joanna

Hannah read the entire document a second time. Then she carefully placed it back into the envelope. Dropping it back into the file folder, she quietly closed the file cabinet. Switching off the light, she stepped into the hall and closed the door, locking in its secrets.

CHAPTER SIXTY-ONE

When Abby got back to her room she found another letter from Dad.

My dear Abby,

We are fully into the Witness Protection Program now. The trial is over and Frankie was sentenced. At least that part of our lives is over. Now we have to begin the next chapter. I'll never be safe as long as the mob knows where I am. The federal marshal who is in charge of me is moving me to California.

They have found a place for us to live and I will need a new career. They will give us a monthly stipend until I find a job. I might have to start a different type of career. We will be assigned new names and the government is taking care of all the arrangements to give us new identities. I know this is going to be hard, but not as hard as the last year. I have missed you terribly. If you have survived a year in a convent in South Dakota posing as a nun, I think you can survive living in California, hiding on the beach! The marshal will contact you and he will bring you to California to our new home. We still can't use the phone, but we can continue to write. Oh how I miss you.

Your loving Dad

Tears poured down Abby's face. Sobbing, she read and reread the letter. Her heart ached. She thought of all the things they had done together in Chicago as a family. Pulling out writing paper, she began.

Dear Daddy,

You know how much I love you. I want to be with you. I want my life to be like it was before. But you never told me that I would have to change my name and never acknowledge my past. I thought we were just going to have to move to a new state. I am scared. This year has been really hard, but I have new friends. Do I have to leave them too, and never talk to them again? Daddy, how many times do I have to start over? Are you sure this is the only way?

I love you, Abby

The girls had finished their classes for the school year, and continued their jobs throughout the summer. Catherine felt that they deserved an outing. She spoke to Leah about another trip into the Badlands.

"That's a great idea, Catherine. Especially for these girls who have no plans to stay with us. I think they have felt like captives in our midst at times. It will be good for them to get off our grounds and feel free, even if briefly."

The cook packed another picnic lunch for the girls. She stuffed chicken salad between thick slices of homemade bread and put together a green salad filled with berries and nuts. As a surprise, she tucked in chocolates made in the convent kitchen. This was a special excursion, and cook had hidden more of her peppernut cookies in the bottom of the basket.

Rising extra early, the girls assembled outside the front entrance while darkness still wrapped itself around them. Catherine backed her minivan from its parking space and pulled up near the door.

"Leah is waiting for us around back," she announced as the girls piled inside.

Driving around the building, Catherine stopped close to the kitchen entrance. The girls' favorite teacher was waiting with a large picnic basket and a cooler. Catherine popped the lift gate, and Leah stowed the containers inside. She quickly walked around to the front of the car and joined Catherine.

It had been months since Abby and her friends had enjoyed a trip into the Badlands. The sun was beginning to peak over the horizon as they headed toward the unusual formations.

"You are in for a real treat," announced Leah.

Catherine parked her car at a scenic lookout and the girls jumped out to get a better look. As the sun was rising, the view was spectacular. Even these teenage girls didn't have any words for this overwhelming experience.

"The higher the sun climbs, the more changes you will notice in the colors," Catherine softly announced.

This time Catherine had decided to take the Sage Creek Rim Drive. She turned onto the gravel road, and announced that they would be traveling off the beaten path. She wanted the girls to see some of the wildlife found here. They scanned the horizon for signs of bison.

"Oh look at all the sheep. They are really close to the road," exclaimed Emily.

"And do you see the Pronghorn out there?" questioned Leah.

"What are Pronghorn?" asked Hannah.

"They are antelope. And if you keep looking, you'll see mule deer too." The girls were all amazed that they could see so much wildlife from the windows of the car. Catherine pulled off the road and stopped several times for the girls to scan the horizon. They competed for who could find the next sheep or antelope. The rock formations seemed to change color before their eyes as the sun climbed higher. After Catherine had completed the entire Sage Creek Rim Drive, she continued onto the Scenic Loop.

"There are the fairy castles again," pointed out Abby.

"I still think it looks like we are on the moon," grinned Hannah. Turning their heads to the right and then back to the left, all the passengers took in the beauty.

"I am watching for prairie dogs," said Emily.

"Over here to the right, Em," Abby motioned, as they passed mounds of the little lively creatures, standing up and staring back at them.

Catherine found just the spot she favored. She pulled the car off the road and slowed to a stop. "This looks familiar," said Abby.

"Isn't this where we had our picnic before?" Catherine smiled at Abby and nodded.

"You had been here before, hadn't you?" asked Emily.

"Yes, I told you I had hiked out here while in college."

"I remember you told us about your boyfriend. He had a nickname. What was it?" asked Hannah.

"I think you are referring to Tyee. I called him Ty." Leah glanced at Catherine, a questioning look in her eyes. Catherine carefully avoided the glance as she opened the lift gate of the van. "Okay, girls. Why don't you unload the food and we'll carry it out a ways until we find our perfect picnic spot." Abby reached for the large picnic basket and Hannah quickly took one of the handles. Emily and Leah managed the beverage cooler while Catherine led the way.

After hiking about a quarter of a mile, Emily announced, "My arms are about to fall off. Can't we stop here?"

Catherine laughed. "Sure, this is a good spot. There are enough flat rocks for a picnic table and I think each of you can find one to sit on." Leah opened the basket and found a tablecloth tucked on top of the cache. She unfolded the bright red cloth and spread it over a large flat boulder. Catherine unpacked the sandwiches and salad while Leah handed out plates and utensils.

"I do love it out here," Leah said as she breathed in the late summer air. The girls crowded around and began helping themselves to their picnic lunches. Emily and Hannah found a low flat rock large enough for both of them.

"I just wish we could have worn blue jeans and a tee shirt," complained Emily.

"I think I have heard that before," chuckled Catherine. "Soon enough you will be going home and leaving your habit behind. By the way, what are you planning after you leave here?" Emily looked at Catherine, remembering all the kind support she had received when she had come here, seeking a safe environment.

"I plan to attend college. I'm not sure yet where I will go. I want to talk it over with my parents first."

"I'm so glad you have chosen college, Emily. You will discover a wonderful world waiting for you out there."

Emily nodded. "I know I will. I hope to become a doctor. And I hope someday to fall in love with a man and get married. I want to have children too."

Catherine turned to Leah. "Well, Leah, tell us about your new brother!" A huge smile spread across Leah's face. By now, even Hannah had heard about the triplet brother that Leah and Lydia had found.

"He's wonderful! Not only is he handsome, but he's very funny. And smart. And kind. And gentle. And strong."

Catherine laughed. "Then I am sure he is your brother. So many family traits."

"Catherine, are you teasing me?" asked Leah.

"Of course not. I have always known that you and Lydia are all of those things too. Have you met any of the rest of his family?"

"His adoptive mother died not too long ago. He has a very kind aunt. She has invited us to come spend a weekend with her and her husband. We have only spoken to her on the phone yet. We are waiting for that family to get used to the idea of Mike having identical twin sisters who are nuns! And Lydia had to explain to her how triplets can be made up of identical twin girls and a fraternal triplet boy. I guess she has been researching it on line. She knows it's true from the DNA tests, but you can imagine that it is a little hard to comprehend."

"It is a little hard for any of us to comprehend," smiled Catherine.

"I will really miss all of you," Emily announced. "But I sure do look forward to getting out of this cumbersome habit and into my jeans again."

"I don't think the habit is so bad," Hannah volunteered. "I love wearing something new, even if it is a nun's habit. I never had anything new before, except for the things Danielle bought for me on the way here."

"Who is Danielle?" asked Emily.

"She is the woman who came along with Sam when he drove me from Chicago to South Dakota. We went to a store one evening and she bought me pajamas and a new blouse. She was really nice. I think she is a U.S. Marshall, too. She really seemed to like Sam a lot. So did I. He was so nice to me."

Catherine stared across the buttes as she listened to Hannah, trying to hide the wistful look in her eyes. Catherine stood and walked a few steps toward the cliff.

"The Native Americans called this a holy site. Can you girls feel the spirituality of this place?" Abby joined Catherine. They stood side by side for several moments.

Hannah said, "I wouldn't mind staying in South Dakota. This is the first time in my life that I have been happy." Leah moved over and sat down beside Hannah, putting her arm around the young girl.

"And I believe we are all better for having known you," she gently whispered.

"What about your plans, Abby?" asked Catherine. "Is your Dad settled anywhere yet?"

"He wrote that the trial is over and that the Witness Protection Program is relocating him. I can't tell you where. Of course he wants me to join him and I do miss him terribly."

"Why can't you tell us where?" asked Hannah.

"Because the Witness Protection Program hides people who are in danger by giving them a new identity. That includes new names and even past histories. You are coming out of your hidden life, and I feel that I am entering mine. We will never even be able to contact old friends."

Emily spoke up. "But, Abby, you can eventually look forward to being married and having a child. Don't you want that?"

"Oh, sure, someday I suppose I will."

Hannah glanced at Leah, then out across the majestic Badlands. "I hope to have a child too someday. In this holy place."

NOTE FROM THE AUTHOR
LJ HEMMINGSON

Even though I don't live there currently, my roots remain firmly planted in my beloved South Dakota. I always look forward to taking a drive across the state, from Sioux Falls to the Black Hills. If you have never been there, it is a trip worth taking.

As you near the Missouri river, the farmland begins to diminish, and gives way to rolling plains. In a good year, the grazing land is green. In a dry year, well, not so green. But there is always that catch in my heart as I gaze across the prairie. There is an old saying that out there you can see the farthest, and see the least.

It becomes easy to imagine the years when wagon trains rolled across, filled with hopeful people; some very young, and some not so young. I can feel that unique quality of spirituality permeating my every breath.

All the tiny towns mentioned in 'west river' country are factual. Sam's home, The Pine Ridge Indian Reservation, is a real place. And then we see the Badlands. What a shock it must have been to those early travelers to see in the distance such bizarre formations. And of course, they could see them from quite a distance. I'm sure they agreed with the native population who termed them *makosica*.

While I was writing this book, I cajoled my dear husband into driving down gravel roads, the car tires kicking up dust as I searched for my imaginary setting for the convent. Although I didn't actually see it, I envisioned it behind a particular butte However, the deserted town of Scenic was right there where the map said it would be.

I especially want to thank my husband for his unwavering faith in my ability to bring this story to its end. Also, many thanks to my family and friends who were gracious enough to read my first drafts and give me feedback.

Maybe, dear reader, we can share pie and coffee at the Purple Pie Place someday!